The
Stranger
on the Ice

D0188234

ALSO BY BERNADETTE CALONEGO

Stormy Cove
Under Dark Waters
The Zurich Conspiracy

The Stranger on the Ice

Bernadette Calonego

Translated by Gerald Chapple

Bernadette Calonego (signature)

This is a work of fiction. Names, characters, organizations, places, events, and incidents are either products of the author's imagination or are used fictitiously. Any resemblance to actual persons, living or dead, or actual events is purely coincidental.

Text copyright © 2016 by Bernadette Calonego
Translation copyright © 2018 by Gerald Chapple
All rights reserved.

No part of this book may be reproduced, or stored in a retrieval system, or transmitted in any form or by any means, electronic, mechanical, photocopying, recording, or otherwise, without express written permission of the publisher.

Previously published as *Die Fremde auf dem Eis* by Edition M in Luxembourg in 2016. Translated from German by Gerald Chapple.

First published in English by AmazonCrossing in 2018.

Published by AmazonCrossing, Seattle

www.apub.com

Amazon, the Amazon logo, and AmazonCrossing are trademarks of Amazon.com, Inc., or its affiliates.

ISBN-13: 9781503904255
ISBN-10: 1503904253

Cover design by PEPE *nymi*, Milano

Printed in the United States of America

For Rosa and Peter

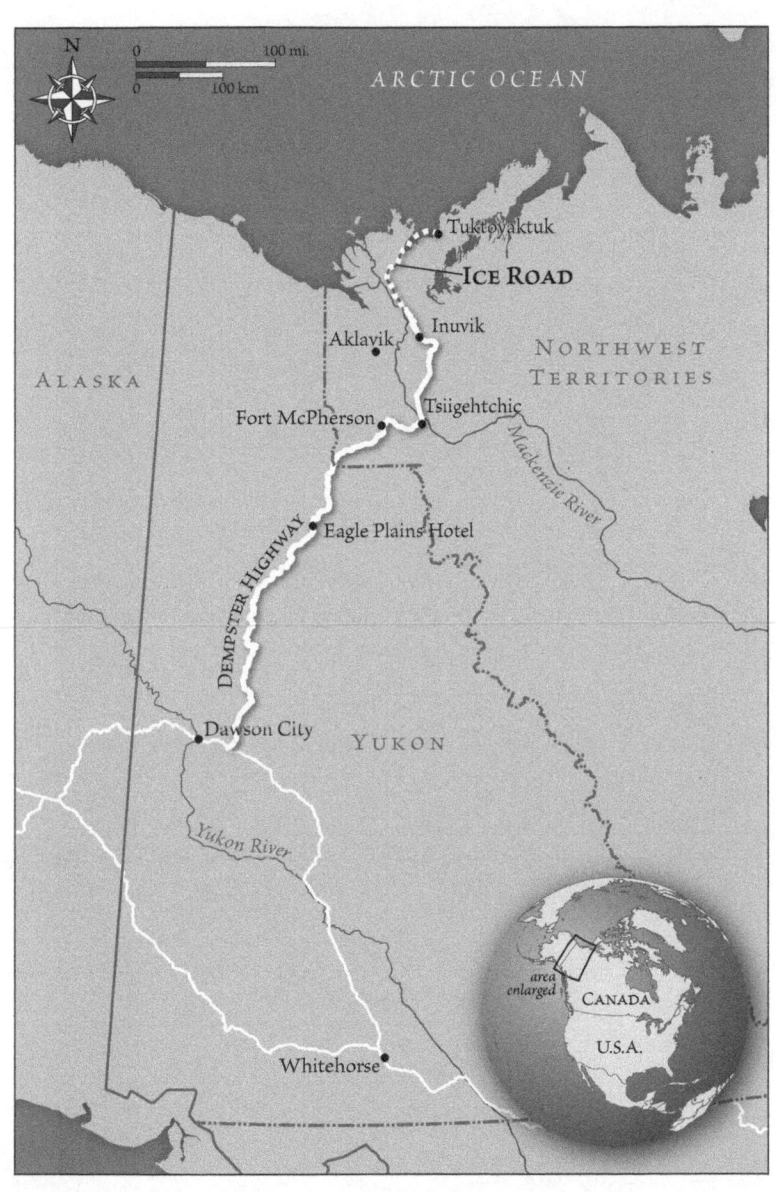

CHAPTER 1

It caught his eye at once. Just off the Ice Road.

A tiny point at first. He drove several feet closer. Dark blue. Couldn't mistake it in this white wilderness. He certainly wouldn't. His eyes picked up anything unusual here.

He was constantly on the ice in winter. Day after day. Him and his truck. A powerful machine that could lug sixty tons. Today he was pulling a trailer with housing for the new foreign workers. Those guys from the south get on Skype to their families back home and say they're drilling for gas in the Arctic Ocean. Not that people three thousand miles away have the slightest idea what that means.

Must be a blue pickup. Probably did a pirouette on the ice. Sure didn't mean to, unless the driver was just playing around. He already knew what to expect. The hood plowed into a snowdrift. Wheels pulled away like dislocated shoulders. Seen that all too often.

The usual yahoos, for sure. Goddamn amateurs. City types with giant egos inflated like a frog's throat and with an even bigger lack of experience. Highway cowboys out of Calgary. Or Vancouver.

Maybe an engineer from LRLS Gas & Oil. Or some jerk of a globetrotter from Italy. Even worse, an American from Texas. Last year it was Brits wanting to film musk ox. Not here, on Banks Island. Of course they just *had* to race down the Ice Road. Instead of musk ox they got themselves a broken axle.

Those idiots haven't the foggiest idea how to drive a vehicle on glass fifteen feet thick. They'd laugh him out of court if he told them, "That glass is alive. It's called ice."

He knew where those big-city babies get their crazy ideas from. TV, of course. *Ice Road Truckers*, a reality show. He'd never have watched anything like that himself. But his wife, Judy, talked him into it. "Just so's you see how they do it," she'd said.

His eyes almost popped out of this head. Those TV people really lay it on thick: "Polar Sea Adventure! Only for the boldest and most daring drivers. They risk their lives on the winter road over the frozen delta of the mighty Mackenzie River. They drive to beat hell, and with a sixty-ton load. They could fall through the ice at any moment."

His pal Poppy Dixon had dropped in with a case of beer, and they'd howled with laughter. Poppy pounded him on the back so hard that he almost fell off the sofa.

"Wow! We're big, fuckin' heroes, eh, Todd? And we didn't even know it!"

Adventure? Bullshit! Last year Poppy's truck had gone through the ice. Eighty tons went down. Rebar for a gas company way out there somewhere. A couple of Helvin West's men hoisted him out with a crane. Poppy hadn't laughed at the time. His face was white as snow.

Now he could clearly make out the blue pickup. Nose first, deep in the wall of snow bordering the road. What a mess. And what was that in the snow? A reddish-brown shape. A dead moose. Or what was left of it: the head. The long tongue hanging out of its mouth. Red streaks all over the place. Red as Judy's nail polish.

His foot tapped on the gas pedal. He couldn't risk going more than thirty with that heavy load. End of March and sun already—sun, sun, sun. Nothing but sun for four days. Four damn days in a row. The ice was still holding. But who knew for how long? Only Clem Hardeven, the ice master. If he said the ice road was closing, then it would be closed. Even Helvin West listened to Clem. And Helvin was Clem's boss.

He geared down. Slow, slow, slow. Todd, my friend, enjoy the spectacle of this idiot who dug his own grave in the snow. The blockhead braked too hard on the ice when he saw the moose's head, I'll bet.

You gotta learn how to brake on the ice. A rookie, was all he could say, a beginner. Maybe the guy had had a few beers too many in the Crazy Hunter. Big mistake. You don't play with fire on the ice.

Suddenly, even before he'd stopped, a lightbulb went on in his head. Blue! The pickup was a shiny dark blue! With white lettering. He didn't even have to read it. Holy shit!

He put on his gloves and fur hat and zipped up his down jacket. He climbed down from his truck and waddled over the sparkling ice like a curler. It was easier for him to drive than walk. The Ice Road was slippery as wet glass.

Axle wasn't broken. He could see that right away. He adjusted his sunglasses. Too much sun and too much white around for his liking. Nothing moved inside the car. He tried to open the door. Couldn't. He tried the other side. He pulled and twisted until the door popped open, and he almost fell over. He peeked inside. Nothing. Not a soul. The bird had flown the coop.

What to do? Best hightail it to Inuvik. Wasn't far. The cops would certainly know what was up. He'd lost enough time as it was.

As he drove on, the pickup gradually disappeared in the rearview mirror. Too bad the wreck didn't vanish into thin air. He didn't want anything to do with it.

One more long curve, and he could almost smell Inuvik.

But there was something else. A dark heap beside the road. What the *fuck*! He knew it wasn't a moose. His truck skidded to a halt. Out into the cold again.

It took some effort to work his way over. A woman. Lying right on the ice. Curled up like a fetus. Not moving. Her head lying on one arm, eyes closed. Her cap still on her dark hair. Her hood flipped back. Like she was asleep. He bent down and shook her. Shouted, "Hello, hello!" But he already knew. So stiff and ice-cold. She was young. And she was dead.

He didn't know the woman. Just the pickup. And he couldn't make any connection.

Penguinlike, he waddled over the ice back to his truck and reached for the satellite phone.

CHAPTER 2

A tight steel band was wrapped around Valerie's head. At least that's how it felt. Her stuffed-up nose almost made breathing impossible. Her body shook with fever. She'd finished the tea hours ago that her neighbor Faye had made. She tried to get up to go to the kitchen—but as soon as she did, everything went black before her eyes. She helped herself to an herbal lozenge, then she gasped for air.

If only her sleepless night would just disappear and the pain in her head and limbs with it.

But she was secretly happy. In two weeks she'd be guiding six clients from Whitehorse to Inuvik and then to the Arctic Ocean. Her flu was sure to be over by then. It had better be. A sick tour guide would mean the death of a company that consisted only of a single person.

She tried once more to lay her head down flat. An evil hobgoblin was hammering on the top of her skull. Her long brown hair clung to her temples. Her heart was pounding as if she'd just sprinted a mile. She wasn't up to taking her temperature yet again.

Suddenly, her tootling cell phone woke her up. She must have finally dozed off. The light was still on. Everything was blurred, but she could still make out the Accept button on the phone. She hit it, robotlike.

"Hello?" Her voice sounded as rough as sandpaper. Words swam toward her ear from far away.

"Val? Is that you?"

She squeaked out a yes.

"Val, it's me, Sedna. I need your help. It's urgent. Do you understand?"

Sedna, wouldn't you know it. Her new friend who wasn't a friend anymore. They'd had a falling-out, and Sedna had taken off to who-knows-where five months ago.

"No. I don't."

"You've got to help me, Val. I'm in serious trouble. Where are you?"

Where do you think?

"I'm in bed. I'm sick."

And it's the middle of the night.

"You've got to get help, Val. I need help—right now!"

"What? But . . . I'm in bed with the flu."

Her head was pounding, her pulse racing. She had a hard time thinking.

What she really wanted to say was: Sedna, call somebody else. I can't help you. Not this time. I warned you, but you wouldn't listen.

"Val, pull yourself together! It's an emergency. Somebody's trying to kill me!"

What did she say? Valerie's nose was dripping. Where was that damn box of tissues?

"Where are you, Sedna? Why don't you call the . . ."

There was a loud crackle at the other end of the line.

"Sedna, call the police."

"I can't, I . . ."

More static. Then the line went silent.

Valerie sat there as if struck dead. Red lightning flashed through her aching head. She closed her eyes to shut out the bright light coming from the lamp on her night table.

She waited. No point trying to sleep.

Sedna would call back. Or she really would call the police.

What did she say? "Somebody's trying to kill me."

Typical Sedna. Dramatizes everything. The queen of conspiracy theories.

She'd warned Sedna. You do *not* simply walk into a gold mine where people have guns and alcohol under their cots. And absolutely not if you're a woman all by yourself. The mines are a magnet for crazies and misfits who have nowhere else to go. Nobody's going to protect an innocent woman there, even if the mine owner's her friend.

Maybe Sedna wasn't in a camp at all. It was the middle of March. No mining for gold in March. Every place in Northern Canada was still snowed in or iced over. And Sedna liked to make things up.

Maybe that's why she was so fascinating. Valerie thought eccentrics were exciting.

When they first met two years ago, she discovered that Sedna was different.

Her hair color, for starters. Valerie was sitting across from her on the Horseshoe Bay ferry from Langdale. A fashionably dressed woman, maybe midthirties or a bit younger, with unconventionally short, colored hair that Valerie secretly called "that precious-metal look": hair streaked with silver, copper, gold, and cobalt blue.

They struck up a conversation on their way to Vancouver, and after twenty minutes the woman said, "My name's Sedna."

Valerie knew the origin of her name, and Sedna was impressed. If that's not a coincidence, she thought, then it's Divine Providence.

Sedna, the goddess of the Alaska and Greenland Inuit. The mighty goddess of the ocean, who lost her fingertips in a tragic boating accident.

They were transformed into whales, seals, and other denizens of the deep. Valerie's stepmother, Bella, had often read to her from a book of myths of the Arctic people, childhood stories that were as familiar to her as *Alice in Wonderland*. Valerie loved the character of Sedna. By contrast, another goddess, who created the fish but sacrificed her own children so that others might live, she found scary.

She told her new acquaintance this as the ferry sailed by small wooded islands with frame houses. Sedna made no reply, merely staring at the water where the wind billowed the sails of a few boats.

Then she suggested having something to drink in the cafeteria.

The snow-covered peaks of the coastal mountains came into view. Valerie asked, "How did you come by that name?"

Sedna sipped her cappuccino.

"My parents were hippies. They hunted around for an out-of-the-way name. My mother found Sedna in her oracle cards, under 'goddesses from ancient cultures.'" She rolled her eyes, which said it all.

Valerie smiled.

Sedna emptied her cup.

"Well, there are worse names than mine."

"For instance?"

"Edna."

They giggled like teenagers.

Not long afterward she bumped into Sedna at the farmers' market in Gibsons, a peaceful port village crowded with yachts and a few fishing boats. Shortly after her divorce, Valerie had moved a few hours away from Vancouver, to the Sunshine Coast, to start a new life. Her plan was to concentrate her travel business on hale and hearty seniors. And in the rural idyll of the Sunshine Coast, with its mild winters, there were hordes of them.

Sedna convinced her to volunteer for the neighborhood watch. This meant driving along the streets and keeping an eye out for suspicious characters. At the time Valerie would have done anything to make friends, even joining a hula-hoop club and marching through town in the annual parade with a fluorescent hoop around her waist. Patrolling in Sedna's red Mazda was fun at first. Sedna knew almost every house and every person in the neighborhood. Many of her stories rang too good to be true, but being with her was never boring. She changed her hairdo every few weeks. Valerie, on the other hand, would simply do up her long chestnut hair in a ponytail every day because it was so practical. She cut her bangs herself. Sedna experimented with makeup and sometimes wore false eyelashes. Her pretty face would turn into a thousand tiny lines when she laughed, but it was completely smooth when she was serious.

She had these wonderfully crazy conspiracy theories. For example, she believed that the village authorities were deliberately polluting the drinking water, which was long recognized as the best drinking water in the world: it always took first place in international competitions. For generations anybody could fill canisters of it from the community well for free. When the local authorities suddenly slapped a fee on this, Sedna and many fellow citizens were enraged. Their anger boiled over when pathogens were discovered in the water, and people had to buy mineral water at the store.

"They did that on purpose," Sedna said. "The authorities contaminated the water to get back at us."

"Don't you think that's a bit farfetched?" Valerie inquired.

Sedna shook her head like a parent dealing with an unreasonable child.

"Maybe your take on the world is a bit naïve, Val. You probably believe what the newspapers say about who destroyed the Twin Towers?"

Valerie was smart enough to keep quiet.

She continued to consider Sedna a friend. She took an exploratory trip the following summer to Inuvik, a village in the Arctic, and Sedna came along. Valerie normally took tours on the Ice Road and to the Arctic Ocean at the beginning of April, but they were so successful she decided to plan a summer tour to the Arctic as well.

The trip with Sedna didn't work out. The problems began as soon as they reached the Yukon Territory. In Dawson City she disappeared for a whole day and didn't turn up until that evening, without a word to Valerie about where she'd been. In Inuvik it was worse. Valerie found a hastily scribbled note one morning telling her not to worry, Sedna would be back at the hotel in three days.

Valerie was furious. Sedna accused Valerie of treating her like a toddler in a playpen, arguing that they hadn't agreed to do everything together. That was the beginning of the end of their friendship. Valerie knew it, but for some reason, she kept going on the neighborhood patrols with Sedna. The death knell finally sounded when a friend of Valerie's saw Sedna in Cardero's Restaurant in Vancouver. With Valerie's ex. The friend didn't have any idea who the woman flirting with Matt Shearer was. But her account didn't leave any room for doubt: a woman with a dozen colors in her hair and silver earrings shaped like Indian canoes. Earrings like Sedna's.

Valerie phoned her ex.

"Are you alone?" she asked—and immediately regretted her awkward gambit.

Matt said nothing.

She sighed. "That didn't fly. Can I start over?"

"Sure," he said, sounding surprised. And wary.

She was twenty-one when she'd accepted Matt's proposal of marriage. Ten years later she didn't want to be married anymore. Not to Matt, not to anyone. She wanted to be free and try out all the potential roads that life was supposed to offer her. The thought that she'd be intimate with only one man for the rest of her days terrified her. She wanted a life that would spread out before her like an uninhabited prairie, where she could choose several different paths to take. Not just the one she'd traveled until then; to her mind it was completely predictable.

She still loved her husband, but when he wanted them to move to Paris because of a job opportunity, she panicked. She chose the dumbest excuse to escape her marriage: an affair. The assignations meant little to her, apart from the fact that they were a novel experience. When Matt found out she'd been unfaithful, he said, "You're not the woman I used to know," and moved out of their apartment. She still felt an attraction toward him afterward, but there was no going back. She no longer trusted herself in matters of the heart. She wished she could have asked Bella, her stepmother, for advice, but the first symptoms of Alzheimer's were already apparent, and Valerie didn't want to bother her with it.

Matt quietly waited for her response on the end of the line.

"I'd like you to tell me something. Why did you go out with my friend Sedna Mahrer?"

"She got in touch with me and asked me," he said without hesitation.

"How . . . did she find you?"

"I assumed you helped her."

"No, I had no idea."

"Isn't she a friend of yours?"

"I'm not so sure at this point." Valerie was at a loss about what to think.

Matt continued.

"I met up with her, we went to Cardero's, and I haven't laid eyes on her since."

"She didn't try to contact you again?"

"No. She didn't seem very interested in me."

"Oh." Valerie struggled to find the right words. "How—"

Matt cut her off.

"I had the impression she wanted to talk about *you*, Val. She asked me lots of questions about you. And about your family. I have to say, she was very clever about it. Still, I caught on and wasn't very forthcoming. So you don't have to worry."

She knew exactly what that last sentence was meant to convey. Valerie and her twin brothers had had more than enough public attention.

"What did she want to know about me?"

"Your background, your parents, how you grew up—Val, I'm very sorry, I've got a meeting. Maybe you should talk to Sedna about it and not me."

And he was gone.

Valerie waited until the next patrol to confront Sedna. She knew Sedna couldn't avoid her while sitting in the car.

"Were you with my ex in Cardero's?" she asked the moment she got into the passenger seat.

Sedna waited just for a second.

"Yes. Why?"

"Why? What were you thinking?"

"I went out with him." Her voice was perfectly calm.

"Don't you think that's a bit . . . out of line?"

Sedna looked her straight in the eye.

"Out of line? Just because you were once married to him? You're divorced, Val. You left him. He's free to do whatever he wants."

"But I confided in you! I told you things about me and Matt."

"Yes, that's right. You told me a lot of very nice things about him. So I thought it would be fun to get to know him."

"You could've at least asked for my opinion. That's what I'd have done if I were you."

"Val, you'd have found a way to stop us from meeting if you'd known about it beforehand. That's why I didn't ask."

Valerie stared at Sedna. Sedna stared right back with her intense blue eyes.

"If looks could kill," she muttered.

Sedna stopped the car, and Valerie opened the door and got out.

It crossed her mind too late that she hadn't asked Sedna why she'd wanted to know so much about her family.

She found out two weeks later that Sedna had gone off on a long journey. And nobody knew where.

CHAPTER 3

Clem Hardeven prowled like a tiger around his little row house from the kitchen to the living room and back because he'd forgotten what he wanted to do. Meteor, his Husky-Labrador mix, lay on his doggie bed, lifted his head, and watched him. Clem was irritated but couldn't do a thing about it.

Damn, damn, damn.

He couldn't get anybody on the phone, and if he did, they'd know diddly-squat, just like him. Times are hard when you can't slam down the receiver in a rage. Would make him feel a lot better right now.

Something was brewing in Inuvik—he'd never felt such tension in the air. He was the man in town who was supposed to know what's up. He was the manager of the Ice Road. The ice master, the go-to guy. But ever since they'd found that body, he was out of the loop. Literally left out in the cold. It drove him nuts.

He *had* to know what was going on. Helvin, his boss, was nowhere to be found. Incommunicado. For hours! He wasn't in the office or at home. Supposedly. His secretary played dumb.

If anybody would know that a dead body had been discovered, it was Helvin West. Nothing happened on the Ice Road without Helvin's say-so. Clem couldn't even go out to drill holes to check the ice thickness and see that the Ice Road was safe for heavy trucks without Helvin's

OK. And the secretary told him: No drilling until further notice. And no vehicles on the Ice Road until further notice. It drove him bananas. What the hell was going on? Todd, the truck driver, was keeping his mouth shut. Not a peep out of him about finding the body. Not because of the police investigation either. For sure. Bullshit. There were forces more powerful than the dozen cops stationed in Inuvik. Todd was keeping mum because Helvin had told him to. And that really made Clem antsy.

Otherwise news flew around Inuvik as fast as a seal can dive. It wasn't so hard in a village of thirty-five hundred people. Maybe Hisham had gotten wind of something.

He put on his snowmobile suit and picked up his jacket. Meteor was already at the door, his tail wagging faster than a windshield wiper in heavy rain. The dog knew what was coming. Clem walked out into the snow and scanned the sky. Gray, but no sign of an approaching storm. The winter had tested the character of Inuvik's residents more than once. Power outages and frozen pipes. Sometimes for days. Not only the pipes for drinking water but also the sewer pipes that were above ground.

Inuvik seemed to Clem like a mock-up in a human anatomy class: all the pipes and tubes ran outside in front of the buildings for all to see. Like a passel of giant snakes, the interlocking circulatory system was several feet above ground, courtesy of the ever-present permafrost. And the layer of soil above the permafrost moved like a live beast; it froze and expanded in the cold, thawing and contracting when it turned warm again.

Clem's eyes didn't burn in the cold as much as they had a week ago. Four sunny days in a row. Maybe spring was actually on its way.

He drove his snowmobile up to a green building where a sign read, COMPUTER-REPAIRS@NETPOLAT. If rumors were flying around, they made their way to Hisham, the village's computer-repair technician. Hisham was one of Inuvik's Muslims who prayed in the northernmost mosque in North America. "The world's first mosque on permafrost," Hisham would boast to the tourists. The house of prayer had been donated by a charitable organization in Winnipeg and built in that city, almost twenty-eight hundred miles away. It was then trucked sixteen hundred miles before being floated downstream on the Mackenzie River for the remaining twelve hundred miles. It was the last barge to make it before winter arrived.

"I'd never have allowed that thing on the Ice Road," Clem had joked, trying to get a rise out of Hisham.

Hisham had responded coolly, "That wasn't your call. We'd have asked Helvin."

When Hisham opened his shop door for Clem and Meteor, he didn't appear to be in a particularly good mood.

"Why am I told nothing?" he shouted. "Did I break the law? I should know exactly what's happened—I've got three daughters after all. They could be in danger!"

How the hell would I know? Clem wanted to say but bit his tongue. *He* wasn't used to having to ask for information either.

"The police are investigating, so they can't go around telling the whole world about it," Clem said.

"The whole world?" Hisham tossed a computer cable into a corner. "I couldn't care less about the police investigation. I'm interested in blood."

Blood. Exactly what Clem now smelled. "Who said anything about blood?"

"Todd found the body. He says he'll be as silent as the grave. But you know what?"

He spread his arms as if wanting to hug the broad-shouldered man in front of him.

"Todd talks in his sleep!"

He looked at Clem in triumph.

"He spilled the beans in his sleep—his wife heard it."

"Hisham, for Chrissake, where did you get this crap?"

The pious Muslim ignored Clem's choice of words.

"She was here with her iPad. Todd talked about a lot of blood. In his sleep. In his sleep!"

Clem got angry all over again. Dammit, that might have been a murder, a murder on the Ice Road, and he knew fuck all about it.

"Is that everything you know?"

"Isn't that enough? A dead woman and lots of blood! How are my daughters supposed to feel safe from now on?"

"Lock them up in the house, the way you always do when I show up."

"*You* can talk, Clem; you don't have any daughters. Maybe it's about time you got around to finding a wife. You can't marry your dog, you know."

Clem never saw Hisham's daughters when he went to the Netpolat store, even though they were computer savvy and often helped their father out. His buddy Phil Niditichie, a First Nation Gwich'in, once teased him about it: "You're a Christian and just too good-looking." That cost Phil a round of beer in the Crazy Hunter. Clem didn't take remarks about his good looks lightly, although he was aware that the women in Inuvik—many younger than his thirty-six years—noticed his tall, muscular build and attractive face.

Around the Mackenzie Delta, there was no bad blood between whites and Muslims or the Gwich'in indigenous people, nor between whites and the Inuvialuit, as the Western Arctic Inuit called themselves. No malice, just a whole lot of good-natured joking. And they all were united in the collective implementation of "Delta Time," which didn't exist as a time zone in reality but was the universally accepted custom of always being late.

No, there was hardly ever a fight. But now there was a dead woman.

And all Hisham knew was what Todd had supposedly blabbed in his sleep.

Clem opened the door to leave, and Meteor ran out ahead of him. "Give me a call if you hear something."

"Inshallah," Hisham replied.

Meteor had reached the Crazy Hunter before Clem pulled up. The dog was sniffing out the surrounding area as much as possible before the familiar motor of the snowmobile started up again. Clem went into the watering hole that from the outside resembled a garage more than a bar.

The air stank of damp clothing, barbecued hamburgers, and alcohol-soaked breath. Clouds of smoke obscured his sight in defiance of the no-smoking signs.

The customers were crowded around the bar, and it wasn't yet five o'clock. Clem noticed one pair of eyes after another following him. Everyone looked curious, hungry for news, and more than a few patrons eagerly asked him what he knew. He wouldn't find the answers he was hoping for in the Crazy Hunter. He quickly scanned the crowd for a face that might promise some more information, then waved to the bartender before making a quick departure.

Outside, Meteor was nowhere to be seen. Clem called him and started his motor. The dog came running and immediately dashed over to the other side of the street where a man was standing. Clem recognized the face under the wolf-fur-lined hood. Lazarusie Uvvayuaq, an Inuvialuk from the town of Tuktoyaktuk, greeted him with a broad grin. Clem drove over and gave him a friendly clap on the shoulder.

"Hey, Laz. Looking for a warm bed?"

Clem prided himself on having discovered Lazarusie's talent as a hunting and fishing guide for tourists. Maybe not discovered it, but certainly promoted it. He used his connections elsewhere in Canada, especially Ontario, to drum up business for him.

Laz needed the money for his seven children and thirteen grandchildren. Only his adopted daughter, Tanya, and his son Danny were still living at home as far as Clem knew. But Inuvialuit families were tightly knit communities, and grandparents were often the main providers for the children who left home. Clem was deeply indebted to Lazarusie, who had once saved his life when his snowmobile fell through the ice.

"Can't go home," Lazarusie said with a laugh, showing several gaps in his teeth. He'd come from Tuktoyaktuk by snowmobile, the whole way across the Ice Road. It was five hours there and back.

"I know, the Ice Road is closed," Clem said, not revealing that he wasn't the man behind the closing. Lazarusie knew he could stay at Clem's; it was a ritual for them.

"The door's open. Make yourself at home. I'll be there in half an hour."

He turned his snowmobile around, but had a sudden thought and stopped.

"When did you leave Tuktoyaktuk?"

Lazarusie casually looked away as he climbed onto his own snowmobile, as if he didn't know why Clem was asking him that.

"Yesterday."

A few seconds of silence. Then Clem spoke: "Go to my place and wait for me."

Lazarusie nodded, and Clem watched him drive away. Meteor followed Lazarusie for a while, then came back panting.

"Meteor, go with Lazarusie, go home," Clem ordered. "I'm going into the lion's den."

CHAPTER 4

"It's probably garbage. Nevertheless, we still have to tell the police."

Faye, Valerie's next-door neighbor in their duplex, sat in an armchair, far enough from Valerie's bed to avoid breathing her flu germs but near enough not to appear insensitive. She eyed the pile of trash in the room without comment: orange peels, empty yogurt containers, crushed tissues, and damp washcloths. Faye was more than just Valerie's neighbor: she was worth her weight in gold. When Valerie moved into the left half of the duplex, Faye had introduced herself at once.

"We single women have to look out for each other. We might be lying hurt or dead in the house, and nobody would notice," she'd announced. Valerie was newly divorced at the time, and this horrific scenario struck a nerve. She'd hardly ever lived on her own. But she didn't want to cling to Faye and vice versa; she made that clear to her right away. Faye just gave a chirpy laugh and said, "You Canadian women really are afraid of relationships. There's a practical side to that kind of help."

Faye did *not* become a clinging vine. Valerie hadn't really found out much about her in all their time together, other than her family had escaped poverty and the dictatorship in Haiti and immigrated to Canada. Faye had been a social worker in Toronto before moving to the

Sunshine Coast in her early forties and taking up painting. She couldn't live off her art so she got by doing modest house renovations.

Valerie often caught herself gazing at Faye's face for too long, because it was a delight to the eye. Valerie envied her neighbor's long, thick eyelashes, her big eyes, and her sharply defined, full mouth. Faye's impeccable skin was a shimmery, warm tone like dark honey (Valerie couldn't describe it in any other way, although it sounded like a cliché). At some point the genes of white colonizers must have mingled with her family's genes. Her body appeared strong and muscular. Not only did Faye work hard, she really liked to do weight training.

With her slight frame, Valerie would have profited from some muscle training, but she disliked all sports other than badminton and Zumba. Long, strenuous walks were part of her routine, but she felt they didn't count. Her skin tended to burn in the sun, and she continually applied lip balm to prevent chapped lips. She'd have loved to project the image of a tanned, tall, athletic, blond tour guide in a khaki tropical outfit. She saw herself instead as a fragile ballet dancer, with thin arms (Matt had called them "swan necks") and small feet. In spite of how she looked, she wasn't at all fragile, which was something she constantly had to prove to others. At least she'd been blessed with perfect teeth, olive-green eyes, and evenly arched eyebrows, attributes inherited from her mother, whose beauty had beguiled the best-known athlete in Canada.

But Faye wasn't aware of all that.

Valerie drew the covers up to her chin.

"It was a weird telephone call," she said.

"With Sedna, weird is normal; *that* we know."

Faye had met Sedna at a Toastmasters club meeting where the women honed their public-speaking skills. Sedna stood out because of her peculiar interests. Such as, why every family ought to own a gun to defend itself.

"She begged me to help her," Valerie repeated.

"To save her from the clutches of some backwoodsman?"

"She said somebody was trying to kill her."

"Are you certain that your fever didn't make you hallucinate?"

"I don't think so."

"Where is she?"

"I asked her that but couldn't hear her response very well. Her voice faded in and out . . ."

"Have you got her cell number? No, wait, it's in my phone."

Faye pulled out her cell, typed, and waited, tapping her feet in their black-and-white polka-dotted stockings.

"I texted her. Let me see your phone. I want to know where that call came from."

Valerie did as requested, but after looking at the display, Faye frowned.

"Unknown number. Not exactly helpful."

She looked around as if there were a clue somewhere nearby.

"We've got to tell the police. And her family. Know anything about Sedna's family?"

"No."

Valerie felt like a log drifting helplessly on the ocean. Faye regarded her sympathetically.

"I'll take care of it. You look like death warmed over. You need to rest and have no more excitement."

Rest. Music to Valerie's ears.

Faye shouldered her handbag and was already in the hall when she stuck her pretty head in the doorway again.

"Just in case the police ask me: Why in the world did she call you of all people?"

Yes, why? She hadn't heard from Sedna since October. Almost half a year. Valerie had dropped the neighborhood watch because she'd been on the road with tour groups in British Columbia, Quebec, and Ontario. She'd invested a lot of energy and preparation in her cultural tours; they were well received, to her great satisfaction. She'd hardly given Sedna a thought. And nobody had mentioned her. Not even Faye.

Valerie thrashed around restlessly. Sedna really knew how to dream up outlandish scenarios. Valerie recalled a visit to her last spring. She found Sedna crafting pottery in her shed. Sedna was forever taking up new hobbies that she'd pursue for several months then suddenly abandon. For example, Valerie had met her when she was knitting with giant needles; later Sedna gave her a glass mosaic she'd made herself; after that she'd poured chocolate into metal molds with erotic scenes (and sold them at the Christmas market in Gibsons). She'd also sewn beach bags out of old parachutes. When Sedna took up pottery, Valerie bought three huge flowerpots, though they cost five times more than at the garden center.

Sedna was sitting at her potting wheel that day and immediately put a finger to her lips, where it left a gray streak. She wiped her hands on a bleached-out towel, then picked up a ballpoint pen. She laid a finger on her lips once more, as if somebody had forbidden her to speak. She scribbled something on a piece of old newspaper and beckoned to her visitor to come closer. At first Valerie found it hard to decipher the scribbles.

She finally made out the words: "Have you got your cell phone?"

Sedna's strange fussing about intrigued her in spite of herself, and she nodded.

"Put it in the hallway in the house," Sedna wrote.

Valerie took the pen out of Sedna's hand and wrote one word: "Why?"

Sedna wrote three words below that: "Just do it."

Valerie went back to the house and put her cell phone on a little table by the front door. Then she went back to the shed.

"Now I can explain everything," Sedna said, resuming her work at the potting wheel.

Valerie heard a crazy story that began with a CIA agent, apparently a fascinating man who was in love with Sedna, though she wasn't really interested in him. She said the guy stalked her and spied on her through her computer and with listening software on her cell.

Valerie was amused but feigned interest.

"Spyware on your cell phone? How does that work?"

"These guys can eavesdrop using your cell phone and hear everything going on around you. You can only block it by taking your battery out."

Valerie said nothing. Sedna was intelligent—that, she knew. So why would she invent stories like these? Sedna evidently sensed her skepticism.

"I went to the Vancouver Police Department. I asked if I was right in thinking it is actually possible to spy on people in their own homes by accessing their cell phones."

She gave Valerie a meaningful look.

"They agreed. They said yes, it's technically possible."

"How?"

"You can program it by remote control."

Valerie paced back and forth in the shed. She'd planned to buy a new pot—and now this.

"How'd you get to know this CIA agent anyway?"

"On a website for . . . interesting political theories."

"And you arranged to meet him?"

"Of course. In Seattle. I met him several times. We had some interesting conversations."

"Sedna, why would you want to meet with someone like him? Someone who spies for a living?"

"Because agents are human beings, too, and they do important work. I used to be a private detective. We talked shop a bit—that was fun."

"What? You never told me that."

An enigmatic smile played around the corners of Sedna's mouth.

"Well, you haven't said much about *your* early life."

The remark was tossed off lightly. Not seriously enough to make Valerie suspicious. That wouldn't come until later.

The hammering in Valerie's head started up again. One thought took root firmly in her mind: I'm not going to let Sedna into my life ever again. No matter what crazy thing she says or does.

CHAPTER 5

The Ice Road's fate was sealed. Clem was reminded of this whenever he drove to Helvin West's company buildings. In a few years, nobody would travel over the frozen Mackenzie River delta in winter. Soon there'd be no trucks with twenty-foot-thick ice under them, and below that the waters of the river and the Arctic Ocean. No truck or car wheels would roll along the second-largest delta in North America, and neither would any snowmobile runners. Farewell Ice Road, and so long ice master Clem! Pretty soon nobody would be there to supervise the formation of the glassy roadway, to measure the echo electronically, and to have holes drilled deep down to find out how thick the ice is over all those 115 miles. Nobody to deploy the graders and snowplows. Or send out rescue teams if a truck occasionally did something stupid and fell through the ice.

There was no going back. The new overland route between Inuvik and Tuktoyaktuk was almost completed. A road on permafrost, which is just ice with a thin layer of soil over it. Ground that expands and contracts. Those construction guys could only work in winter when it was frozen. That's why Clem preferred the Ice Road a hundred times more.

His boss was of a different opinion. Helvin West had moved his company buildings to the newer part of Inuvik at the right time. A good move, Clem had to admit. Absolutely nobody had shown any interest in that part of town until then because there was no road to it. Now the head office of Helvin's company, Suntuk Logistics, could easily be accessed from the new highway. West had snapped up some land early on along the future site of the overland road and built dozens of identical prefabs for his construction workers on it. He'd guessed where the new road would be located. Now he was building part of it. The previous Canadian government welcomed all this activity and approved the plans because they were anxious to reinforce their presence in the Arctic. Didn't a Canadian prime minister once say about the Arctic, "Use it or lose it?"

Clem passed by the usual array of vehicles in Helvin's depot. Sixty-ton trucks, graders, and excavators. When he caught sight of the police car at the entrance to Suntuk Logistics, he briefly wondered if this was an opportune time or not. At least he now knew he'd find Helvin in his office. He dismounted from his snowmobile and rushed into the building. The secretary protested—her name was Laura Minetti—but he bypassed her with a determined stride, knocked on Helvin's door, and barged in.

Three heads turned toward him, two policemen whom he knew and a person he'd never seen before. Helvin West didn't have to turn his head because he was leaning back in his office chair facing Clem and looking ostentatiously relaxed. Clem's boss was sturdy but not tall, about a head shorter than Clem was. Valerie Blaine had once confessed to Clem that she found Helvin rather intimidating. A square face with a jutting jaw. If he'd had a darker complexion, he could have passed for half-Gwich'in. But Helvin was a blond descendant of Scottish whalers who, unlike other European settlers, had never intermarried with the Inuvialuit or the Gwich'in.

Clem saw his boss's eyebrows slacken—was it out of relief?—when he said, "Clem, as you can see, I'm busy. Can you come back later? Let's say . . . around six?"

"OK," Clem said and left, but not before again quickly scanning the other people at the unexpected meeting. As he headed for the building's exit, the secretary's eyes shot burning arrows at him, but to his amazement none of her famous tirades followed. Laura Minetti was originally from Italy and hadn't adapted to friendly Canadian manners as quickly as she had to the winter cold in Inuvik. Helvin tolerated Laura's snootiness because he wasn't her main target and because other imported secretaries had fled Inuvik posthaste.

Clem hurried out before he could further ignite Laura's anger. The bitter cold air filled his lungs as he breathed deeply. He'd seen what he wanted to. That meeting didn't look like an interrogation. Nevertheless, he couldn't describe what it *did* look like.

His snowmobile glided past the colorful facades of the prefabs that seemed like Monopoly houses. He heard the agitated barking of dogs in the distance; it sounded like the chorus of a sled dog team before the musher gave the signal to start. That must be Alana Reevely and her boyfriend, Duncan Divinsky, who were training for the dogsled race in two weeks. Alana was very pretty, and Clem wouldn't have been averse to a closer relationship, but Alana's passion was mushing and dogs. She talked about almost nothing else. Clem loved Meteor, but his interests were broader. Men had broken Alana's heart time and again. Then Duncan appeared on the scene, and she fell head over heels in love. Duncan was outrageously handsome, and Clem expected Alana to get hurt yet again. But he was wrong. The two had been together for three years, and Duncan had proved to be a calm, reliable guy and a musher heart and soul, just like Alana.

Clem turned left and headed down to the frozen Mackenzie. He knew where he'd find the two. The tracks for the race were being prepared on a flat part of the bank. He saw the trailer loaded with small crates for transporting the dogs. Straw stuck out of some openings. Alana took one of her four-legged friends out and calmed him down with gentle words. It was her great talent, the envy of many mushers.

She disciplined her dogs without shouting or beating them. And she had a sixth sense when matching up dogs into a good team.

Something was in the air. Clem picked up on it right away as he parked his snowmobile. Duncan kept a tight leash on a lead bitch. But it wasn't Booster, the dog Alana had named her outdoor business, Booster Adventures, after.

"Where's Booster?" Clem called.

Alana tied the dog up to the trailer.

She looked at him, her expression sad.

"Dead."

Tears rolled down her cheeks, but she brushed them away at once.

Clem was shocked. Booster had been a strong, intelligent alpha dog that the other dogs deferred to. She was Alana's best chance for a win at the Muskrat Jamboree, the spring festival.

"What happened?"

"She had cramps yesterday. Out of the blue. She writhed on the floor and foamed at the mouth. We took her to the vet immediately. She died last night."

"What did the vet say?"

"He'd like to have an autopsy done. In Yellowknife. To find out what it was."

"Wow!" Clem wanted to sit down, but there was no place for him to. "I'm terribly sorry for you both. Booster was a fantastic dog."

"She was the best lead dog I ever had." Alana's voice took on a defiant tone. "I'm in the race regardless; the dogs are still young and inexperienced but have speed and stamina. I've made Bolter the lead dog. Duncan trained him."

Then she said in a near whisper, "Duncan believes somebody poisoned Booster."

Clem looked at Duncan. He looked crushed.

"A terrible loss," Clem said with sympathy. "And so close to the race."

"We've still got a chance. Raven Link from Alaska is unbeatable for now; I really want to beat Cole Baker, from Dawson City. The damn loudmouth."

"I can only say you're right," Clem replied. He'd never heard a good word about Baker.

Alana petted the dog on his chain.

"When's Valerie coming?" she asked Clem.

"In twelve days, I think."

"She's booked a dog-trip with us. She loved Booster too."

"Alana, we've got to get a move on!" Duncan said.

Clem waved to them both and continued on his way.

His thoughts wandered. The festival. Valerie Blaine.

Four times she'd brought her tours to the annual Muskrat Jamboree of the Mackenzie Delta residents. He couldn't imagine the spring festival without her. And he didn't want to. When the sun returned to Inuvik after continuous winter darkness, he'd always look forward to Valerie's reappearance. He visualized her getting off the dogsled, with ruddy cheeks and a beaming smile for him, who just happened to show up at the right place. He thought about how she teased him in the bar of the Great Polar Hotel because he wanted to win the snowmobile race so badly.

Last year he managed to sit beside Valerie at the pancake breakfast, a fundraiser for Inuvik's soup kitchen. They talked about the past and the future of the Arctic and its inhabitants. He was amazed at how well read and articulate she was, but she never flaunted her knowledge. Instead of the familiar ponytail, her lustrous hair hung loose over her shoulders. Her olive-green eyes sparkled in her narrow face, and her fragrance reminded him of the flowery meadows of his home province, Ontario. At the same time she was also on her guard, which didn't escape his notice; she quickly defused crackling tensions with a dry remark. Maybe the scars from her divorce. Or a new man.

He was beset by a subtle fear. Had Sedna betrayed something? He'd thought until now that Valerie didn't suspect anything. She hadn't given any hint of it during their long phone calls after her trip last summer. Sedna's name never came up in their communications.

And now Valerie would return and hear about the dead woman on the ice. It was only a matter of time before she found out about it. He knew he had to call her as soon as he'd sized up the situation.

A snowmobile came nearer. He recognized the driver from a long way off. Pihuk Bart. A serious contender in the upcoming snowmobile race. Nobody wanted to have him as an opponent. Pihuk was a shaman.

He was also the sole survivor of a mysterious tragedy that still shook people in the Canadian Arctic years later. Clem had heard the story soon after moving to Inuvik seven years earlier. He himself had suffered a very personal tragedy, one that had resulted in his fleeing to the Arctic. But he told nobody about it.

Pihuk's terrible tragedy struck the tiny settlement of Inuliktuuq in the winter of 1989, when two dozen Inuvialuit living about a hundred miles from Inuvik were not heard from for a week. Finally, a party of four men set out from Inuvik to check on them. More out of curiosity than concern, they crossed the frozen tundra. It wasn't until they reached Inuliktuuq that they had a disquieting feeling. Something wasn't right in the settlement. There was no smoke coming from the chimneys; doors had been left open in spite of the brutal cold. The party had the impression that the inhabitants had left their houses in great haste. They found dirty cups on the tables, sleds leaning against walls, and *kiiyallak* left behind everywhere, as if a person could walk through the snow without those warm sealskin boots. The men followed the tracks in the snow, tracks made by bare feet, not boot soles. They walked for just over half a mile before they found the corpses. Some simply lay in the snow, as if asleep. They'd nestled together, at the mercy of the cold, inadequately dressed, all barefoot, many without gloves. Fourteen adults and ten children. All dead, all frozen. Everyone except an infant they found back in one of the shacks, hungry and crying in a box under some reindeer hides. Almost like Moses in the Bible. The infant Pihuk was taken to the hospital in Inuvik, and he survived. Depending on whom you ask—his friends or his critics—that was the beginning of Pihuk Bart's rise to becoming a powerful shaman, or the start of his descent into a dungeon of darkness.

When the awful story went out from Inuvik to the whole world, it was not front-page news. Because on that very day, the Berlin Wall came down, bringing an end to the Cold War. *The Cold War*—what an interesting term, Clem thought, as his snowmobile skirted the heap of snow beside the Hungry Bear Market in the center of town. Maybe the Cold War was over in Europe and the United States. But in the Arctic it kept on going; it just wasn't called that. Still, during arguments in the Crazy Hunter and the Great Polar Hotel bar, Clem kept his opinion to himself.

He could only hope that the police would get to the bottom of the woman's death on the Ice Road faster than they had in the Inuliktuuq tragedy. Investigators at the time didn't come up with a conclusive explanation for the extraordinary behavior of people who had evidently fled their houses in panic and walked to their certain death. Many in Inuvik believed that armed intruders had forced the unfortunate occupants out of their homes. But nobody could figure out why those unknown people didn't leave any tracks. Speculation and theories about who or what caused the tragedy flourished: a plane flying too low and terrifying the inhabitants; an earthquake—although there'd been no sign of one; drugs; a ritual murder (the favorite theory in the tabloids); or a panic caused by high-frequency sound waves, an explanation that emerged on the twentieth anniversary of the tragedy.

Pihuk expressed no opinion about the events. But some speculated that somehow he knew something, that he was keeping a deep, dark secret.

This thought brought Clem back to Lazarusie Uvvayuaq.

When he got home, he found the Inuvialuk in the kitchen still in his anorak.

"Laz, for God's sake take off your bear skin, or isn't the house warm enough for you?"

Laz grinned as he took off his anorak while Clem put the kettle on. Meteor was barking and running around like a chicken with its head cut off, but Clem hushed him. He put two cups down on the shiny Formica of a round table, a relic from the sixties.

"Any news for me?"

Lazarusie shrugged. He didn't like direct conversational gambits.

Clem sat down and stirred sugar into his steaming tea. A glance at his guest told him that something was wrong. He picked out some cookies from a green tin and pushed them across the table.

"How was the trip over the Ice Road?"

Lazarusie sat there in silence, eyeing the cookies.

"Help yourself, my friend."

"Unpleasant. It was an unpleasant trip," Lazarusie responded.

Clem cast a baited hook.

"See anything funny?"

More silence.

"Laz, you know that nothing goes beyond this kitchen without your say-so."

Something flickered over the dark face at the other end of the table. Lazarusie took his time, sipping his tea as if it wasn't boiling hot. Clem observed him, fascinated. He must have the rough tongue of a whale. Suddenly that tongue was loosened.

"A woman," Lazarusie said.

Clem put down his teaspoon.

"The dead woman?"

"Yep."

"Nobody tells me anything, Laz. What did you see?"

"I was watching out for moose, with binoculars. Then I saw something."

He paused, and Clem waited.

"A head."

"What? The woman's head?"

"No, a moose head."

"Jesus, Laz! And the woman?"

"I saw her too. Farther along. About two miles."

Laz rubbed his face with his hand.

"She wasn't alive."

"Did you know her?"

Lazarusie shook his head.

"A white woman. Never saw her before."

"Blond? Dark haired?"

"Don't exactly know."

Laz paused again and thought about it.

"Not blond."

"What else?"

"Saw a pickup too."

"Where?"

"Not far from the moose head. Stuck in the snow by the roadside. I thought the guy saw the moose and got stuck in the snowbank."

"What guy? Did you know him?"

Lazarusie slid forward on his chair.

"Blue pickup. Helvin's pickup."

Clem gaped at him.

"No!" he exclaimed.

"Oh, yeah. 'Suntuk Logistics' written on the side."

"No way that's true," Clem said. Then, almost soundlessly, "Now we're really in deep shit."

CHAPTER 6

Valerie looked at the expectant faces before her while trying to appear enthusiastic and composed at the same time, though she was anxious and tense. And yet she had real reason to feel relieved. Faye had brought her some good news three days ago: the police had tracked down a brother of Sedna's who sounded the all clear. He said Sedna was fine, he was in touch with her regularly, and there was no cause for worry. The police saw no reason to pursue the matter further, especially since Valerie had been running a high fever the night of Sedna's phone call and might have imagined it all.

"You see," Faye said, "that was just one of Sedna's more artful dramatic performances."

But Valerie wasn't so sure. Sedna had never mentioned a brother. She knew about Valerie's twin brothers, Kosta and James. So wouldn't she have said *something* about her own siblings at some point?

Valerie repressed the thought and faced her audience with a smile. Almost fifty people had come to the library in Gibsons for this event, and they were too important for her to appear preoccupied. She was there to drum up business, to advertise future tours. Valerie had observed that elderly people like to plan far in advance because anticipation of the tour gave them almost as much pleasure as the trip itself. Her customers read up on things and did their homework; many of them put together a booklet with pictures and facts beforehand. Valerie was always impressed.

She began her slide show with pictures of three Inuvialuit women who made up part of the Inuvik council of elders. She'd photographed the trio two years earlier. She knew their names and many members of their families and had listened to their stories while sharing sweet bannock and even sweeter tea with them.

Valerie showed slide after slide as she led her audience through the most important stages and high points of the Arctic tour: arrival in Whitehorse in the Yukon; travel by dogsled along the Takhini River; and on to the gold-miner town of Dawson City via the Alaska Highway. Sorry, no gambling in the casino, and no long-legged cancan dancers performing in Diamond Tooth Gertie's gambling den. It was too early in the season for all that. There was a trip instead to Rabbit Creek where gold had been discovered in 1896, touching off a great gold rush. A stop-off at a gold miner's tent. And then drinks that night in a historic brothel.

Laughter and murmuring interrupted her talk, as she'd expected. It had become a bit of a routine, a ritual she liked. She resumed her talk about the Dempster Highway, 460 miles of snowy, icy dirt road with breathtaking views of lakes, rivers, and mountains.

"And if we're lucky, which is often enough the case, we'll see wild animals—a few caribou, ptarmigan, moose, and maybe even a lynx."

At this point she always inserted the story of Jack Dempster, a member of the North-West Mounted Police in the Northwest Territories, who in 1911 led a rescue team out in the dead of winter to find a lost police patrol. The "Lost Patrol" was a name that went down in the history books: four bold policemen who delivered the mail by dogsled to isolated communities and kept watch over the people in these remote areas, thereby shoring up Canada's claim on Arctic territory. In 1910, the four had gotten lost in the Ogilvie Mountains—Valerie showed a slide of the area—and in March of the following year, Jack Dempster's team found them, all dead. Four had starved to death, and one had killed himself in despair. They were a mere thirty-five miles from the manned trading post of Fort McPherson, where their lives would have been saved. But the poor men didn't know it; they'd probably become completely disoriented.

"They were *so* close—what a tragedy!" Valerie exclaimed.

She found the story just as gripping every time, and nobody in the room had any idea why. At least that's what she thought. An elderly man put up his hand.

"Why is Jack Dempster celebrated as a hero? After all, he didn't save the five missing men. They were dead when he found them."

Valerie was briefly taken aback.

"You're right, he wasn't able to save them. But an attempted rescue in the Arctic winter—and a bad winter at that—is an act of heroism all the same. Dempster and his men could easily have died themselves. Don't forget how brutal the climate is there. I'm talking about snowstorms, icy cold, whiteouts, and possible injuries that couldn't be treated."

She stepped closer to the audience.

"If conditions are nasty enough, it's often impossible to find the bodies of the missing, so their relatives never find out what happened. So many men disappear on the ice without a trace, their fates forever unknown. Jack Dempster risked his life, and at least the policemen's families were spared the uncertainty of not knowing."

The man thanked her, and she proceeded to show pictures of the northern lights, which elicited oohs and ahs from the audience, then switched to pictures of the Muskrat Jamboree, the Inuvialuit spring festival. She showed the dogsled races and the snowmobile trip out onto the estuary of the Mackenzie, Canada's longest river. Then the exploration of a traditional Inuvialuit ice cellar, or ice house, below the permafrost, where families stored supplies, particularly beluga—the white whale—fish, seal, caribou, moose, and goose. And lastly the climax: the

Ice Road from Inuvik to Tuktoyaktuk, a village on the Beaufort Sea that the locals simply called "Tuk."

"The Ice Road runs for one hundred and fifteen miles and is the longest nonprivatized ice road in the world and the only one over fresh and salt water," Valerie said in conclusion.

When she turned on the lights, she saw amazement in the audience members' faces. The silent magic of the Arctic had seized many of them, and, as she knew full well, it would never let some of them go.

Answering the call of the Arctic never came cheaply; in fact, throughout history, many had paid with their lives. The Arctic had been a dream for her own mother, Mary-Ann Strong, and one day she didn't wake up from it. She pursued her dream even after her children were born, leaving them behind, but not the temptation of everlasting ice.

It cost her her life. How exactly was something that even Valerie didn't know.

She was invariably plied with questions after her presentation, or with tales of travels that she listened to attentively. A woman friend had confessed to her once that she simply could not deal with seniors. Valerie forgave her and resisted reminding her that she too would be old someday. Valerie had a soft spot for the elderly. While her parents were trekking around in the Arctic, she'd spent most of her childhood in her dear grandparents' care—until fate dealt her a cruel blow.

Valerie put away her laptop and the brochures. Eleven people had tentatively signed up for the Ice Road tour the following year. That was five more than she'd be leading in a few days. She left the library to find a gray-haired woman in a pale yellow raincoat waiting for her outside.

"I've always wanted to meet you," the woman said in a soft but confident voice.

Valerie wasn't surprised. There was almost always somebody who wanted to talk to her after the others had gone.

"I knew your mother quite well," the woman said.

Valerie looked at her, puzzled. Which mother? Her stepmother? Or her biological mother, Mary-Ann?

"She was a friend of my youth. We spent a lot of time together—those were lovely days. We went to Paris, to learn French."

A warm smile spread over the woman's face.

Paris. Mary-Ann Strong, Valerie's biological mother. Did the older woman know that she was dead?

"You've probably never heard of me. I'm Christine Preston."

"No," Valerie responded, tightening her grip on the handle of her small briefcase. "I can't say that I have."

"I live in Ontario. I'm visiting my daughter in Vancouver. I'm retired and spend my time traveling these days. And so I heard about your presentation. I thought to myself, Here's an opportunity to see Mary-Ann's daughter."

Valerie tucked away a loose strand from her ponytail.

"How . . . how did you find out I'm her daughter?"

She had always tried to hide her identity, to avoid being recognized as the daughter of her famous father. Peter Hurdy-Blaine was still a household name: he was once Canada's best hockey player. And his story was well known. Married a young beauty. Later, a failed Arctic explorer. A terrible human tragedy.

She couldn't listen to another word.

"Mary-Ann was an important part of my life, so naturally I was curious about what happened to her children," Christine answered.

This will never end, Valerie thought. People hunting down my brothers and me. Not because of who we are; it's always because of our parents.

Christine appeared to read something in Valerie's face.

"I won't keep you," she said. "But I would like to give you something. It might be of interest to you."

She pulled an envelope out of her handbag. Valerie accepted it without thinking.

"Should you wish to get in touch with me, my address is in there," she said kindly.

Valerie thanked her and struggled to find suitable words of goodbye, but Christine Preston had already turned around and begun walking away.

Valerie thought about telling her brother Kosta in Vancouver about the unexpected encounter. When she arrived home and shut the door behind her, she remembered that she hadn't turned on her cell phone after the presentation. She pulled it out and discovered a message waiting for her. Clem Hardeven.

She hung up her jacket and called him right away.

Her ears and eyes in Inuvik, Clem always knew what was going on. To be sure, she distrusted his attractive, roughneck charisma, which exuded a love of adventure—a mistrust that surely went back to her father. A man like Clem could be a woman's ruin. Alana Reevely had once told her at a boozy farewell party that white men in Inuvik came there to run away from something, were incapable of relationships, or didn't know what women need. And they were incorrigible machos. But Alana was obviously happy with Duncan, a musher, who seemed to be capable of handling a relationship. Valerie intended to worm more details out of Alana on that topic in two weeks.

For all her leeriness, Valerie had to admit that Clem was always supportive whenever something was troubling her and was friendly and reliable. And he also hadn't responded to Sedna's flirting last summer.

Clem's voice coming through her cell phone snapped her out of her thoughts. She was lucky to get him immediately, something that almost never happened. His cell had no reception on the Ice Road.

"I'm in the office because the Ice Road is closed," he explained.

Valerie knew that whiteouts and blizzards repeatedly made temporary road closures necessary. Nevertheless she was surprised because she'd read on the Internet that the forecast for Inuvik was favorable. The undertone in Clem's voice made her suspicious.

"Is something the matter?"

"Don't tell anybody you got this from me. A person was found dead on the Ice Road. Frozen to death."

Her heart skipped a beat.

"Who? What happened?"

"The police aren't releasing any information, but word is, it's a young woman."

"Was she found in a car?"

"No, she was lying on the ice."

"Oh my God! Was she run over?"

"It's not official, but according to the grapevine, she seemed unharmed. Might have frozen to death. Please, Val, this is all confidential, OK?"

"Yes, you can count on me. My lips are sealed. But . . . is there any danger? Should I watch out?"

"You *know* we're all dangerous up here. Don't forget your shooting iron."

When she didn't respond immediately, he continued, "My little joke; I didn't mean it seriously."

She hoped he didn't hear her deep breathing.

"Tell me—the woman . . . Is she a local or a stranger?"

"A white woman. Apparently very young. Dark hair. That's all I know."

Sedna was not very young, and her hair was strikingly colored. Still, Valerie had to let Clem know about the recent call.

"Sedna phoned me a few days ago. Just a short call. We lost the connection after a couple of sentences. She told me she needed help because somebody was trying to kill her."

There was a pause at the other end. Valerie could visualize Clem sitting at his desk, which was much too low for his six-foot-two frame—a desk covered with papers and all kinds of tools. She envisioned his attractive face, with its eagle eyes and long, straight nose, his expression showing total concentration (she liked that look more than she wanted to) on what she was confiding to him. After Sedna's futile, seductive dance around Clem, she had declared him "arrogant" and "humorless." But Valerie knew Sedna was dead wrong.

"Might you perhaps entertain the idea that he could have a girl-friend?" she asked Sedna at the time.

"Might you perhaps entertain the idea that he could be a homo-sexual?" Sedna countered, mimicking Valerie's tone of voice.

As far as their new friendship was concerned, that trip had been an absolute flop.

"Where was she calling from?" Valerie heard Clem ask.

"That's just it. I haven't a clue. She disappeared from here about five months ago."

"And nobody knows anything? She didn't tell anybody where she was going?"

"Not that I know of. I haven't been in touch with her since last fall. I was annoyed because of . . . something she . . . Oh, that's neither here nor there. But she'd told me before that she felt like spending a couple of months in a gold-miner's camp. She'd apparently met somebody, a man who persuaded her to do it. Maybe somebody in Dawson City."

"I haven't heard a word about her," Clem added in his matter-of-fact way. "And you can bet I would have if she'd been in the area."

"I called the police, but her brother apparently told them he was in touch with her and that she was fine."

Clem cleared his throat.

"Got a call on the other line. We'll talk for sure before you leave. So long."

She held her phone in her hand and stared out the large living room window. A gentle breeze was stirring in the branches of the mighty yel-low cedars. A hummingbird sipped sugar water from the feeder she'd put out on the patio. Spring had come to the Sunshine Coast a good while ago. The fresh grass shimmered, a lush green. Contrast that with Inuvik, where they had to expect fifteen to twenty-five degrees below zero.

What could have happened to that young woman on the Ice Road? Should Valerie inform her tour group about the incident? What should she tell them? Clem seemed irritated that he hadn't been better informed about it. She could empathize: the Ice Road was his turf, and he felt responsible for it. She was glad he'd confided in her. It would have been distressing if a participant in the upcoming tour had blind-sided her with the news.

She discovered another message on her phone's display.

Oh, no, she thought, not this too!

She listened to the message from the tour-bus driver she'd hired for the upcoming trip. When she'd finished, the doorbell rang. It was Faye. They'd arranged to go for a walk in Cliff Gilker Park.

"You look worried," Faye said. "Aren't you glad you don't have to worry about Sedna anymore?"

Valerie sighed.

"I'm still looking for a tour-bus driver because my first guy broke his arm. Now the next one has just canceled. If that's not Murphy's Law, what is? Now I've got exactly one week to find somebody."

"Good grief! What lousy luck! Come on, get your running shoes and we'll go get some fresh air. I've got something to tell you."

Fifteen minutes later they turned onto a path in the woods that led over roots that looked like huge blood vessels. They ignored the WARNING: BEAR SIGHTINGS! sign. The air smelled of damp moss and rotting cedars. Loud squirrel calls trilled through the silence.

Out of the blue Faye said, "Sedna cleaned out my bank account."

CHAPTER 7

Valerie stopped in amazement.

"*What* did she do?"

Faye kept running, and Valerie stumbled along behind her.

"I never told you, but she wanted to help me renovate my place."

"Sedna? Why Sedna?"

"She'd helped Emily renovate. Emily Sears. You know her. Sedna did good work, so Emily recommended her."

"*You* are the craftswoman, not her."

"Yes, but Sedna has an eye for design. That's different from the actual renovation work. What Sedna did at Emily's place looks fabulous."

"Really? I didn't know she could do that. She told me she was a private eye once."

Faye gave a dry laugh. She was wearing a colorful scarf on her head and looked like an Abyssinian princess. A princess in running shoes.

"I'd say she was pulling your leg. But the laugh's *really* on me because she fleeced me, damn well fleeced me."

"How so? How'd it happen?"

Faye lowered her eyes and stopped, then scraped her shoes on the soft forest floor.

"She said she could get a special price for the parquet flooring and tiles and all the stuff I needed for the new kitchen. And everything for the new bathroom. Said she had good connections to wholesalers and got discounts. And it was all true—Emily confirmed it. Sedna wanted me to put money into an account that we both had access to."

Valerie half suspected what was coming next.

"But you surely didn't do that, or did you?"

"I did."

They'd come to the bridge over the waterfall.

"How much?"

"Twenty-five thousand."

Valerie's jaw dropped.

"You're kidding, right?"

Faye shook her head sorrowfully.

"Now the account's empty, and Sedna's gone. And we haven't even started renovating."

Valerie stared at the flowing water foaming up as it skimmed over a rocky ledge.

"Did you go to the police?"

Faye made a face. Valerie had never seen her so ashamed.

"No, of course not, because—look, I gave her access to my account, voluntarily."

"That's a pile of money! Did you sign a contract?"

Faye's contrite expression delivered the answer.

They leaned over the railing as the water roared beneath them.

"I suppose," Faye said, "it was an act of desperation. She . . . she simply borrowed it. She must have needed it very badly."

Valerie slowly shook her head and said nothing. So Faye talked instead.

"I believe Sedna's somewhere around Inuvik. She often talked about Inuvik after your tour."

"What did she say?"

"That she liked it up there, the wild-country atmosphere . . . the people. Nothing specific."

Valerie started walking. She could have told Faye about her conversation with Clem, that he hadn't heard anything about Sedna, but something held her back.

Faye suddenly asked, "Can I go on your tour? Maybe I can find Sedna."

"Faye, look . . . you've just . . ." Valerie groped for diplomatic words. "I mean, the trip's expensive and . . . and you . . . you're short twenty-five thousand dollars."

"Take me along as a driver. I have a license and bus-driver's license."

Valerie didn't know how to respond. It sounded like an unexpected solution to an urgent problem. But after her experience with Sedna, she'd sworn to never again take a friend on the tour.

Holy shit! Twenty-five grand.

Faye was otherwise so reasonable and thrifty. Valerie couldn't understand it. Maybe this odd story had sides to it that her neighbor wasn't telling her about.

"You don't have to pay me," Faye offered. "I only want a separate room. So that we don't get in each other's hair."

Valerie had to laugh in spite of herself.

"I'll think about it," she said.

They quietly turned around to go back.

When they got to the car, Valerie said, "You might be sorry if you go with me. Just look at how it turned out with Sedna. I'm not good with friendships and relationships in general. I cheated on my husband even though he was faithful to me."

Faye threw up her hands in feigned despair.

"Can we drop this self-pitying, oh-I'm-such-an-awful-person farce? We . . . we'll get along no matter what, because your customers will be with us. And I promise not to skip out on you."

As Valerie was having her yogurt in the kitchen afterward, she noticed Christine's white envelope on the table. At first she just left it there and wandered idly through the house, taking the garbage to the garage and bundling up old newspapers, before picking it up and carrying it to the living room, where she settled down on the sofa. She heard a noise on the patio. Probably raccoons. Ignoring it, she stretched her back and opened Christine Preston's little gift.

Christine's name and address were indeed on a little card attached to a thin plastic file folder. Valerie opened the file and thumbed through photocopies of pages that appeared to be from history books, descriptions of Inuvik and the story of the Dempster Highway. Did the Lady in Yellow—as Valerie secretly called her—think that she didn't own these books herself or hadn't read these stories? Then a newspaper clipping caught her attention. It included a photograph of her mother that Valerie had never seen before. It had been taken before her marriage. The caption read, "Mary-Ann Strong as a Student in Paris."

Had Christine provided the newspaper with that picture? Another photograph showed her parents before leaving for the famous Dempster Memorial Trek, as the photo caption said. Their faces could just be made out beneath their fur-trimmed hoods. A third picture showed a native boy beside a tent: "Siqiniq Anaqiina, the Boy Guide for Peter Hurdy-Blaine."

What? Nobody had ever mentioned a boy. She thought her parents had gone all by themselves on their famous trek to trace the trail of Jack Dempster's rescue party.

She felt butterflies in her stomach.

So in that case, maybe there was a witness, still living, to her mother's mysterious death. The boy in the picture looked about fourteen years old.

Her father had never, not one single time, spoken to his children about the tragic event. "He's too upset to talk about it," was the standard explanation she heard from her grandparents and other relatives. She'd gotten the same response from Bella Wakefield, her stepmother, later on. Peter Hurdy-Blaine had married Bella two years after returning from that fateful trip to the Arctic. The Arctic he'd thought was a paradise had turned into his very personal hell.

Valerie only knew that thirty years ago her parents had set out on that fateful snowmobile trip. Several days after they left, Mary-Ann Strong was killed by a bullet. The exact details of what had happened were never made public. Valerie was still unclear as to who had ordered the matter kept under wraps.

She and her brothers had never undertaken extensive research on the matter: the unwritten law in the family was to let sleeping dogs lie. But the twins agreed with Valerie's suspicion that it might have been suicide. And now, the news that an Inuvialuit boy had accompanied their parents was weakening Valerie's inclination to bury her head in the sand over this question.

Where was Siqiniq Anaqiina from? Was he still alive? And why didn't he appear in other reports at the time? The name of the paper had been cut from Christine's copy. Valerie had the impression it was some minor local rag. How did Christine come by this article? And why, given all the news coverage back then, did she want Valerie to see this particular article?

Valerie couldn't ask her father anymore. He'd died from a lethal virus in West Africa fourteen years after her mother's death. The Arctic didn't kill him, but a vacation in the savanna heat did. And she couldn't ask Bella—Valerie called her "Mama"—because Alzheimer's had robbed her of her memory. One day, a neighbor had called to tell them that Bella couldn't find her way home. A few weeks later, Bella confided that she couldn't recognize numbers anymore. After numbers, it was letters that became an unsolvable riddle. And then she lost her sense of time. Instead of reading, now she listened to the radio. But before her illness, Bella had read at least two books a week. She tried audiobooks but was soon unable to understand them. Valerie and her brothers were shocked and in denial at first. Thankfully, Bella still had enough of her wits about her to sign herself into a nursing home. That's the way she'd always been—practical. And determined to do what was best for the children who weren't her own.

That seemed the natural thing for Bella to do. She loved Peter Hurdy-Blaine and therefor his children. Valerie and the twins reciprocated without reservation.

Valerie had tried to ask Bella some questions the last time she'd seen her. For instance, where could she find her father's missing diary? But Bella had just smiled at her. And time and again, she'd shout out the word *waterfall*. First softly, then more and more urgently. Valerie couldn't make heads or tails of it. When she saw that her questioning was upsetting Bella, she took her in her arms and rocked her like a baby, telling her, "It's all right, it's all right."

Valerie closed her eyes. Her stepmother's gradual retreat into an inexplicable, dark world pained her. A second mother gone out of her life. Should she tell Kosta and James about Christine Preston? And about the existence of a possible witness to their mother's death?

She suddenly felt tired and hungry. She nestled down on the sofa cushions. Time for the TV evening news.

A report about the young woman in Inuvik followed a story about a terrorist attack and another on a disastrous avalanche in the Rockies. An excerpt from a press conference in Inuvik made her ears prick up. The dead woman on the Ice Road had been identified as twenty-one-year-old Gisèle Chaume from a small town in Quebec. Her body had been found by a truck driver not far from a pickup that Helvin West, the manager of Suntuk Logistics, had reported stolen.

Cause of death was still to be determined, the newscaster said. The police were treating the situation as "suspicious," he said. A special investigator had been called in from Yellowknife.

The place where the body had been found was shown. And then— Clem Hardeven.

Valerie gave a start. Clem was standing somewhere on the Ice Road, looking concerned. He was expressing his sympathy for the young woman's parents and saying he hoped the case would be cleared up quickly.

"We're doing everything to ensure safety on the Ice Road," he stated. "It's a mystery how something like this could happen. This young woman's death has profoundly shaken the citizens of Inuvik and Tuktoyaktuk."

With that, the report was over.

Valerie turned off the sound. It had grown dark outside.

Cause of death unknown. Suspicious circumstances. Special investigator.

That certainly sounded like . . . murder.

CHAPTER 8

The polar bear was emaciated; it moved ponderously and slowly. It squatted before a large breathing hole in the ice where the two hunters had seen seals surface just a few minutes before. Nuyaviaq Marten wasn't after *natchiq*; he delegated seal hunting to his sons. This man from Tuktoyaktuk was the most successful polar-bear hunter in the region—a reputation that filled him with pride. He'd killed his first *nanuq* when he was thirteen. His father had taken him out on the ice and taught him how to detect the tracks of the powerful predator. They were out on the frozen Beaufort Sea for four days, then moved westward, at first on snowmobiles, then on foot. His father not only showed him how to find *nanuq* tracks; he also taught him patience. "*Nanuq* has sharp teeth and claws, but we have patience"—that's what his father had drummed into him.

His cousin who was with him today, Henry Itagiaq, was short on patience. Instead, he had a fever—burning buck fever, the nervous excitement that novice hunters feel when they're close to game. Nuyaviaq could nearly smell it. They lay on their stomachs on the ice and observed the bear through binoculars. It was just over a hundred yards away, upwind so it couldn't pick up their scent. Henry tried to crawl closer on his stomach, like a seal. Nuyaviaq held him back with a hand signal. He knew when the right moment would come. He just knew.

He noticed something else. *Nanuq* was nervous. Distracted. Did the bear suspect that hunters were on his tail? Nuyaviaq watched the yellowish giant, fascinated. Why didn't it seize one of the seals that periodically popped their heads out of the hole? *Nanuq* must be very hungry. Its flanks were hollowed out in spite of the abundance of seals that winter. Its coat was shaggy and dull. Nuyaviaq knew he wouldn't get a good price for it. It pained him to see *nanuq* in such a state.

All of a sudden the bear sprang to its feet. Something had frightened it. Then it began to run in the direction of the hunters. Nuyaviaq murmured, "Stay down 'til I—"

Too late. Henry was already up on his feet. Nuyaviaq had no choice but to jump up himself. They stood stock-still, rifles at the ready. The bear turned to the right and ran faster. "Shit!" Nuyaviaq said to himself. Then, suddenly, a cracking sound came from the ice.

Boom! An earsplitting bang!

They instinctively threw themselves down on the hard ice as the echo from the blast sped through the air like flickering northern lights. The ice quaked.

And then silence.

Henry spoke first.

"What the hell . . . !"

Nuyaviaq cautiously raised himself to a kneeling position and looked around. At first he couldn't see anything. He scanned the horizon through binoculars.

"Over there!" he shouted. "Smoke!"

A distant, dark, giant cloud of smoke billowed up to the sky. A strange odor hit their nose. Henry grabbed his binoculars.

"What the hell . . . !" he repeated.

When he realized that something had happened that deserved more than mere curiosity, he shouldered his weapon.

"Run!" he exclaimed.

They sprinted back to their snowmobiles as fast as they could.

From a distance they could see a gray veil hanging in the air over the ice for a long time. And a distant yellowish dot.

Nanuq was fleeing, just like its hunters.

It took them over two hours to reach Tuktoyaktuk, where they headed directly for the shed with a green metal roof. A light was on in the little window. Nuyaviaq turned off his motor and bounded up the steps. Inside the office, a squat man who was on the phone—an Inuvialuk like himself—looked up in surprise. Roy Stevens, the man behind the desk, could tell from Nuyaviaq's excitement that all hell had broken loose somewhere. Stevens was a ranger stationed in Tuktoyaktuk, a member of the Canadian army volunteers, a troop formed primarily from the indigenous population and charged with patrolling remote stretches of the Arctic.

Nuyaviaq gave the ranger an unambiguous hand signal, and Stevens abruptly ended the call.

"There was an explosion," Nuyaviaq said. "Out on the ice."

Nuyaviaq spoke with a quick urgency that was entirely uncharacteristic. Being an Inuvialuk, he always gave his words just the weight that was necessary.

"A huge explosion about two hours to the northwest," he added. "Enormous."

Henry Itagiaq had come in as well and nodded vigorously in agreement.

"And then we saw black smoke like an enormous cloud. Gigantic."

Stevens blinked at the two men. His brain was still processing the news. But his body reacted faster: his insides were already knotted up.

"Who was with you?" he asked.

"Just us two."

Stevens couldn't overlook the fact that the hunters were shaken. And normally it wasn't easy to see that an Inuvialuk was scared. He himself was an Inuvialuk but with a bit more ambition flowing through his veins. And when the Canadian government was looking for people to serve as scouts and watchdogs in the Arctic, he seized the opportunity. Inuit and Inuvialuit rangers had skills that normal soldiers could only acquire with enormous effort. It took an experienced man of the Arctic like Stevens to find his way around in the emptiness of that frozen universe, to survive the brutal cold and the endless darkness in winter, and to avoid the permanent threat of death by starvation and thirst.

Stevens picked up a pen and a printed form.

"I'll make an official report, OK? Like some tea?"

The men looked at him. They made no move to sit. He poured three cups of tea, adding sugar and condensed milk. Then he started to piece together the puzzle of their story. As the ranger diligently wrote down all the details, he gradually became convinced that Nuyaviaq Marten and Henry Itagiaq hadn't simply been fooled by a polar fata morgana, an Arctic mirage. What they'd seen and heard was real. A gigantic explosion.

Roy Stevens tried with all his might not to think about what that could mean.

CHAPTER 9

Clem Hardeven slammed down the tailgate. Lazarusie Uvvayuaq's snowmobile was tied down in the truck bed. Meteor ran around inside the back of Clem's four-door cab from one window to the other in anticipation, sticking his moist nose in the back of Lazarusie's neck, who was in the passenger seat. The Ice Road had been reopened, and Clem wanted to drive to Tuktoyaktuk as quickly as possible.

He drove down to the frozen Mackenzie. A transparent white veil hung over the blue sky, thin as tissue paper. As soon as it dissipated, the sun would shine on the ice unobstructed.

They drove past tugboats that had been pulled up on the bank at the beginning of winter. On a hundred-foot-long barge, a two-story, boxlike structure with little windows was waiting for the ice to melt. Floating accommodations. It was the least expensive way to create temporary dwellings in a permafrost area. Soon after the huge white storage tanks, the Northwest Territories government road sign appeared on the right, clearly indicating that this was not a private road. What a joke, Clem thought. Of course the Ice Road was administered by the government, but it was Helvin West who really controlled it. He made the rules, and Clem ensured that everyone obeyed them.

Shortly afterward they passed the place where the young woman from Quebec had been found dead. A band of black-and-yellow police tape snaked its way along the side of the road.

"Would you like to get out and show me where she was lying, exactly?" Clem asked his passenger.

Lazarusie shook his head. He was anything but talkative today, unusually so. Clem had to admit that he didn't feel like chatting either. His thoughts were on Valerie. She was sure to have heard the official statement from the Royal Canadian Mounted Police last evening. He'd expected to find out more from the police but was disappointed. He hoped for Valerie's sake that customers wouldn't jump ship at the last minute because of this unfortunate business. Or even worse: that she'd have to cancel the tour altogether. That was the last thing he wanted.

When he talked to her, he was always listening carefully for something in her voice that would tell him if she knew about his one-night stand with Sedna. He'd slept with her the previous summer, but he couldn't tell Valerie that.

A big-city woman from Vancouver wouldn't understand a man's situation in a small community in the Arctic north. In an isolated settlement, with dozens of other single, sexually starved men and only a limited choice of potential bed partners. Not many urban women would want to live in a place like Inuvik where, for example, they couldn't sit on a sunny patio in front of a restaurant or trendy café and people-watch. His most recent girlfriend, a hospital speech therapist and a great animal lover, had said farewell to Inuvik because she could no longer stand the sight of sled dogs tied up on very short leashes day and night in thirty-below weather. Other women who found a job in Inuvik yearned for the fresh fruits and vegetables they were used to finding in other places—bananas that didn't arrive all brown off the delivery truck, for example—or summers without the terror of swarms of mosquitoes. They missed bookstores, fitness centers, the prospect of professional advancement. Joan, a woman from Toronto who'd shacked up for a while with the newly divorced Poppy Dixon, couldn't stand looking like a fat sausage in her down-filled winter jacket and pants. It certainly was easier for women to look sexy by shedding their outdoor clothing, the way Sedna did when she undressed in order to seduce Clem. Of course, she was furious with him the next day, when he went for a spin in a helicopter to see the musk ox on Banks Island—with Valerie, not her.

Not that he had great hopes for Valerie. When she was in town with her tours, she was all business. He'd watched her again and again, in the Crazy Hunter or the Great Polar bar, how she deflected in no uncertain terms any men attempting to hit on her. So no hunting ground there for him; rejection was the last thing he needed. All the same, he liked her.

A snowplow drew near. Clem waved to the driver, an employee of Suntuk Logistics. There wasn't much snow on the Ice Road; it looked like a hockey rink. Considering the possible dangers, the road's reputation was excellent, and he was proud of it.

Patches of blue opened up in the sky, and the sun broke through, making the ice sparkle. Clem put on sunglasses. Lazarusie trained the binoculars he always carried with him on the low white hills beyond the delta, where windswept, bony fir trees stuck out like the stubble of a beard.

"Lynx," he reported.

Clem had never been under the illusion that he'd ever fully understand the Inuvialuit and their culture. Even after seven years among them, he was puzzled by many of their ways. Lazarusie sometimes spent a couple of nights at Clem's place, often with his wife, to get away from the escapades of their untamed, adopted daughter, Tanya. Inuvialuit parents didn't punish or discipline their kids; they simply led by example instead. That was how they'd raised their families since time immemorial.

But at some point the modern world had descended upon the Inuvialuit, and everything had changed. Young people were caught between their ancestors' traditions and way of life, and the lifestyles of the *tanngit*, white people. They started paying little attention to their parents. Lazarusie told him that he'd named his eldest son after his dear grandfather. Inuvialuit believed that this was how a forefather would become a human being again, that his soul would live on in the child. It made perfect sense to Clem that you really couldn't punish or reprimand a beloved grandfather. Nevertheless, he couldn't help thinking that Tanya deserved a tough lesson in how to behave. Lazarusie had adopted her from relatives who had too many children. It came to light later that she had come into the world with brain damage resulting from her parents' alcohol addiction. Fetal alcohol syndrome. One of the many human tragedies in the Arctic, Clem thought.

Pingos loomed on the horizon of the flat tundra—huge, fantastic hills with a core of ice and a skin of earth. Tourists loved them. The government in Ottawa had given eight of them national landmark protection. Still three miles to Tuktoyaktuk. Two snowmobiles came toward them.

"I must talk to these men," Lazarusie said.

Clem stopped the truck and Laz got out.

The men appeared to be Inuvialuit from Tuktoyaktuk. Clem saw Lazarusie gesticulating. The racket from the snowmobiles prevented him from listening in, but the discussion looked like a lively one. The two men laughed, but that didn't mean much. Inuvialuit often softened bad news with humor.

"What's up?" Clem asked Lazarusie when he'd settled back in beside him.

"They saw a gigantic explosion out on the ice."

"Who are they?"

"Nuyaviaq Marten and Henry."

"Henry Itagiaq?"

"Mm-hm."

Clem waited. They could already make out the houses of Tuktoyaktuk, modest dwellings epitomizing human steadfastness surrounded by the infinite polar ocean.

"They were polar-bear hunting. The explosion came right out of the ice."

Clem frowned.

"What do you mean, it 'came right out of the ice'?"

"It broke through the ice, and a lot of smoke went up into the sky."

"Where was this?"

"About two, three hours northeast of Tuk."

Clem thought for a moment.

"There's no gas drilling up there."

"No."

"When did it happen?"

"Day before yesterday. And Ilaryuaq and Brad went out by snowmobile and found a huge hole in the ice, like a small lake."

Yet another incident that was slow to reach his ears, Clem thought.

"That's impossible! Are you sure this isn't one of Henry's crazy stories, Laz?"

No answer. Clem threw Lazarusie a sideways glance and noticed the worry in his face.

"It was a huge explosion, they said. Like a super bomb."

Clem knew what he had to do. He drove to the ranger station at the entrance to Tuktoyaktuk. Roy Stevens was just coming out the door in a heavy red parka. Clem skipped the formalities and wasted no time.

"Roy, what the hell's going on? I just heard about an explosion out on the ice."

The ranger seemed to be in a hurry.

"Can't tell you anything, pal. My boss is on it. You know how it is with rumors like that."

Stevens climbed onto his snowmobile. Clem stood in front of it, blocking the ranger's path.

"When something like that happens, we've got to know about it."

"We" meant Helvin West, of course; Helvin counted on Clem to report to him everything he ought to know. Stevens understood very well what Clem meant. He revved up the motor.

"Helvin shouldn't give it another thought. He's bound to have other problems."

Stevens's machine slid back a bit and turned a corner. Clem swore silently. He wouldn't let himself be blown off so easily. He knew exactly what he had to do when he got back to Inuvik.

Lazarusie helped Clem unload the snowmobile. Before Clem drove away, Laz handed him something.

"I picked this up. It was lying beside the dead woman. You can do what you want with it."

Clem stared at the object. A shaman's rattle.

It dawned on him now why Lazarusie hadn't wanted to get out of the truck at the spot where the body was found.

Because of Danny, his son, the future shaman.

CHAPTER 10

The ferry from Langdale to Horseshoe Bay was a third of the way through the forty-minute trip when Faye brought Valerie a cup of hot coffee to haul her out of her brooding funk.

"I think this will do you some good," she said, sitting down beside her.

Valerie thanked her apathetically. She couldn't get the images she'd seen on TV out of her head. They showed Gisèle Chaume, the young woman from Quebec, laughing heartily with her girlfriends, posing with her parents, visiting Mexico, and riding horseback. The last shot showed her dancing the cancan onstage in Diamond Tooth Gertie's gambling hall in Dawson City. The performance, as the reporter commented, was a favorite with the tourists. Another young woman from Quebec recounted how adventurous Gisèle was, how much she loved the North, which is why she stayed in Dawson City over the winter instead of leaving in the fall as so many people did.

Gisèle's friend cried on camera as she said, "She dreamed of opening a café and a bed-and-breakfast and covering the walls with artwork."

The cause of her death was still unknown. Evidently, the investigators hadn't made much progress.

The segment had ended with the mayor of Inuvik, Marjorie Tama, reading a statement:

"Our sympathy goes out to Gisèle Chaume's family. The death of this young, vivacious woman, who came to our community to make her way in life, fills us all with great sorrow. We will continue to do all we can to keep Inuvik a place where children and adults can feel safe."

Valerie knew Marjorie Tama. They'd become friends over the four years she'd been traveling to Inuvik. Marjorie was an Inuvialuk who championed aboriginal traditions and her people's status. She was a driving force in seeing that the Inuvialuit were awarded rights to their land and more self-government. On top of that, Marjorie helped create a modern economic basis for the inhabitants of the Mackenzie Delta. Valerie admired Marjorie, her energy and competence. She told her as much once and received a surprising response: "Yes, you and me are absolutely alike in that regard."

Marjorie hadn't sounded quite like herself on TV. Valerie was used to seeing her act so much more spontaneous, authentic, and riveting. She'd have liked to talk to Marjorie about Gisèle but felt the time wasn't right. The mayor surely had enough on her plate right now.

Valerie felt the warm coffee hit her stomach. Faye commented on the houses dotting the small islands they were passing. Then she asked Valerie, a propos of nothing, "Why did you give up journalism?"

Valerie almost spilled her drink.

"Who told you that?"

"Sedna."

Sedna. Not again.

"When did she tell you that?"

"Last year. Just before a meeting of our Toastmasters group."

How did Sedna know so much about her former life?

Valerie had published her articles under her married name, Shearer. Did Sedna weasel this fact out of her ex at lunch at Cardero's? She couldn't really imagine that. Matt was discreet and not so easily tricked.

Valerie had reverted to her maiden name after the divorce—at least to one half of it. Because the name Hurdy-Blaine was still too recognizable.

"So is it true?" Faye pressed her.

"Yes, but not everyone has to know."

Valerie realized her voice was edgy. Faye smoothed out the wrinkles in the multicolored wool skirt she was wearing over black leggings and looked at her quizzically. Valerie found herself wondering if Faye had packed all the warm clothes she'd recommended for their Arctic tour—especially the snow boots she'd loaned her.

"Sorry, I didn't mean to hit a sore spot," Faye said.

Valerie flapped a hand around in the air as if shooing away an invisible fly.

"No problem. It's just . . . it turned out to be unpleasant in the end."

"I can believe it. A friend of mine works for the *West Coast Herald*, and she expects to be laid off at any moment. Newspapers are a tough business. It's hard to make a profit."

"I wasn't fired, I quit. And it wasn't here but in Ontario."

"A major newspaper?"

"Yep."

Even after all these years, it was difficult to talk about it. Valerie had been a respected journalist with a very promising career ahead of her. Any number of doors seemed open to her back then. At least that was what she supposed. She dreamed of being assigned a post as a foreign correspondent in Africa. After journalism school, she'd worked for a nonprofit in Senegal. Then she and Matt had toured half the continent on motorcycle. So when the paper's correspondent in Marrakesh was nearing retirement, she applied for the position. Her editor-in-chief led her to believe that her odds were good. When he suggested that she organize a tour to Rwanda as a service for their readers, Valerie eagerly got on board. Most of her working hours became devoted to preparing for the tour. The tour was a hit, and her editor soon offered her the chance to arrange additional tours to South Africa and Namibia. Before she knew it, she'd become less of a journalist and more of a tour guide.

Valerie took four groups to the continent during her final year with the paper, all while still waiting for the Marrakesh appointment. Then one day her editor called her up and broke the news: their publisher had decided to cover Africa from their office in Spain. Cost cutting.

"Are you kidding me?" Valerie shouted.

Fifty-four countries and one measly foreign correspondent who didn't even live on the continent.

Valerie thought about staying in Africa as a freelancer. But in view of the shaky economics of the newspaper business, she couldn't make up her mind. Some weeks afterward she discovered that a correspondent would be working out of Africa after all. Somebody else, not Valerie. The paper planned to share the guy with several other media outlets. The editor wanted to keep Valerie on as a tour guide, so he made her an offer: 50 percent tours, 50 percent journalism. That was the straw that broke the camel's back.

Along with her shattered African dream, Valerie felt her marriage beginning to crumble.

She started mulling over her career and her life. The newspaper world increasingly seemed to be a dead end. Firings, crushing pressures in the office, less and less research funding, one budget cut after another. What hope was there for the future? At the age of thirty, she was going through a severe midlife crisis. Then it occurred to her: instead of guiding tours for the paper, why not work for herself?

In the end she decided to leave the newspaper industry *and* her husband. Soon after that she separated from Matt and moved to Gibsons.

"How bizarre," she confessed to Faye. "I wanted to be an African correspondent, and now I'm going to the Arctic."

Faye stretched her long, strong legs.

"Maybe that reporter's nose of yours could sniff out more about Sedna."

Valerie didn't reply.

Maybe you could employ your journalistic skills to find out more about your mother's life and death.

"Just a thought," Faye muttered in response to her silence.

"You mean I could sniff out your money?" Valerie's tone of voice was deliberately cheerful.

Faye laughed.

"Yes, you'll be my treasure hunter, and I'll be your driver."

Valerie's cell phone played its usual tune. A text message from Glenn Bliss, a tour member. It was the first reaction to her e-mail informing people on the upcoming Ice Road tour about Gisèle Chaume's death.

She read the message: "Saw it on TV. Murder in the northern wilds. Can't wait to go there!"

CHAPTER 11

Kosta was waiting at the Horseshoe Bay ferry terminal.

"Your brother's really good-looking," Faye whispered as they followed him to the parking lot. Kosta walked at a quick pace; he wanted to beat the Vancouver rush hour traffic.

Valerie smiled.

"He's got a clone, an identical twin. But they're both married."

Faye smiled back.

"They all are at that age."

Except divorcés like Matt, Valerie thought. Maybe he'd never want to remarry, thanks to his first, unfaithful wife.

In the car Kosta immediately inquired about the dead woman in Inuvik. They then talked about Valerie's upcoming tour until they let Faye off at the subway station; she wanted to see friends in the East End.

Valerie was glad to have some time alone with Kosta. She was closer to him than to James, for the simple reason that she saw him more often. James was a multimedia artist in Montreal. She hadn't been very close to either as a child, because she was born six years after them and always felt like a fifth wheel.

Kosta was a lawyer and took care of their parents' estate—or, to be more precise, their father's estate. That was fine by Valerie because it was hard enough to live with her father's memory.

She told Kosta at once about meeting their mother's girlhood friend, Christine Preston. She brought up the article Christine had given her and the surprising information in it about an Inuvialuit boy. She could see this aroused Kosta's interest.

"Did you bring the article with you?"

"Yes, it's in my luggage."

He navigated his SUV through downtown Vancouver, where people rushing along the streets ducked their heads and turned up their collars because of the drizzle. Valerie was happy to be escaping the rain for the next ten days.

She studied Kosta's profile. Faye was right. Kosta was good-looking, in a classical, clean-cut way. Not physically robust and at times intentionally disheveled like their father, who had loved to style himself as a fearless adventurer. When she was a teenager, she'd asked him why Kosta had a Greek name.

"That was your mother's idea," he answered. "She sometimes liked exotic things like that. And because they were twins, I let her do as she pleased."

Let her do as she pleased. Valerie wondered at times whether there were other reasons besides the Arctic tragedy for her father almost never mentioning a word about his first wife.

Kosta was still going on about the boy in the article.

"You've got to wonder sometimes why so much misinformation makes it into the newspaper."

"You're telling *that* to a former journalist?"

"Why not? You should know it better than the uninitiated."

Kosta smiled, but he wasn't teasing her. He was serious. In fact, he usually was. Like their father. Their stepmother, Bella, on the other hand, had a ready wit. She could be hilarious at times. But Alzheimer's had stolen her sense of humor. Valerie felt a stabbing pain in her heart. She intended to visit their stepmom right after coming back from Inuvik and the Northwest Territories.

"So you never heard anything about a boy who went with them?"

"No," was all he said.

She knew why he was being tight-lipped. The two of them could never agree on whether they should or shouldn't root around in the past and dig up more facts. If they did, whatever they learned wouldn't remain in the family for very long. The media would be all over them. It was Peter Hurdy-Blaine's express wish to leave the events be. For their mother's sake, he'd told the children. And for his sake too. They never said it, but as the three of them grew older, one word hung in the air, invisible and omnipresent: *suicide*.

Even after their father's death, they couldn't ignore his wish. It was *his* trauma. They still had to respect his feelings. Mary-Ann Strong's death had always been taboo. Their father had never offered the merest details. The urn with her ashes was put in a marble columbarium in Vancouver's largest cemetery. That was not a good way to get over a major disaster. While their father was still alive, it was clear to Valerie and her brothers that any questions about Mary-Ann—especially concerning her death—were not welcome. He wanted to forget—her pain, his pain, the terrible events that had rolled over them like an avalanche of ice. *He* had escaped, but not his young wife. He must have felt guilty about it. Valerie was able to understand that better later on.

"I don't think that boy existed," Kosta declared. That sounds pretty illogical for a lawyer, she thought, biting her tongue.

They crossed the Granville Bridge over False Creek inlet.

Even in the rain, Valerie was enchanted by the view of glassy apartment buildings and the boats in the harbor. She had a sudden urge for an apple focaccia from the public market on Granville Island. But they were on their way to the chic Dunbar area where Kosta and his wife had bought a house twelve years earlier. Clever move. Even a very busy lawyer could hardly afford a nice house there today.

"Who is Christine Preston anyway? Why would she appear out of the blue and confront you with a thing like that?"

Kosta sounded almost angry, which baffled Valerie.

"It wasn't a confrontation. She was very friendly and . . . I think she'd come across my presentation and just wanted to meet her best childhood friend's daughter."

"Her best childhood friend? Why haven't we heard anything about her before?"

Again, she noted his lack of logic.

"Because this sort of thing was never discussed in our family, as you very well know. We really know precious little about our mother."

He didn't answer right away. A heavy rain was now beating against the windshield; the wipers were working nonstop.

"Why? Have you ever wanted to know more?"

She wanted to say, Not for a long time, but I think I do now.

Kosta continued.

"You know, it's interesting that time and again you take tour after tour to an area that isn't all that far from where it happened."

She looked at him in surprise. She was going to Inuvik for the fifth time, and he'd never broached the subject until now.

"Pure coincidence," she responded, as calmly as she could. "I go up there because of the demand. People want to go there, and I've got to make money. I lead tours to Vancouver Island and southern Alberta for the same reason."

At that moment she could convince herself that this was true. But she was also very well aware of the fact that some people in Inuvik could probably still remember her parents and her mother's death. So far nobody there knew she was Peter Hurdy-Blaine and Mary-Ann Strong's daughter. Perhaps Kosta was afraid she'd reveal her identity, hoping for new information. She'd done a little research on her mother in the past months—without her brothers' knowledge. Not much came of it, though. Mary-Ann Strong had apparently left no diaries or other personal documents behind, and their father had largely destroyed his own writings.

Valerie wondered whether she ought to tell Kosta about Sedna, about the inquiries she'd made. But then she'd have had to tell him about Sedna's rendezvous with Matt. Matt was a good friend of Kosta's. Even now. Her brother hadn't been thrilled about the divorce. And what had Sedna really done anyway? Maybe she was simply a bit more curious than other people.

"Where does this Christine Preston live anyway?" Kosta asked.

"In Zurich, Ontario. She was visiting her daughter in Vancouver. She gave me a card with her address and phone number."

"Do you still have it?"

Valerie nodded.

"Did you call her after you read the article?"

"No, I was too busy."

"OK, I'll contact her."

They hit a traffic light. People with umbrellas hurried over the pedestrian walkways.

Valerie looked at her brother.

"Are you worried about Christine Preston?"

"Not worried, just cautious."

He rubbed his left hand over his temple. He always did that when he was tense.

"I got an anonymous letter a couple of weeks ago."

"An anonymous letter? What did it say?"

"Just one sentence: 'Peter Hurdy-Blaine, your family is not what it pretends to be.'"

She repeated the sentence in her mind. What was that supposed to mean? Her father had died sixteen years ago.

"The letter was addressed to you but meant for Dad?"

"Yes. Odd, isn't it?"

"I don't get it. Who'd write a thing like that? And . . . who writes letters nowadays? It's so . . . old-fashioned."

"It was written on a computer. There are surely other ways to communicate that would leave fewer traces," Kosta said, once again the consummate lawyer. "It's as if the sender wanted us to find him. Or her."

"Are you going to do anything about it?"

"I'm not going to the police, if that's what you're thinking."

No, she didn't think that. Sometimes Kosta still treated her like a kid sister.

Their conversation ended abruptly as they turned into Twenty-Third Street West and stopped in front of a two-story building with some rosebushes. She got out and climbed the steps to the entrance carrying a heavy backpack. The door opened, and a little boy pushed ahead of his older sister.

"Auntie Val, are you going to shoot a polar bear?" he shouted so loudly that half the neighborhood could hear.

"No, my little bear," the blond lady who appeared behind the children answered. "The best Auntie Val can do is to shoot pictures with her camera."

Valerie grinned and dropped her backpack on the floor. Sandy, her niece, hugged her at once. Her little brother fumbled around with a toy pistol that shot foam-rubber bullets.

"You can take it with you," he said, swelling with pride. "I'll loan it to you."

"My darling, we've got a flare pistol that makes a lot of noise and a little flame and scares the bears off but doesn't hurt them."

Valerie stroked Sandy's soft hair and felt the girl's warm head against her stomach. For a moment she felt weightless and happy.

Then she heard a still, small voice in her head.

"Don't forget your shooting iron."

CHAPTER 12

"Stay! You've been outdoors long enough today." Clem gave the command to Meteor, who was trying to leave the house with him.

His cell phone rang at that moment.

Ottawa returning his call.

"They're sending a long-range plane to investigate the explosion. An Aurora," the voice on the other end of the line announced.

"Who? Who's sending the Aurora?"

"The army."

"Sending it from where?"

"From the Yellowknife unit."

"Wow! That means they're taking this seriously."

There was a pause on the line.

"It's being treated as a routine operation, and there'll be a brief press announcement tomorrow. A radio reporter in Inuvik got wind of this so they had to do something."

"When will the Aurora be up, exactly?"

"Dunno. That's all I can say. Can you keep this under your hat until the media are informed?"

"Sure."

"Are you coming to Ottawa soon?"

"Possibly. A family visit is long overdue."

"We'd have a job for you. The new government is looking for good people like you."

"Whenever I hear the word *government*, I feel sick to my stomach."

"The climate here is very different now, much more open. The people who made life hard for you are gone. Drowned in their own insignificance."

"But everybody still knows what happened . . . back then."

"The key people know the real backstory. Hey, man, you don't still feel guilty?"

No, not guilty, not anymore. But still bitter.

"Let me know when you're coming. We could get together."

"A class reunion?"

"Right on."

"I'll bring the caribou steaks."

They laughed and signed off.

Clem drove to the Great Polar Hotel. His cell phone alerted him again. A text message this time.

"Am in Whitehorse. Nobody pulled out. Valerie Blaine."

Only six more days until she was in Inuvik. She'd reserved rooms at the Great Polar, unlike previous years when she put her customers up in log chalets with woodstoves. The chalets had been booked out for the winter by a Dutch travel agency. Clem could imagine that the hotel, with its modern look and amenities, didn't square with the image adventurous tourists had of Arctic lodgings. But Valerie wasn't down about it because they could get to the Muskrat Jamboree on foot from the hotel.

It occurred to Clem that she hadn't heard about the weird explosion on the ice.

Inside the hotel bar, Clem and his buddies didn't spend time talking about the explosion—or the mysterious death on the Ice Road. Instead they planned their strategy for the upcoming snowmobile race. Given the dramatic events of late, Valerie would have found their chosen topic of conversation odd, to be sure. Vancouver women didn't understand such things.

Clem's team had lost to Paulie Umik's men the year before. Umik owned a company that was angling to dominate the construction sector in Inuvik. Clem, the favorite, came in third on account of a bad flu. He should have been in bed, but racing fever held the upper hand. Clem's friend and teammate, Phil Niditichie, a Gwich'in and a teacher at the local community college, was a little ahead of a man on the Umik team, who pulled up even by using a tricky maneuver on a curve. What happened next still triggered controversy and arguments in the delta a whole year afterward. Umik's team claimed that Phil had deliberately caused the other man's machine to tip over. Phil was the first to cross the finish line but never saw the six thousand dollars in prize money: he was disqualified despite a barrage of protests. To this day, anger burned like a glowing ember in Clem and his teammates' hearts.

They were going to win this year's race come hell or high water. Clem and Phil had each bought new snowmobiles, and Clem was free of the flu.

In the middle of their barroom strategizing, Clem's cell phone rang again. Damn! Marjorie Tama's name lit up the display. It had totally slipped his mind.

"Gotta go, people—drum dance at the arena," he explained, grinning in embarrassment. A wave of wisecracks promptly broke over him.

"Hey, Clem, you don't have to go—you can perform for us right here!"

"We'll buy you a round if you're good at it!"

"Remember not to use a turkey drumstick!"

"He's got lead feet; can't even jump through a doorway!"

Clem drained his beer and banged the glass down on the bar.

"OK, guys, it's about the young people in our town. *Some*body's got to do something for them. Who's going to volunteer? You just have to serve dried fish and tea. How's about it?"

He looked around with an intimidating stare.

"Where there's food, there's gotta be Clem," Phil Niditichie crowed from the far end of the bar.

"Where there's Phil, there's gotta be one real sharp mind," Clem retorted. "Real sharp."

Everybody howled, including Phil.

Clem picked up his muskrat-fur hat.

"Well, looks like I'm the only one who gives a damn about indigenous culture. And don't forget, boys: no boozing during the Muskrat Jamboree."

"That's why we're filling our gullets today!" Poppy Dixon shouted. Laughter and hollering followed Clem out the door.

Outside, a white veil of snow flitted like a ghost through the gathering darkness. A strong wind whirled up snowflakes like dry leaves. Was it punishment for the string of sunny days? He dove into the icy elements like a bull into a matador's red cape.

Pickups and SUVs were lined up in front of the arena when he arrived.

Marjorie Tama waved to him as he entered the warm building. She tried to shout at him from a distance, but nothing penetrated the roar of the drums, the singing, and the gusts of laughter. The benches were crowded: a colorful mishmash of Inuvialuit, Gwich'in, Métis, and white people. Before reaching the corner where the mayor was setting up dishes of food and several thermos jugs, he noticed what the crowd found so funny. John Palmer, a Royal Canadian Mounted Police officer, was hopping around the arena with some kids and teenagers. In uniform, ammunition belt and all. Palmer waddled like a goose, flapped his hands as if playing an invisible piano, squatted to the right, then left, and rotated his arms like a windmill. Holy smoke!

Clem had to admit the guy had no qualms about being the butt of all that laughter. The two teens beside him, who were warming up for the drum dance competition, looked positively statesmanlike compared to Palmer. Their parkas sparkled blue and red with traditional embroidery, and they were trimmed with wolverine fur and white piping. The RCMP officer brushed off the laughter, throwing himself into his dance with a look of sheer delight on his face. Palmer was a young man from Mississauga in Ontario and had only been stationed in town for nine months. It didn't escape Clem that the new police officer was making an effort to mix with the native populations and establish a good rapport with their young people.

"Break's coming up. Are you ready?"

Marjorie was standing beside him. She pulled at his jacket.

"Still cold?" she said. "You should dance too." She laughed, and her eyes nearly vanished completely beneath the folds of her skin. Clem followed her to the snack table.

"Do you know what the story's about?" Marjorie shouted in his ear.

"What story?"

"The song, the dance."

He said he didn't know.

She tried to explain it to him, but the noise level was too high. She laughed and shrugged. The Inuvialuit would habitually laugh at any hardship.

It was critical for the police officer, John Palmer, to show his face at this event: somebody might whisper something in his ear. Gisèle's death had scarcely been mentioned, at least to Clem. Maybe the silence was an expression of helplessness. Or maybe everyone thought it was better to keep your mouth shut—especially if you didn't know if a crime had been committed or not. You might say the wrong thing to the wrong person. Clem had heard through the grapevine that many parents were forbidding their daughters to go out at night.

Clem lost sight of Palmer while serving the children and adults their dried fish and tea. Marjorie set another tray down on the table, *maktak* with barbecue sauce.

"Beluga," she explained. "Not for you—after all, the police are here," she teased.

Inuvialuit loved blubber but couldn't legally sell it to tourists and whites. Any whale killed was destined for their own needs. Clem's eyes roamed around the arena. He saw Palmer off in a corner, cell phone to his ear.

"Have you ever hunted *qilaluguq*?" an old man asked him, giggling as Clem piled up the shining, pink-white cubes on a plastic plate. He laughed along with the old man, who knew very well that Clem hadn't killed the whale himself. Only the local Inuvialuit in the Mackenzie Delta had permission to kill belugas. This annoyed some white hunters. Low-class types, as Clem thought of them, who regarded the world as a gigantic hunting ground. The beluga paradise was forbidden to them. Clem didn't give a fig about it, though he owned a hunting rifle. He'd never have dreamed of admitting that he found it more fun to photograph animals than kill them. That did not conform with the image many men in Inuvik projected.

"Why do you think my skin's so white?" he asked the old man, who kept hanging around him. "Because I eat so much beluga *maktak*?"

The old man's face lit up like the sun.

"No, because you eat a lot of snow!"

The people in line behind him snickered, and Clem flashed his broadest grin as he filled up plate after plate.

"One point to you, my friend," he conceded. "Be careful not to eat too much *maktak* or you'll be as white as the *tanngit*."

"Not as white as your toes, you softie!" a teenager shouted; he was wearing a hoodie and sneakers, in spite of the cold. The look was everything.

"Clem, got a minute?"

John Palmer materialized before him.

"Sure, just let me . . ."

He signaled to Marjorie to replace him at the snack table.

Palmer took him over to the bulletin board, away from the crowd. He didn't waste time on pleasantries.

"Do you know where Helvin is?"

Clem saw drops of sweat on John's forehead. Dancing must have been strenuous.

"No. Why?"

"When was the last time you saw him?"

"The day you guys were in his office."

"When?"

"In the evening, shortly after six."

"What did you talk about?"

"John, what's going on? Are we talking about Gisèle Chaume here?"

"Helvin's nowhere to be found. Didn't come home last night, and his wife reported him missing this evening."

"What! That's . . . strange. Why didn't Toria phone me?"

"What did you talk about three days ago?"

"About the dead woman and what we were going to say officially."

"And what about unofficially?"

"I've got nothing to do with it, and he said *he* didn't have anything to do with it either."

"And you two haven't talked to each other since then?"

"We did, once. I called him on my cell phone."

"Why?"

"Well, it's no secret—I've heard his pickup was parked around where the dead woman was. He claimed somebody swiped the vehicle from the company parking lot. And that he had an ironclad alibi: he was at home with Toria that night."

"You've had no contact with him after that?"

"I called him on his cell today. No answer."

"Doesn't that bother you?"

Clem suppressed a sigh.

"That's almost normal for Helv. It often takes several tries to get him."

Clem's eyes traveled around the room. The whole business stank to high heaven. Toria was pissed off because Helvin had stayed out all night, but she didn't even contact *him*, Clem. Helvin was probably sitting in some hunting cabin washing his brain cells out of his skull with loads of beer. And maybe he had somebody with him. He'd heard rumors. About women Helv wasn't married to.

But now was the stupidest time to simply disappear. That really didn't put Helv in a good light.

"Ooookaay," Palmer said slowly. "If you hear anything, let us know immediately."

"Of course."

What the hell was going on? Clem could see many pairs of eyes throughout the arena following him as he returned to his post at the snack table. Who else knew that Helvin had disappeared into thin air? Probably a whole slew of people did. And nobody had called *him*. Now he was really angry with his boss. Clem was fuming inside as he resumed piling food onto plates.

Marjorie seemed to have a sixth sense for a person's state of mind because she was studying him with raised eyebrows. She didn't ask questions; maybe she was already in the know. After all, Toria was her daughter's best friend.

When he left the arena late that night, the blowing snow had stopped. The night was dark and still as a monk at prayer. Another of those amazing, sudden changes in the weather in the delta. As if somebody pulled a lever up and down.

He left the lights of Inuvik behind and took the shortest route to Helvin's house. He circled it several times before admitting that he actually didn't know why he was there. Was it to check on whether Helvin really had gone missing? He couldn't ring Toria's doorbell at this late hour. Besides, she hadn't felt the need to let him know before going to the police. Let her get out of that shit by herself. Herself and Helvin.

On the way back home, he saw something bright flickering in the black sky. The northern lights. Wide green streaks flashed and snaked through the atmosphere. Valerie would be entranced by this spectacle. The northern lights were right at the top of her list of tourist attractions. A trip to the Arctic without northern lights, as she once told him, was like a trip to Canada without bears.

Then she laughed.

"And like Clem without Meteor."

His dog was sure to be waiting eagerly for him. Probably mad at Clem for leaving him alone for six hours. To make up for it, Clem had managed to snag several Styrofoam containers of leftover fish for his dog. And he planned to take him along the next day on the snowmobile. To the cabin where he hoped to find Helvin.

He parked the truck and walked toward the front door, balancing the Styrofoam containers in his arms.

Suddenly, he heard a noise behind him. Something hard banged him on the head. He felt a flash of pain go through him before he hit the ground.

CHAPTER 13

The beast bared its long, pointed fangs. Its bulging eyes were fixed on Valerie. Every time she saw the saber-toothed tiger in the Whitehorse Museum, she felt pleasurable shivers down her spine. She was with her group in the Yukon Beringia Interpretive Centre because it presented the history of the Canadian north much better than anywhere else.

It also gave her the opportunity to sneak a peek at the individuals on the tour, when they were photographing the mammoth, say, or the primeval bear fending off wolves, or the huge bison.

Paula Kennedy, a teacher from Westminster in British Columbia who'd retired at sixty, was listening to the audiotape about Beringia. Paula, a compulsive communicator, would be sure to tell everybody afterward about the Bering landmass that comprised parts of Siberia, Alaska, and the Yukon Territory about ten thousand years ago. It hadn't been covered by glaciers during the last Ice Age; that's why Beringia provided a living space for animals and people alike. Paula was ever the teacher in her retirement, and Valerie appreciated her enthusiasm. She encouraged discussion in the group about the region they were traveling through and its past.

Of course, Sedna couldn't have cared less about the glacier-free Bering landmass when she'd been there with Valerie. Valerie had explained to Sedna that this land bridge had stretched from Siberia to the Yukon River and that animals had first migrated over this route from Asia to the North American continent. And that the first humans had also come to the North American continent from Asia over the same route about fifteen thousand years ago. They had survived in a hostile environment through their extraordinary adaptability. Valerie was fascinated by what the human species was capable of; it had arisen in the African heat, and nevertheless it was able to survive in ice-cold regions near the North Pole. All of it slid off Sedna like water off a duck's back—she fled the museum as soon as she could.

Valerie saw Glenn Bliss going to the reception desk.

"May I take some pictures?" he asked the cashier. He was the one who'd written her that he couldn't wait to travel to the North after the "Murder in the northern wilds." So far Glenn had revealed himself to be a polite, almost taciturn man with an elegant mustache. He looked like an English gentleman but was American. That wasn't the only thing that surprised her. Glenn, at thirty-seven, was a relatively young client, and with his athletic physique, she would have expected to encounter him on a trek through Mongolia instead.

She was about to move on to the next exhibit when a kindly male voice called from behind her: "Ms. Blaine?"

Startled, she turned around to find an older gentleman with a trimmed goatee standing before her.

"I am Ken Gries, the museum director. So nice to have the opportunity to meet you."

Taken by surprise, she shook his outstretched hand.

"I'd like to show you something in my office."

Valerie followed him into a back room in the museum. He closed the door to shut out the sound of the multimedia displays.

His first words said it all.

"I knew your parents."

She tried to play for time by asking, *"My* parents? Are you sure?" The museum director looked taken aback for a moment.

"Your father was Peter Hurdy-Blaine, wasn't he? I met him and your mother when they were in Whitehorse."

"Pardon the question . . . but how do you know I'm their daughter?"

"An acquaintance of yours told us. She was in the museum recently."

"An acquaintance? What was her name?"

He rummaged through the papers on his desk. "Here, I've got it. My secretary wrote it down for me; I wasn't in the office at the time. Phyllis Crombe."

"Phyllis Crombe? I don't know anyone by that name. What did she look like?"

"I'd have to ask my secretary, but it's her day off."

The director offered her a chair, and she sat down.

"I can recall a conversation with your father very clearly. When was it? At least thirty years ago. I was young, probably twenty-eight. Somebody told your father that I'd retraced the long route of the Lost Patrol by dogsled with a few Gwich'in men. You know the story, don't you? It occurred in 1910. Inspector Francis J. Fitzgerald and three men from the North-West Mounted Police undertook a trip in winter. And they all died."

Valerie nodded, which encouraged the director to continue.

"Our expedition took place in 1981. We had three Indian guides and enough provisions, which Fitzgerald and his men did not. Those poor men suffered from terrible hunger. They had to eat their dogs. I'm telling you that four hundred and twenty miles by dogsled is a long, hard slog. It took us twenty-one days."

But his face beamed as he relived it.

"Your father—as you surely know—wanted to retrace the path of the rescue team. Those were the men who found the Lost Patrol all dead. Police Inspector Jack Dempster was your father's hero, if I may say so. I told your father back then everything that was essential—what he ought to take with him: enough provisions, good native guides, fur clothing, strong dogs. Then he told me they'd be on snowmobiles. He and his wife."

He picked out something from the pile of paper in front of him. A photograph.

"That's me with Peter Hurdy-Blaine."

Valerie didn't recognize her father at first. He was wearing a fur hat and a heavy winter jacket. She wondered where her mother was when the picture was taken.

"Your mother was a lively, energetic person. Young and very pretty. Adventurous, too. Gutsy. And practical."

Your mother. The words always sounded somewhat strange to her. After all, Valerie had never really gotten to know her mother. As far as Valerie was concerned, Bella had been the only mother she'd ever really had. Her silence didn't seem to register with Gries. The fact that he had Hurdy-Blaine's daughter before him spurred him on.

"Your mother wrote everything down that I listed. I think she was acutely aware of the risks and dangers the trek involved. Probably more aware than your father."

He studied Valerie's face more closely.

"I can see your mother in you. Especially your eyes. I remember that she had a phenomenal memory. I think . . . if you permit me to say so . . . I had the impression that she was probably better prepared for the trek than your father."

Valerie's ears pricked up.

"How do you mean?"

"Your father . . . he was daring, liked to take risks. Your mother, she was still young, very athletic. Brimming with potential. Your father wanted above all to create a monument."

"You think he wasn't up to it?"

Gries smiled, but his smile seemed slightly pained.

"I hope you will forgive me if I come right out and say that hockey skills don't necessarily count on such an expedition. I believe your mother grasped that very well."

His frankness gave her courage to ask the next question.

"Was there any tension between the two of them before they left?"

Gries bit his lip. He took his time before answering.

"It's possible that she looked up to him at the beginning, when they first met. She was a very young woman at the time, after all. But when I met them, she was anxious to . . . she obviously wanted to be treated as an equal partner in everything, including their Arctic ventures, if you see what I'm . . ."

The cashier opened the door and smiled at Valerie.

"Excuse me. Someone's looking for you."

She and the director stood up at once.

"Here, take this. In case I can ever be of assistance," the director said as he handed her his card.

Valerie thanked him and was walking toward the door when something occurred to her.

"One more question. When was my . . . my friend here, Phyllis Crombe?"

"Last week, Monday or Tuesday."

When they were in the supermarket afterward, Faye asked, "Why didn't you show him Sedna's picture?"

Valerie stopped at the vegetable section. She mustn't forget Trish, who was a vegetarian. Her sister, Carol Simpson, who ran a beauty salon in Vancouver, had brought Trish, a newly divorced mother of five, on the trip and paid for everything; Valerie was moved by that.

"I have a photo on my laptop. Maybe I'll send it to him. He can show it to his secretary."

"You definitely should. Sedna's unmistakable: that colored hair and flashy bling really make her stand out," Faye said. "That, and the fact that she's sexy, charming, colorful . . ."

She searched for more words, then whispered in Valerie's ear, ". . . smarmy, sleazy, swindling . . ."

"Oh, shut up!" Valerie broke into laughter and gave Faye a gentle poke in the ribs.

"You're quite an eye-catcher yourself, Val," Faye murmured. "Take a look at that guy over there who's staring at you. Over there, at the meat counter."

Valerie turned around. She exchanged glances with the man and recognized him immediately. Phil Niditichie, Clem's friend. She waved at him to come over.

"On the way to Inuvik?" he asked.

"Yes, every year. How's the Dempster look?"

"Took the plane. Got a conference."

He ran a hand through his head of black hair.

"Did you hear what happened to Clem?"

"No."

Valerie's mouth turned dry.

"Somebody clubbed him. He's in the hospital."

"Oh my God! Is he badly hurt?"

"Slight concussion. Nothing serious."

"Who did it?"

"Dunno. But it knocked him out of the race."

She had to think for a second about which race Phil was referring to. Then she remembered. The snowmobile race.

Her grip on the cart handle tightened.

"Is he here in the Whitehorse hospital?"

"No, in Inuvik. He just needed some stitches."

Phil's voice showed no anger, but his body language betrayed his nervousness.

Something was going on in Inuvik, something was brewing. She sensed it. First the dead woman. Now the attack on Clem. What next?

"I'll go see him in the hospital in a few days when I'm in Inuvik."

"The Dempster shouldn't be a problem. Good weather coming."

She nodded. A question about Gisèle Chaume was on the tip of her tongue, but she held back, saying instead, "So Helvin West will have to get along without Clem for a while."

"Yeah . . ." Phil hesitated. "Helv hasn't been seen the last couple of days. His wife . . . Toria reported him missing."

"Really?"

Valerie knew Toria; she'd always bring her things from Vancouver that she couldn't order online.

"It's not the first time. He'll turn up again," Phil assured her. "Gotta go. We'll be sure to see each other in Inuvik."

Valerie watched him sauntering over to the cashier.

"That's extremely interesting," she heard Faye say.

Valerie quickly pushed her cart along and resumed their shopping. Better for her to concentrate on the tour than worry about events in Inuvik, she thought.

As they were putting the groceries into the Chevrolet minibus she'd rented, the sun burst through the overcast sky. Patches of deep blue grew larger, like ink drops on a paper towel. She closed the rear door.

"Change of plans. Let's do our trip by dogsled along the Takhini River today," she announced.

"Okeydokey," Faye said, climbing into the Chevy. They had lunch with the group in the hotel restaurant before leaving Whitehorse.

Upon their arrival at the Klatinih Ranch, they were met by a horde of yowling dogs all hoping to be selected for dogsledding. Two men were trying to keep the impatient animals down. Glenn Bliss and Jordan Walker were filming the preparations. Jordan, a passionate amateur filmmaker from Calgary, was eight years older than the thirty-seven-year-old Glenn. They were evidently friends before the trip. A Canadian-American friendship. The oldest participant was Anika Forman, a former lacrosse player and farmer on her second tour with

Valerie. At eighty-seven, Anika didn't let her age slow her down. She was particularly looking forward to the dogsledding jaunt.

"Why aren't they all huskies?" Anika asked.

Scott, a man from the ranch, explained that many types of dogs are bred for the speed and stamina required to run in races.

"These crossbreeds are called Alaskan huskies as opposed to Siberian huskies," Scott said. "The dogs I train run from six to seven hours without extended breaks."

He told the group the different commands for making the dogs run, slow down, and stop. Valerie sat at the back of one of the four sleds with Paula, the retired teacher, in the front. After a loud "Go! Go!" the party started up.

Valerie loved it when the dogs shot over the snow with harmonized movements and noticeable pleasure and energy. They sped downhill to the frozen Takhini River.

The snow glittered in the sun. Skinny, tousled trees stuck up like coxcombs out of the vast plain. When the teams stopped for photo ops, the dogs cooled off in the snow.

Valerie heard Anika's cheerful laugh behind her. Who says that elderly ladies can't have a rollicking good time? she thought, feeling satisfied. The procession started up again. Valerie felt like she was merging with the landscape, the huskies, and the blue sky. She forgot about Sedna and her parents' fate; she forgot about her responsibilities and what might be awaiting her in Inuvik. She felt pure, unadulterated bliss.

The dog teams returned to the ranch after two hours. Valerie took some time to pet Hector, her favorite dog. He licked her face, removing her sunscreen. Just then, Faye appeared at her side.

"Guess what I found out!" Faye asked, her eyes shining. She really looked good with all that white snow around her. "Scott told me that he saw Sedna in Dawson City!"

"Awesome! So he knows her?"

"No, not really, but his girlfriend does. And she also knows Gisèle . . . or did know her."

Valerie scratched Hector behind the ears.

"When was Sedna in Dawson?"

"End of February. He gave me his girlfriend's name. She works as a waitress in the Downtown Hotel. You know the one, where they serve a dead toe in whiskey."

Valerie glanced over to see Trish and Carol disappearing into the main building of the ranch. Souvenirs-and-coffee break.

Faye was very excited.

"She still has her wild-colored hair. He confirmed it. Though he didn't know what she was planning to do."

Faye knelt down next to Valerie and the dog.

"We need to talk to Scott's girlfriend."

Valerie stood up and gave Hector a farewell pat.

Faye was unstoppable.

"You know what this means, don't you? Sedna isn't wearing a wig or something. She isn't in hiding."

They walked on the trampled-down snow to the log lodge, where Valerie took off her hat and gloves.

"So that's the way it is," she said. "Now, who in the hell is Phyllis Crombe?"

CHAPTER 14

The door opened once again.

Clem really didn't feel like having more visitors. The doctor had prescribed rest, rest, and more rest. Why were all these people being let in to see him? He'd really have to complain to the nurse on duty.

All of Inuvik seemed curious to see Clem Hardeven in his miserable state. Even John Palmer of the RCMP dropped by, although that was to be expected. But Clem wasn't much help to the officer. Everything had happened so fast, and all of a sudden, he was unconscious. What could he tell Palmer? He wasn't aware he had any enemies in Inuvik. He always steered clear of brawls and altercations. Nevertheless, could he really say whether or not certain people harbored a secret grudge against him?

Palmer let Clem know that Helvin still hadn't turned up. The RCMP apparently didn't have the foggiest notion where he might be. Clem told Palmer the location of Helvin's hunting cabin, but the police had already searched it. No trace of Helvin West.

Clem welcomed some visitors more than others. Helvin's foreman wanted instructions concerning the Ice Road. The three kids who'd found Clem lying on the frozen ground and had gone for help just wanted to check on him. Good boys. All three were Inuvialuit kids. Clem promised them the new video game they were dying to have.

His pal Phil Niditichie found time for a brief visit before flying to Whitehorse. As always, Phil couldn't hold his tongue.

"So, a concussion. You know what that means? No work, no TV, no racing, no sex."

"Fuck off," Clem muttered.

He was secretly happy that it was only a mild concussion. A snow pile had broken his fall.

The face that came into his field of view was the last one he expected to see.

Toria. Helvin's wife.

She'd thrown her parka and ski pants over her right arm and held her hat and gloves in her left hand. Toria was one of those women who didn't confine herself to shapeless winter clothing; she dressed in fashionable, revealing clothes. She was wearing a tight, melon-colored cashmere sweater with a plunging neckline. Toria had once been the reigning beauty in Inuvik. Her ancestors were German and Inuvialuit, and this mixed heritage had found its supreme combination in her. But her generous consumption of alcohol and nicotine had begun to leave visible traces in her evenly proportioned face. As she neared Clem's bed, he couldn't help but notice her swollen eyes.

"You look awful," she said. "Did somebody kick your face in?"

He wanted to shake his head but remembered in time that anything of the sort was prohibited.

"No, I simply hit the ground . . . after somebody whacked me on the head."

She stopped at the end of his bed.

"Jesus Christ, Clem! What the hell's going on in this damn town?"

"*You*'re asking me, Toria?"

He avoided eye contact and looked out the window at the blue-and-red facade of the other hospital wing. The sky was overcast, but there was no wind. The flag of the Northwest Territories drooped from the flagpole.

"I want to hear it from you. Where's Helv?"

"No idea. Wish I knew. Why didn't you phone *me* first, before the cops?"

She crossed her arms, emphasizing the curves of her breasts.

"This time it's different. I don't think he's chasing a woman."

Clem slowly turned his injured head in her direction. Their relationship had been awkward for some time. Ever since she'd thrown herself into his arms and tried to seduce him because Helvin had once again picked up a tourist from Sweden or Switzerland or wherever the blondes of this world come from. Clem had only wanted to comfort her. Not that it hadn't been enjoyable when Toria's body snuggled against him. She made no bones about desiring even more concrete comforting. But she was his boss's wife, for Chrissake! That was a problem he could very well do without.

She walked to the other side of the bed. For a few seconds, he was afraid she'd sit on it. But she began pacing up and down the room instead.

"I don't know what he's got up his sleeve. He . . . he thinks the gas pipeline will never get built. He's bet all his hopes on it. And his money. Our money. All those outlays for machines that are rusting away before his very eyes."

None of this was news to Clem. He'd warned Helvin time and again not to invest any more cash until it was clear that the oil company would go ahead with the project. Helvin just laughed at him.

"You've got to think big, man. You'll never have any success if you aren't the first to get in there. If you hesitate, then other people are gonna shoot right past you. And I know how to prevent that, believe you me."

Clem waited for Toria to divulge more. But she held back.

He tossed out a baited hook.

"Did you get the pickup back from the cops?"

"You can't really believe he had anything to do with that woman! With that Gisèle. He was in bed with me the whole night. He's got an airtight alibi. She stole our truck."

Her face crinkled up with rage.

"And just so you know: the RCMP has hauled Pihuk in for questioning. That Gisèle woman went to have a rendezvous with him that night on the Ice Road."

Clem was silent. He cursed his helplessness. He wanted more than anything to get up and run out of the room.

What Toria told him made no sense. Gisèle was interested in shamans like Pihuk and in meeting him, but how could she have stolen the truck? How could she have gotten into the Suntuk Logistics compound all by herself? Maybe somebody took her there. And then there was Pihuk. If he really was a suspect, then he was caught in a trap. Somebody had to help the poor bastard. And Clem knew exactly who could do it. But for that, he'd have to get out of this damn hospital.

Toria was now in high gear.

"Helvin's an idiot at times, but he never does anything illegal. Last summer he lent his pickup to that woman from Vancouver," she said, smoothing down her sweater. It was not long enough to cover her derrière or anything else in those revealing leggings.

Was she talking about Valerie? He felt a pain in his stomach.

"Didn't Val tell you? She'd get so upset when her friend would disappear for days at a time."

Sedna. Toria meant Sedna. So Helvin had a hand in that. Toria's anger revealed more than she'd intended. When he looked at her exhausted face, he found more than worry over Helvin's probable dalliance with a woman. He could see that she was genuinely afraid of something. Before he could drill down, the nurse appeared.

"Visiting hours are up, sorry," she announced.

"I'm on my way," Toria said, picking up her winter clothes.

"I can't go looking for him with this concussion," Clem said apologetically. "Not for the next several days."

Toria looked at him with a mysterious glint in her dark eyes.

"Better for you to stay here. You wouldn't want to be where I suspect he is now, believe me."

With those cryptic words, she left him to himself.

CHAPTER 15

Anika Forman carefully placed one foot ahead of the other. She insisted on treating herself to a stroll along the wooden sidewalks of Dawson City to admire its buildings. Glenn Bliss and Jordan Walker each held an arm so that she could keep her balance on the icy boards. Valerie had never had a single person on her tour who didn't love the atmosphere, shrouded in mystery, of this historic gold-mining town. And everyone loved the raised pedestrian sidewalks, which looked just the way they had in the pioneer days, when asphalt streets didn't exist—just dirt on fine days and mud on rainy ones.

Anika refused to be treated like an old lady. But she liked the "Calgary boys," as she called them.

Valerie led her tour through the streets, past buildings from the gold rush years. Her favorite photographic subject was the old bank by the iced-over Yukon River. In Dawson City—shortened to "Dawson" by the locals—there were several carefully restored dwellings; others were near the point of collapse, but they helped keep the city from looking like a sterile, open-air museum. In the golden evening light of the winter sun, the decaying mustard-colored facade of the former bank was resplendent in its former glory, in spite of the boarded-up windows beneath the neoclassical molding. Like an aging actress in flattering light is how Valerie saw it.

Her group was in a good mood. Valerie heard lively chatter and laughter, which cheered her heart. They walked past large heaps of snow bordering the streets until Valerie stopped in front of a frame house that had lines of poetry painted on the wall. The poet's name, Robert W. Service, was written under them; he was obviously known to her little group. "The Spell of the Yukon." Paula Kennedy recited the inscription as if she were in front of her class; nobody interrupted her.

The poem told the tale of a prospector who grubbed around in the muck like a slave for years, suffering sickness and hunger, sacrificing his youth to the gold rush—all in the mad hope of getting rich. This fable had lost none of its appeal after more than a hundred years. The narrator in Service's famous ballad finally made his fortune in gold—and was disenchanted all the same. Gold and wealth didn't deliver the contentment, happiness, and joie de vivre he'd been promised.

"And somehow the gold isn't all." The first stanza ended with this line. Paula recited the rest of the ballad, resolutely and with the pathos of a star onstage. She even took off her cap in spite of the biting wind. Anywhere else she might have been embarrassing, Valerie thought, but here, where the drama had played out almost a hundred and twenty years ago, everybody was all ears. After Paula spoke the final line and tossed back her gray pageboy haircut to great effect, the tour members all applauded with enthusiasm.

"Just think: that guy wasn't even a prospector," Jordan piped up.

"Who? Robert Service?" That was Trish.

"Yep. He worked in a bank in Whitehorse. He wasn't in Dawson for the gold rush but only several years later. He could very well claim he didn't give a hoot about gold. It was with his poems that he made his fortune so he could retire to the French Riviera."

Valerie was impressed. She'd recommended Service's works to everyone, as well as the books of the legendary Jack London, who tried prospecting for gold in Dawson for a short time.

After Jordan's remarks Paula followed suit, adding, "That's right. He came to Dawson later, when he was already a writer. When was that, Valerie?"

"Nineteen oh eight," she replied, retaking her role as tour guide. "The Klondike gold rush lasted from 1896 to 1899. During that time, over thirty thousand people lived in Dawson, mostly Americans. There are only about two thousand people living year-round in Dawson today."

Then she added a juicy detail that always elicited bemused amazement from the tourists: "During the gold rush, there were only three toilets for all those people."

The group's lively reaction didn't disappoint her.

"Only a very few got rich . . ."

"Besides Service and Jack London," Jordan interjected.

"That's right. Most of them came to Dawson too late. The land claims had already been granted by the time they arrived. And of the hundred thousand people who tried to get here, only half of them made it to their destination. As few as twenty thousand registered their claims around the creeks. Even those men came away empty-handed. Perhaps three hundred of them found enough gold to get wealthy. And just like lottery winners, most of these lucky devils squandered their wealth right away and wound up with nothing in the end."

While she was talking, she felt the tip of her nose getting colder and colder. But since six pairs of eyes were on her, she concluded her little speech.

"The people who really earned a lot of money were the owners of the brothels, shops, and saloons. Many of them lived far away in Vancouver and Seattle and San Francisco. That's where the prospectors had to buy their gear and food supplies."

Paula piped up again.

"The police forced the prospectors to buy enough food and equipment to survive the winter, right?"

"Unless they died in ships' accidents or in the mountains before winter even started," Anika chimed in, indicating that she too had done her homework for the trip. "I need an invigorating brew, or I'll freeze on the ground."

"Well, it might be time for the sourtoe cocktail," Glenn shouted, though he was otherwise reserved; frost had formed on his mustache again. Valerie was convinced he was kidding because she couldn't imagine that he was so keen on this bizarre tourist ritual.

But everyone else was for it. They didn't meet a soul on the icy path to the Downtown Hotel. After they'd turned onto Second Avenue, a dark SUV overtook them, then parked behind another dark SUV at the curb. Valerie saw a man get out of the second vehicle and go into the first one. Her temperature shot up. In the milky glow of the streetlights, she thought she recognized a face. But she couldn't make out any faces behind the frosted-up windshield.

In the hotel bar, she quickly drew Faye aside.

"I need to make an urgent call," she said quietly. "Can you watch my group?"

"Of course." Faye gave her a thumbs-up. "I confess I haven't a clue how this crazy ritual with a toe in whiskey works."

"Don't worry. The bartender will regale you with the history of the old custom and teach you how to deal with the mummified toe."

"You mean we don't chew it up and swallow it?" Faye grinned. The whole business was obviously fun for her, Valerie noted with relief.

One less thing to worry about.

The tour group was already encamped at the bar inside, where a young female bartender Valerie didn't know was reciting the legend about the wizened toe. Valerie had heard it over and over. A human toe was preserved in salt when not in use, and then, when the tourists showed up, it was dropped into a whiskey-filled glass, where it swam around merrily. A customer wishing to become a member of the

Sourtoe Cocktail Club had to drain the glass to earn the appropriate certificate.

"The toe must touch your lips," the woman behind the bar said emphatically.

The whole group accepted the dare, and Jordan and Glenn continued shooting a video to document it all for posterity. Valerie sneaked out into the corridor and called Clem's number. If he didn't want to be disturbed, she could at least leave a message. But he answered quickly and seemed pleased to hear her voice.

"Finally, a ray of light in my drab days."

"How are you doing? Are you still in the hospital?"

"No, they kicked me out as fast as possible. Too many patients, too few beds. Where are you?"

"I'm in Dawson, and I think I saw Helvin."

A few seconds of silence. Then Clem said, "Tell me exactly what you saw."

Valerie tried. Clem's voice seemed to come from far away.

"What did he have on?"

She gave it some thought. Nothing that had attracted her attention.

"Anything on his head?"

"No."

"So he climbed out of one car and got right into another?"

"Yes. I only saw his face for a split second. Maybe he's got a double."

Now she was having second thoughts about whether she should have alarmed him. But Clem was hooked.

"Can you go back and get the license plate numbers on the cars? And can you inform the Dawson police?"

"The police? Oh wow! Clem, I can photograph the license plates. But I'd rather not have anything to do with the police."

"You did absolutely the right thing. Keep me posted, Snowy Owl."

He'd given her this nickname when she first came to Inuvik in a white ski suit with black piping. He'd teased her, saying, "Good camouflage for the snow, but unfortunately not the best color if you want them to find you in the Arctic." The next year she wore a bright orange down jacket.

Valerie glanced back at the bar, where the sourtoe madness was going full tilt. Anika posed for Jordan's camera with her whiskey glass and the mummified toe to her lips.

"Touch it! Touch it! Don't bite!" the rest of them yelled. Glenn was the only one hovering in the background; a cautious smile played around the corners of his mouth—just the way she'd imagined an English gentleman would smile. Faye was directing the whole show, and Valerie felt a warm wave of gratitude rising in her.

She hurried out onto the street, where she saw one of the SUVs some distance away. When she got close, she didn't see anything moving or hear a sound. She took her cell phone out of her purse, where she'd wrapped it in a warmer, and had just bent down when she heard the car door open. She quickly stood up and saw two men coming at her. Neither one was Helvin. She slid her hands in her pockets because she had no gloves in spite of the cold.

"What are you doing there?" one of them asked. "Are you photographing the car?"

She'd learned as a journalist that it was often best to be honest.

"Yes, as a matter of fact I was going to. I didn't know anybody was in the car."

She tried to stay calm. Nobody was in the streets at that moment.

"Can we see the pictures?"

The men were standing in front of her now. Very close. Threateningly close.

"I never got that far," she said. "I didn't take any pictures."

"Were you trying to photograph the license plate?"

"Yes. Because it's shaped like a polar bear, and I've never seen anything like it."

"Anyways, we'd like to take your cell phone."

The man stuck out his hand, and Valerie instinctively took a big step backward. Her pulse was racing. It didn't look good.

Suddenly, one of the men said something to the other in a language she didn't understand. The second man uttered a monosyllabic answer, and they disappeared into their vehicle. The doors slammed shut, and the motor kicked in. Half a minute later, she lost sight of the SUV. Then she heard another car coming. She turned to find a patrol car. It stopped beside her, and the passenger window slid down.

"Everything OK?" one of the cops asked.

She nodded vigorously and managed to get seven words out: "On my way to a sourtoe cocktail."

Valerie waited until she found a secluded spot in the hotel before she let Faye in on everything.

"Is that all the police asked you?"

"Yes. I think they thought the men were drunk and were hassling me."

"Shouldn't you have told them what actually happened?"

"I can't get dragged into this. I'm traveling with a group I'm responsible for. I'll keep my eyes and ears open, that's—"

"Got it, got it. Why did Clem want a picture of the license plate?"

"That's easy. He wants to find Helvin."

She suddenly felt very tired. Whereas Faye still seemed to be bursting with energy.

"It's kind of funny that Helvin disappeared after Gisèle's death. And then you see him here in Dawson. Why is he hiding like that and not telling his wife anything?"

Valerie found other things odd too. Why would Helvin risk being declared a missing person by the police? Or had he counted on Toria putting up with his occasional hide-and-seek games, as she always had? It was an open secret in Inuvik that fur often flew between them.

"I wonder . . . ," Faye began. ". . . I can't get it out of my head that Sedna's going into hiding is somehow involved with those incidents in Inuvik."

"What makes you think that?"

"Dunno. Kind of a feeling."

They came to Faye's hotel room.

"My gut tells me that we'll know more in the morning. Good night."

CHAPTER 16

Valerie and Faye stood in front of a large, sturdy tent the next morning. The tour group inside the tent was enthralled by Curdy Finch, a prospector who loved to have tourists flocking around him. He was the proud owner of a claim not far from Bonanza Creek, formerly Rabbit Creek, and Eldorado Creek. These were the two creeks where gold was first discovered in 1896. Valerie took a big, hot swallow of coffee from her thermos, and Faye tried to smoke one of her rare cigarettes—a project she soon gave up in the relentless cold. For a woman born in Haiti, she was surviving amazingly well in the Canadian North.

Valerie's gaze wandered over the frozen winter landscape, which showed no signs of life. Scrawny brush poked through the snow cover as if the twigs were gasping for air. Even the sky seemed frozen. They escaped into the tent where a woodstove in the corner radiated warmth.

Curdy Finch held a prospector's pan in his hand and gave a long-winded explanation of how he washed away sand and gravel from the creek in it.

"The heavy gold particles sink to the bottom of the pan, and that's how they get filtered out," he said.

Curdy emptied a Mason jar into his hand and displayed to the wide-eyed audience five gold nuggets.

"Last summer I found a hundred fine ounces of gold," he announced, "but nuggets are worth the most because you can use them in jewelry."

Paula couldn't resist the temptation to touch the nuggets.

"How much are these five worth?" she asked.

Curdy grinned, showing his worn-down teeth.

"Several hundred thousands of dollars."

This elicited oohs, wows, and a nervous giggle—that was Trish, who probably figured she could pay for her kids' education with that much gold.

Valerie looked at the circle of people. Curdy knew how to fire up his audience's imagination; it was a gift from heaven. With his creased, weather-beaten face and his rough work clothes he was the very model of a prospector. As always, Valerie would slip him twenty dollars.

Faye tapped her on the shoulder.

"We still have to talk to Scott's girlfriend," she reminded Valerie.

But first on Valerie's to-do list was the giant excavator from the second phase of the gold rush. These electrified giants would dig their buckets into the earth, down to great depths. It was like putting the soil through a meat grinder. Every time she looked from the hill above Dawson City down onto the floodplain below, it pained her to see how this landscape had been destroyed during the feverish search for gold. The damage was still clearly visible, more than a hundred years later.

After a museum visit and a quick lunch, she dismissed the group for the rest of the day. Valerie and Faye drove to the Downtown Hotel and asked for Grace Wilkins. The nice receptionist informed them that Grace wasn't on that day. She offered to call her at home and reached for the phone.

"She'd like to talk to you," she said, handing Valerie the receiver.

"We met your friend Scott in Whitehorse," Valerie explained. "We'd like to ask you about a woman you know and saw in Dawson."

"Yes. Scott told me about it," Grace responded. "Can you come to my place?"

The receptionist pointed out on a city map where to find Grace's residence.

The house, a bungalow with a purple front and lime-green window trim, was at the Dawson city limits. The long-legged woman who opened the door was maybe twenty. She wore an extra-long, soft, cuddly sweater, jeans with glittery embroidery, and knee-high, soft-leather brown boots. She gave them a friendly smile and took them into a living room that looked like a boudoir. Colorful East Indian tapestries were draped on the walls and bedecked two sofas. It smelled of incense.

"Unfortunately, I have to go in half an hour," Grace said apologetically. "A rehearsal for our cancan show this summer. Have you ever seen our act?"

Valerie said she'd seen the cancan dancers in Diamond Tooth Gertie's gambling hall last summer, with a girl she knew, and that they'd been impressed.

Grace beamed.

"This summer's show will be real cool. New costumes and choreography. It'll be more erotic. And I'm gonna sing! Just a sec."

She disappeared briefly and came back with an ensemble that she held up against her body. Valerie and Faye struggled a bit to admire the sparkling, ruffled bustier and the gaudy, wide, flouncy skirt whose function was to be gathered up to expose what was underneath.

"You've gotta try the tea," Grace said. "I've just had it sent direct from India." She filled the kettle and asked about Valerie's travel plans. When she heard the words *Ice Road*, the smile left her face.

"You must have heard about Gisèle's death. Isn't it terrible? We're all in shock, devastated. How could that happen? Poor Gisèle!"

"You knew her well?" Faye asked.

"Of course! We often hung out. She even danced at Diamond Tooth Gertie's with us."

Grace put three cups down on a painted box that served as a coffee table.

"Try it. I plan to import tea from India and sell it all over the Yukon." Her face brightened. "Gisèle was always interested in these kinds of experiments, you know."

"What do you mean?" Valerie asked.

"She liked novelties. She liked new places. Before she came here, she'd really only been in that hick town in Quebec; I can't even remember the name. And she'd been to Montreal once." She brushed her henna-tinted hair over her shoulders.

Valerie blew on her steaming tea and wondered what it was that drew pretty young girls like Grace and Gisèle to a remote city like Dawson. Even if only for a few months. What was so exciting about dancing the cancan for tourists? Or were there other, much greater temptations?

"Is that why Gisèle went to Inuvik?"

Grace stopped moving for a brief moment, and Valerie noticed her moist lips twitching a bit.

"Dunno . . . She never said she wanted to go to Inuvik. Maybe . . . she just wanted to see the Igloo Church. It's famous. Gisèle didn't tell me everything."

She looked at Faye, then Valerie.

"How do you like the tea?"

"Interesting," Faye replied diplomatically. "I've never tasted anything this exotic."

Grace once again beamed with pride.

"So you're looking for Sedna?" she asked.

"Scott told us you'd seen her," Faye replied.

"Yeah. In the Alchemy Café."

"When was that?"

"About five weeks ago. I also bumped into her last August at the annual Prospectors' Dance Festival in the hockey arena. That's where I first met her."

Valerie was surprised.

"At the Prospectors' Festival. She went *there?*"

She'd had no inkling about Sedna's intentions. How could she allow herself to be so effortlessly deceived!

"It's a big event in town. All the mine owners are there, and everybody and anybody with the right status and name. Lots of rich people. You can buy raffle tickets and win a solid-gold bracelet. A thing like that sets you back six grand in the store," Grace said, rolling her eyes. She obviously didn't approve.

"What were you doing there?" Faye held her teacup firmly with both hands.

"Waitressing. Sedna came with Richard Melville. I know him, and he introduced me. You can't show up with Richard at a ball and not turn heads. Particularly if you're a woman."

Valerie took note. Richard Melville. Who'd have thought it.

Grace rattled on.

"He's got two or three mines here. Gold. He's kinda like a big shot in town. And sorta old. Over fifty. Richard's been in Dawson forever. Everybody knows him."

Valerie leaned forward.

"What have you heard about Sedna since then?"

"Hmm . . . Just that she wanted to take a chopper somewhere in the tundra. Kinda weird. They cost a bundle here. And why'd she want to go up there all by herself? A bit dangerous, if you ask me."

"So did she actually take a helicopter up there?"

"Dunno. You'd have to ask the guys at Blue Eagle."

"And where can we find Richard Melville?"

"He's probably long gone by now, off to where it's warm. The Maldives. Or Barbados. Or Florida, for all I know. Somewhere I'd like to spend the winter. But I can't leave because of Scott."

Valerie pressed on. "Do you know where we can find Sedna?"

Grace shook her head.

"Maybe she doesn't want to be found. People come to Dawson to leave their family sometimes. Or their spouse. It's par for the course."

She looked at her wristwatch. A staggeringly expensive watch, Valerie estimated.

"Oh, before I forget. Can you take a little package to Inuvik for me?"

Grace jumped up and took something off a shelf on the wall. Faye accepted the package and squinted at Valerie. The name on the wrapper: "Clem Hardeven."

"You know him?" Valerie asked as she stood up.

"Naw. Somebody left it for me with a note. For me to give it to him. No idea who."

"May I see the note?"

"Threw it out."

Grace tugged at her soft sweater.

"Is there a problem?" she asked.

"No," Valerie heard Faye say. "Not at all. Many thanks for the tea."

Once they were on their way in the Chevy, Valerie blurted out, "Faye, we simply cannot take this package with us. We don't have the slightest idea what's inside. It could be drugs."

Faye laughed.

"I think there was something in the tea, too; it tasted a bit like hash."

Valerie looked at her, baffled, and Faye laughed even harder.

"Val, you know what we'll do? You call up your good friend Clem and tell him we'd like to open the package before bringing it to him. Then we'll see what he says."

"You are one smart lady," Valerie acknowledged. "You know, I'm beginning to think girls like Grace have something up their sleeve far more dangerous than Indian spices from Rajasthan."

They parked in front of Brown's Tack and Saddle, and Valerie called Clem. Once again, he answered promptly. The poor man must be desperately bored.

Valerie came straight to the point with a concise report about the package.

"May I open it to see what we're schlepping?"

He seemed genuinely surprised.

"A package? Tell me again who gave it to you."

Valerie repeated the story.

"I'm not expecting any packages, and I don't even know a Grace Wilkins. It's fine for you to open it. Maybe it's got something to do with Helvin."

"Yeah, but what if it contains a deadly virus or anthrax? Do you have enemies, Clem?"

Out of the corner of her eye, Valerie saw Faye make a face.

"Val, I'll open it, if you want, and you can stay outside the car until the coast is clear."

"What's that I'm hearing?" Clem asked.

"That's my friend Faye. She's making fun of me."

Nevertheless, Valerie gave Faye the package. Faye took off the brown wrapper to reveal a small, shiny box.

Her eyes widened.

"Oh, an engagement ring?" she said jokingly.

Clem heard her.

"What? A ring?"

Valerie gave her the finger.

"No, she's just kidding. C'mon, Faye."

Finally, Faye opened the box. She and Valerie stared at a small object lying on a dark velvet cloth.

"What is it?" Clem asked.

Valerie whistled.

"A gold nugget," she shouted.

"A *big* nugget!" Faye exclaimed.

Silence at the other end.

"Did you hear what she said?" Valerie asked.

"Yeah. This isn't a joke?"

"No, it's definitely not. What should we do with it?"

"There's no sender's name?"

"Uh-uh."

It took him a few seconds before he spoke.

"Pack the thing up exactly the way it was, paper and all. And bring it here."

"You're going to owe me big-time," Valerie warned.

"Is a White Russian in the Crazy Hunter good enough?"

"I don't want a drink; I want a helpful explanation."

"I'll try to impress you with a dazzling eye-opener. But my brain's somewhat fuzzy at the moment."

"Clem, did you ever meet Gisèle when she was in Inuvik?"

"Me? No. No way. Where . . . who said I did?"

"My inquisitive brain."

A pause.

"Wait till you get here and we'll talk it over," Clem said. "The two of us."

"Aye, aye, sir."

She wished him a speedy recovery and ended the call.

Faye looked at her and shook her head.

"Now I'm absolutely sure there was hash in that tea."

Both of them burst out laughing.

Valerie had let the group know that evening what to expect on the Dempster Highway the next day. The weather forecast was fantastic: sunny and only thirteen below. She was looking forward to going to bed early and was brushing her teeth when there was a knock at her hotel-room door. It was Faye.

She had excused herself from joining them for dinner that evening. "I was at that helicopter company Grace mentioned," she said. "Remember? Blue Eagle. I inquired about Sedna."

Valerie gripped her toothbrush; her lips were smeared white. Faye was unfazed.

"She wanted to fly to a place in the tundra. A very particular spot. Where a man and a woman had camped thirty years ago. Rather well-known people apparently. I didn't really get what it was all about, but I wrote down their names."

She took a piece of paper out of her pocket.

"We've got to find out who those two are. The Blue Eagle guys said Sedna hadn't booked in the end because it cost too much. What a laugh! Too much! As if she didn't steal enough of my money."

Valerie felt as if someone had kicked her in the guts. She glanced at the piece of paper and sat down on the edge of the bed.

"No."

"No, what?" Faye stared at her.

"We don't have to find out who these people are. I know who they are."

"Really? Who?"

"My parents."

CHAPTER 17

Clem awoke with a start. Meteor was growling at the front door. He returned to the sofa when his master got up.

"Good doggie," Clem said, patting Meteor lovingly on the head. "Let's see what's up."

Now *he* heard a noise. Somebody was prowling around outside. Since the attack, he'd kept the front door locked, for the first time ever. He also kept a revolver within reach. Meteor growled again and shot into the kitchen.

Whoever was out there couldn't see any light inside because Clem had turned off all the lights before going to bed. He looked out a kitchen window. Was that a knock? Meteor ran to the door again. Clem opened a window and shouted, "C'mon out, you yellow rat!"

A familiar voice rang in his ears.

"Uqaqtaukun uqaruktuami." I want to make a phone call.

Clem turned on the light switch, then headed to the front door to open it.

"Why the hell are you sneaking around out there? Meteor's balls were in an uproar."

Loud crunching sounds in the snow. Then Lazarusie Uvvayuaq stepped into the light. Meteor recognized him and stopped growling. Lazarusie followed Clem into the kitchen.

"Qiqitaani," he said. I'm freezing.

"Well now, that's really a disgrace for an Eskimo," Clem said. He could get away with saying that to Laz, who often called him a paleface in good fun.

Clem filled the kettle and put it on the stove.

"How long have you been hanging around out there?"

Lazarusie pulled off his hood and sat down, still wearing his parka. "No idea."

Clem should have known: never ask an Inuvialuk about time. He put a sugar shaker on the table.

"Why didn't you just knock on the door?"

"I didn't see anybody. And your pickup isn't here."

"It's still at the hospital. The doc wouldn't let me drive. Maybe in a week, he said. So you need a phone?"

Lazarusie nodded.

"Gotta call my wife."

"Good idea. What happened anyway? More problems with Tanya?"

The kettle whistled, and Meteor lowered his ears.

"The cops wanted to talk to me, but I wasn't home."

"I see. You're here."

Clem poured black tea into two cups and plied Lazarusie with the inevitable cookies. Laz shook a huge amount of sugar into his tea.

"Why don't you go to the station and talk to the RCMP? I bet they found boot tracks around the body. And your snowmobile tracks. It's better if you tell them what you know."

"No. I've got to talk to you first."

Clem sat down, feeling uneasy.

"Because of the shaman's rattle."

Lazarusie didn't say anything. They sipped their tea in unison. Meteor looked from one man to the other, hoping for a cookie. Lazarusie often slipped him one in spite of Clem's protests. Not that the

Inuvialuit spoiled their dogs. But Meteor wasn't a sled dog in Lazarusie's eyes, nor a working dog, just the pampered domestic animal belonging to his white friend.

Clem suspected what was driving Laz. He felt a touch of cold in spite of the hot tea. He stalled for time, played with a cookie. Silence wasn't necessarily a void that the Inuvialuit had to fill with conversation. Clem had seen it often. They sometimes waited for a long time and said almost nothing. But Clem had to bring up the subject before it was too late.

"They took Pihuk Bart in for questioning. Won't you tell the RCMP about the rattle?"

Lazarusie immediately turned his head away and pretended to be distracted. Clem knew exactly what that meant: he'd treaded on a taboo. And yet he couldn't avoid it. This was serious business.

"Laz, I wouldn't have asked if there wasn't a murder investigation going on."

"I need to call my wife," his visitor said.

Clem handed him his cell phone. He went to the bathroom and held the door shut to fight off Meteor's snout. Clem could hear Lazarusie's voice and some words in Siglitun, the dialect of the Tuktoyaktuk people. He didn't get the exact words but got the gist of what they were talking about.

Danny, Lazarusie's son who still lived at home with Laz and his wife, was for some reason raised to be a shaman. That was why Danny—Clem knew him by his Christian name—was not allowed to play with other children in school or at home, or to watch TV or listen to music. The family insulated him from unwanted influences. When Danny was fourteen, he began to rebel. Time after time he would escape from home, get involved with drugs, and declare he wanted to sing in a band. He didn't give up his role as shaman-in-waiting entirely because it garnered him admiration and approval. But he fooled around with it in ways that didn't conform to tradition and certainly not to his parents' and the Tuktoyaktuk council of elders' beliefs. Clem guessed that Danny must be sixteen by now. He'd heard recently that he was taking part in a government job-creation program.

He went back into the kitchen. Lazarusie looked up.

"I'll talk to the police. What am I supposed to tell them?"

Clem filled Meteor's water bowl and took out the shaman's rattle Lazarusie had given him for safekeeping. He held the gorgeous carving in his hands. A bird's head with little pointed teeth in an open bill. On the elongated body, but not the handle, hung dozens of tiny bone attachments that Clem recognized as baby seals only after he'd scrutinized them. Shaking the rattle made the little bones produce a sound like the wild wind over the ice. A masterpiece—Clem appreciated that at once.

"One of your relatives carved this, didn't they?"

Lazarusie nodded.

"My uncle made several rattles for Danny. They resembled his grandfather's very much; he was a shaman, too. Tanya says Danny started to sell them. He'd discovered that collectors would pay a lot to own one. But that's probably not true."

"Laz, how did Gisèle happen to get this rattle?"

Lazarusie bent his head.

"Danny says that Tanya stole it and sold it."

"There's a rumor making the rounds that Gisèle was going to meet Pihuk Bart on the Ice Road that night. If that's really so, she was evidently interested in shamans. Did she ever get in touch with Danny?"

"My wife asked Danny that, and he said no."

Clem rubbed his tired face. He ought to get some rest and stop racking his brains.

"You *must* tell the police everything when you talk to them, Laz, including the business with the rattle. I don't see any other way."

Lazarusie clenched his fists and pressed them down on the edge of the table.

"That will make the spirits angry. Bad things happen when sacred rattles fall into the wrong hands."

Clem looked at him in amazement. It wasn't the police his friend was scared of; it was the power of ancient ritual. The revenge of the spirits.

"That's why we've got to stop this, Laz. You're doing exactly the right thing. And whatever happens, I've got your back, OK?"

Clem picked up his phone. He called John Palmer and let him know Laz was there and ready to talk.

"Have him come here; I'm in my office," Palmer said.

"He feels safer at my place, John. Would it be possible for you to come here?"

To his surprise, Palmer agreed.

Palmer appeared in ten minutes with a second officer, who introduced himself as Franklin Edwards from the Yellowknife RCMP. Clem had a vague recollection of seeing him in Helvin's office. Meteor couldn't make up his mind whether to be on guard or thrilled. Clem commanded the dog to lie down on his mat in front of the stove.

Clem was amazed that the Inuvik police had brought in a man from the capital of the Northwest Territories as backup. Was Gisèle's death behind it? Or maybe the explosion on the ice? So far there'd only been a dry press report that had downplayed it.

Palmer asked the questions and Edwards took notes. Lazarusie began to talk, haltingly, omitting nothing he'd told Clem. Edwards put on rubber gloves and dropped the rattle into a transparent bag.

Then Lazarusie said, "I found something else."

His hand disappeared into his pants pocket. He laid something on the table, palm-sized, wrapped in a damp, tattered cloth, tied with a string.

Edwards removed the cloth. When Clem saw the box, he caught his breath.

"Where did you find this, exactly?" Palmer asked.

"Between my snowmobile and . . . the dead woman."

"How far from the body?"

"About seven arm's lengths."

Edwards carefully opened the box. They all stared at the gold nugget.

It took a few seconds for Palmer to speak up again.

"Why did you pocket this?"

"I forgot to put it back. After I saw the body, I got scared. And then, later, when I remembered it, I thought it was too late."

Edwards spoke next.

"It's not every day that a gold nugget is found on the Ice Road, right? A person would remember that, don't you think?"

"I didn't know what was in it. I never opened it. I just remembered it today."

Clem thought it was time to get the police off Lazarusie's back.

"Somebody's sending me a nugget, too. Just heard about it yesterday."

The policemen's eyes turned toward him, as did Lazarusie's.

"A friend called me from Dawson. A young woman gave her a package with my name on it and asked her to bring it to me. My friend is coming up the Dempster today. I told her I wasn't expecting a package, so we decided she should open it to see what was inside. And there it was. A gold nugget in a box."

"Where's it now?" Edwards wanted to know.

"My friend's bringing it."

"Where is she?"

"She's planning to leave Dawson today."

"What's her name?"

"Valerie Blaine, from Vancouver. She's a tour guide bringing a group to Inuvik."

It didn't escape Clem that Edwards waited a beat before writing down the name.

"Who was the woman who gave your friend the package?"

"Grace. Grace Wilkins, if I remember correctly. She works as a waitress in the Downtown Hotel."

Clem had the sudden feeling that the investigators knew more than they were letting on.

"What the hell's going on with these damn nuggets, John?" Clem asked Palmer.

"That's what we're trying to find out."

"Lemme guess: some more of these nifty presents have turned up, am I right?"

Edwards stood up and Palmer followed suit.

"Lazarusie, we'll have to take down your statement officially at the station," Palmer said. "Not today, tomorrow."

Then he turned to Clem.

"Don't forget to hand over the nugget to us."

"How could I forget?"

Clem stood up and stretched his back, as if attempting to appear even more imposing than he already was, given his height.

"What's happening around here is quite extraordinary, you might say. A massive explosion in polar-bear country; a dead woman on the Ice Road; somebody whacks me on the noggin, dammit, and now somebody's paving the streets with lumps of gold. Helv West has vanished off the face of the earth for days now. And nobody can tell us what gives. Pretty nice state of affairs. Truly reassuring."

He crossed his arms over his chest.

"Know anything about Helvin? He was spotted in Dawson, by the way. And what about the idiot that knocked me out?"

John Palmer adjusted his fur hat.

"We're pleased that you've given us this information," he said. "We're doing everything in our power."

The officer from Yellowknife nodded. He wished Clem a speedy recovery. "And call us if you hear anything."

"*What* am I supposed to hear?" Clem muttered after the RCMP officers had left the house.

"From your friend on the Dempster," Lazarusie said, spelling it out.

CHAPTER 18

They left Dawson at eight sharp. Breakfast had to wait. The Chevy took its own sweet time to warm up. A few minutes later somebody—Valerie thought she heard Carol's voice—started shouting and others immediately joined in.

"Dempster! Dempster! Dempster! Dempster! Dempster!"

Even Faye bellowed along with them. Valerie felt like she was in a football stadium full of excited fans. The boisterous mood in the bus was irresistibly infectious. She turned around and saw a sea of happy faces despite the early hour. A tour guide's boon. She laughed and shook her head as if to say, "You guys are really something."

They stopped at the entrance to the Dempster Highway and studied the checklist for drivers on a bulletin board. FIRST AID KIT, WATER CANS, EMERGENCY FLARES, SPARE GAS. IN WINTER: SHOVEL, SLEEPING BAG, COLD-WEATHER CLOTHING, STOVE AND MATCHES, AND A VEHICLE IN GOOD CONDITION AND THOROUGHLY INSPECTED. Valerie had the bus pull over in front of two other boards: EAGLE LODGE 363 KM, INUVIK 735 KM. But the final board, a warning, fascinated the group: NEXT GAS 370 KM.

The minibus moved on ahead, and everybody started talking loudly at the same time.

"Do we get a danger allowance?"

"Val, did you bring enough antifreeze?"

"I'm already sweating in my thermal underwear."

"Keep your batteries warm, people!"

"Why aren't you wearing your Hawaiian shirt, Jordan?"

"Does a satellite phone work on batteries?"

"How cold is it outside, Val?"

"Minus twenty-two, but it's supposed to be minus thirteen later. You've really lucked out."

She didn't tell them that the water in the canisters and the chocolate bars had turned hard as stone in the minibus overnight. They'd have to melt snow to make their coffee when they stopped for a break.

Mercifully, the frozen dirt road was almost ice free. Valerie told the group that the climate along the Dempster was surprisingly dry because the Pacific coastal mountains held back the moist air. Unlike other parts of Canada, the northern region of the Yukon Territory had not experienced prehistoric glaciers or ice sheets.

"But you already know that from the Beringia Museum," she said. "There's not much snow in winter, and it thaws quickly in the spring, as you can see by those deep gullies." She pointed to the ditches running along the side of the road. "The water can run off there, and the road doesn't get flooded. Otherwise it would freeze, and we'd be on an ice rink."

She'd already lost her audience during that last sentence because Glenn Bliss had spotted a red fox.

"Photo stop!" he shouted.

Now Valerie saw the fox too, lying beside a fir in a hollow. When the bus stopped, it bounded off.

A fine mist had covered the landscape so that only the shoulders of the road were visible. An occasional fir rose out of the milky soup like a scrawled black-ink drawing.

Once they hit the hard gravel, they made better time. They encountered a road service SUV, the only vehicle they saw on this stretch.

While the voices from the seats behind her chattered away, Valerie and Faye talked only when necessary.

Faye was focused on the road; she took her position very seriously. Valerie remembered how she'd traveled the same stretch last summer. Sedna had slept through the early morning hours. Sleeping off her hangover, Valerie supposed, because though she herself had gone to bed early, Sedna said she was going to make another pilgrimage to the Downtown Hotel. For a nightcap, she said. Valerie now knew that Sedna had spent that August night dining and dancing with Richard Melville, the gold-mine owner, at the Prospectors' Festival.

Valerie's thoughts turned to her brother Kosta; she'd sent him a long, detailed, newsy e-mail that morning. There was no reason not to tell him about Sedna, and Faye's discovery at Blue Eagle. She asked him, "Why do you think Sedna is hunting down our parents?"

Valerie was suddenly struck by the thought that Sedna wanted to know more about her biological mother than she did. But why?

Peter Hardy-Blaine, your family is not what it pretends to be.

Faye interrupted her ruminations. "You look good in that jazzy jacket."

"Oh, thanks." Valerie turned toward her in surprise. "I want to be visible in the snow. Yellow or pink—that was the question."

Faye had on a bright green jacket. Nobody could accuse them of not leading by example.

"Then get out into the snow so those guys up there can see you."

"Those guys up there?"

Faye pointed with her chin toward the windshield.

Valerie leaned forward and saw a helicopter making an arc before disappearing from view.

"Somebody's keeping an eye on us," Faye said.

Valerie leaned back.

"Probably the highway patrol."

"Probably," Faye said, not entirely convinced.

The group behind them was discussing Jack Dempster's life. Paula was once again in her element, plying her fellow travelers with information from a pamphlet. Valerie had been saving it for the next picnic stop but was happy to turn it over to Paula.

"The men of the North-West Mounted Police patrolled the northern part of the Yukon Territory and the Mackenzie Delta on dogsled. Their patrols maintained the links between Dawson City, Fort McPherson, Herschel Island, and Rampart House. They sometimes traveled for months on end. Inspector Fitzgerald and three men never came back from a patrol in 1910, and it was Jack Dempster who found out what had happened to them."

Paula had barely finished the sad conclusion of the Lost Patrol's story when a babble of voices started up.

Faye whispered something to Valerie.

"I don't know if I'm crazy, but it's as if I can smell Sedna. As if she's nearby."

"Are you psychic? Because that would be very practical. Too bad I couldn't pay you more if you were, though."

"You're not taking me seriously, Val. I just have this feeling."

Valerie put her hand on Faye's arm.

"Sorry. I'm a little tense. And my stomach's growling. We're almost at the spot for our break."

"Just one car in the last forty-four miles." Faye whistled through pursed lips.

Valerie smiled.

"It doesn't get any better, believe me."

They turned into the Tombstone Mountain campground ten minutes later. In an open log lean-to, they fed the cookstove with shavings and logs. They melted snow in aluminum pots on the grill for their coffee. Everybody pitched in. They roasted little curried sausages, plus tofu for Trish. They took turns standing at the stove to warm their hands. Valerie spread out pineapple, Camembert, baguettes, potato chips, carrots, and ham slices on the wooden table. After the meal, she brought out a bottle of Baileys that she'd kept warm in her room overnight. The group's reaction was one of delight as they waved their paper cups. Only Faye, as their driver, conscientiously refused it.

Valerie surveyed the group. A person was missing.

"Where's Trish?"

"She was going to go out back, to the bathroom," Trish's sister Carol shouted.

"She went there with me and Paula," Glenn said.

"How long ago was that?"

"Fifteen minutes maybe."

Valerie didn't waste a second.

"C'mon, let's check on her."

"Can I go, too?" Faye and Glenn asked simultaneously.

Valerie thought for a moment. Faye had to stay with the group, but Glenn was strong and might be useful. Then she changed her mind. She didn't want to risk having an American citizen get himself into trouble. "No, please stay here for now."

She took Carol by the arm. As they turned to walk away from the group, she reminded her, "In this climate, we can never leave anybody alone outside. We always go out in pairs, OK?"

Carol nodded, looking a little embarrassed.

"I didn't really think . . . even to the bathroom?"

"Always," Valerie said firmly as they stepped onto the snow.

The outhouses were scattered around the area, but Trish wasn't in any of them. They discovered footsteps, too many to differentiate. Carol called her sister's name over and over, hesitantly at first, then louder and louder. They circled the area in the snow and broke through some underbrush, Valerie in front, Carol close behind.

Suddenly, they heard a weak voice from a hollow, about two hundred yards away. They fought their way toward the voice.

Once they reached the hollow, they spotted a blue-green spot in the white. Trish. She staggered toward them and began to cry even before Carol took her in her arms.

"I . . . I couldn't find my way back," Trish sobbed. Her head was uncovered, and her hair was damp and pressed against her face. Valerie noticed she wasn't wearing gloves either. She wrapped her own scarf around Trish's head.

"But the outhouses are so close to the lean-to," Carol said, every inch the older sister.

"I don't go in toilets like those," Trish stammered. "They're . . . disgusting."

"But why'd you go so far away?"

Valerie cut off the interrogation.

"We'll get you warm as quickly as possible," she said.

The small crowd was waiting for them with inquisitive faces and steaming cups of coffee. The hot liquid soothed Trish. She gave Valerie back her scarf and explained to the group that she'd gone into the bushes so she wouldn't have to use the outhouse. Then, she said, she'd followed some tracks back, thinking they were hers, but that turned out to be a mistake. She suddenly didn't recognize her surroundings. And then she heard a noise: someone tramping through the snow.

"Every time I stopped, the noise stopped, too," Trish said. "It was creepy." Her otherwise rather pale face was now aglow. "And when I walked ahead, I heard it again, every time. I was really scared."

"Maybe you heard our footsteps," Carol offered, putting an arm around her sister.

Trish shook her head.

"No, I heard you two later. It felt like an eternity." She shuddered.

Valerie also put a comforting arm around Trish's shoulder. You can never predict how people are going to react in unfamiliar surroundings.

Trish pulled something out of her inside jacket pocket.

"I found this in the snow," she said.

They all stared at the longish object in her hand. It looked like a miniature ukulele with a narrow neck and a curved body, but with a carved head at the wider end. Tiny things resembling wooden toothpicks were stuck into the sides, with stylized fish and seashells attached to them.

Valerie's heart began to palpitate. She couldn't believe what she was seeing.

Anika was the first to regain her speech.

"What is it?"

"An instrument?" Jordan asked while reaching for his camera.

Valerie snatched the object out of Trish's hand.

"Where did you find this, exactly?"

"Hmm . . . not far . . . just a few steps from the second outhouse. Just before the brush starts."

She still seemed out of it.

"What's that?" Paula asked, so close to Valerie that she could smell the Baileys in her coffee. She felt that all eyes were glued to her.

"A shaman's rattle," was her hasty answer. "Inuit shamans use it to summon spirits."

"A souvenir somebody lost?" Glenn reached out to touch the rattle, but Valerie took it away.

"It looks authentic, but an expert will need to see it to be sure," she said, wrapping her scarf around the rattle. Then she forced a smile.

"Enjoy your coffee, everybody, while Faye and I take the leftovers back to the bus."

Glenn called out after them: "Don't forget to go to the outhouse in pairs!"

Valerie gave him a thumbs-up in affirmation.

They were scarcely out of earshot when she said, "I've seen this rattle before, I'm sure of it."

"Wow! And where?"

"Sedna brought it home last summer. She showed it to me on the way back from Inuvik but didn't tell me where she got it. You can't normally get your hands on one of these."

Valerie's words were tumbling out.

"This rattle is probably very old. You can't simply go and buy one."

Faye opened the hatch of the Chevy and stowed away a box of groceries. Then she pulled her hat down lower on her forehead.

"And you laughed at me when I said I could smell Sedna around here somewhere," she boasted.

Valerie nodded absentmindedly.

"C'mon," she said, "let's make a quick search of the place. Maybe we'll find something else."

CHAPTER 19

Meteor bounced along like a rubber ball beside the snowmobile Clem was driving down to the frozen Mackenzie. He'd had it with staying in the house like a prisoner within his own four walls. The ice-cold air in his lungs and brain felt like a liberation. The sun beamed as if it had to compensate for the rotten winter weather, enticing the residents of Inuvik out of their homes.

On the ice, the preparations for the Muskrat Jamboree were moving at full speed. Men were rapidly hammering boards to the platform for the spring festival's muskrat-skinning competition. Clem had entered it several times, but like many of his sex he'd failed miserably against the skilled Inuvialuit women. His forte was snowmobile racing, but not this year because of his concussion. He hoped the doctors and hospital personnel wouldn't catch him driving his snowmobile onto the frozen river today.

The mighty Mackenzie. Canada's longest river, powerful and wide as a large lake in summer, and occasionally torrential and dangerous on its way to the Arctic Ocean. In winter it was transformed into a white, unending plain—frozen immobility, a metamorphosis Clem found captivating even after seven years in Inuvik.

Opposite the platform stood a tent with poles made from thin, unpeeled tree trunks; a smoking stovepipe jutted up from it. Clem parked there just as an Inuvialuit woman emerged wearing a Mother Hubbard–style parka—with fur inside and colorful fabric and trimming outside—and a wool hat over her black hair. She had a shiny pink placard in her hand. Marjorie Tama. Clem didn't often see her in traditional dress. The mayor halted.

"Clem! What a surprise! Did you escape from the hospital?"

"But of course, Marj, somebody's got to catch the criminal who clobbered me."

"Maybe he got the wrong man," Marjorie speculated. "Nobody here has anything against you, Clem. It's beyond me."

"Dunno, Marj, a little too much bad stuff in too short a time, don't you think?"

Clem knew that Marjorie was worried about the recent violent incidents in her community. If conflicts threatened, she knew how to calm things down and mediate. She believed in professional negotiations at the bargaining table, of course, but also in the healing power and wisdom of her people's ancient myths that she passed down to children and adults. When she spoke about these, Clem felt reminded of the fairy tales his parents had told him as a child. But instead of evil witches or man-eating giants, it was *qallupilluk*, the Kidnapper, that stimulated his imagination: a monster with slimy fish scales and webbed fingers that would hide near ice cracks during spring breakup and drag down children who dared to walk out on the floes. He was especially fascinated by *mahaha*, the Tickler, who terrified people with his manic giggling and eagle's talons; he would ambush unlucky people caught in a blizzard then tickle his victims to death.

There were no monster legends pertinent to Gisèle Chaume's death. Something intangible, menacing, was in the air that Marjorie and Clem couldn't identify. But it wasn't in the Inuvialuit's nature to be consumed with fear. There was hardly anything that they couldn't counteract with humor, courage, or equanimity.

Marjorie broke into a broad grin.

"Why do I always bump into you where there's food to be had?"

"People gotta survive, Marj. What's on the menu?"

She handed him the placard.

The offerings looked familiar—no different from the previous year. Roast muskrat with potato salad. Flour soup with *balowak*, rabbit; *maktak*, whale blubber; *uqsuq*, seal blubber; plus soup with goose meat, chili con carne, and rolls. And pancakes and muffins with coffee.

"Who catches the muskrats?" Clem inquired.

She was looking past him. He followed her eyes. Pihuk Bart was hanging around a shed built just for the festival. He also wore a knitted wool hat, with strands of hair on it resembling a horse's mane. Leather fringes were sewn all over his jacket; embroidered flowers decorated his chest. He'd tied a black-and-white bandana over the lower half of his face like a train robber in the Old West.

"Cowboy rags," Clem declared.

Marjorie shot him a withering look.

"Don't tell *him* that. He's a shaman."

"Will the RCMP leave him alone now, do you think?"

"He's said to have a solid alibi."

"And what else do people say about this shaman of ours?"

"He has his followers. Maybe he made a big impression on Gisèle. Laz Uvvayuaq is most certainly not a fan of his. As far as the people in Tuktoyaktuk are concerned, Danny's the next great shaman. Coffee?"

Clem followed her into the tent. She filled a paper cup from the thermos as she spoke.

"Danny can't take the pressure anymore. He's had enough. Not just because he's young. No music, no dancing, no friends, no parties. Rumor has it that he sometimes sneaks out of the house at night. And people in Tuktoyaktuk think Pihuk's to blame because they need a scapegoat."

Clem took the steaming cup. He felt its warmth even through his glove. He wanted to change the subject because Lazarusie was a friend.

"What do you think happened back then in Inuliktuuq? Why did everybody run out into the cold, to certain death? And why leave the tiniest baby behind?"

The helpless infant, the sole survivor, Pihuk Bart.

Marjorie swayed her head back and forth.

"Maybe they were scared."

"Scared of what?"

"The child."

"Why—"

Clem was cut off by a commotion in front of the tent. He knew immediately what had happened.

He stormed out, yelling, "Meteor!" But it was too late. Men were running from every direction at a wild pack of wailing, growling, slobbering dogs entangled in their dogsled harnesses.

"Meteor!" Clem screamed again when he saw a man swinging a stick at the roiling pile of dogs; loud howling and whimpering followed. Meteor broke out of the bunch and ran like crazy around the place until his master's commands steered him to his proper spot. Blood shimmered below the dog's ear. Clem gave him a scolding, but he was just as mad at himself for letting Meteor out of his sight. The sled driver used the stick to disentangle the harnesses of the agitated dogs. Clem recognized him: Nuyaviaq Marten, a hunter from Tuktoyaktuk. He fastened a leash to Meteor's collar and walked back toward the tent.

Marjorie intuitively sized up the situation.

"Nuyaviaq is bringing us *maktak*," she said. "Here, give him a cup of coffee. That'll calm him down."

"I'm such an idiot," Clem confessed as he passed Nuyaviaq his coffee. "I shoulda paid more attention to Meteor."

The Inuvialuit hunter's face showed no sign of resentment. Rather, mischief was in his eyes.

"I've heard that you're not right in the head since somebody bashed it in."

Both men laughed.

"And I've heard you're supplying the blubber for us."

Nuyaviaq grinned.

"Only for Inuvialuit, not for *tanngit*, eh?"

Clem held his smile.

"I didn't know you were out whaling, Nuyaviaq."

A shadow crossed the hunter's face.

"Somebody's killing whales with explosives, but it's not us."

"Who . . . what do you mean?"

Nuyaviaq took his time before answering, yelling at his fidgety dogs.

"That explosion . . . nobody wants to kill whales that way."

He wiped his nose with his glove.

"Who says somebody's killing whales with explosives?"

Nuyaviaq looked at his boots, then at the dogs.

"I only saw it from a distance. Ilaryuaq and his brother went out there the day after. They saw a giant hole in the ice—huge. Why a big hole like that? Somebody's after our whales."

"I've heard the military's sent a plane to find out what's going on."

"Why a plane? They'd have to send a sub."

"Did you go out on the ice, to the hole?"

Nuyaviaq shook his head.

"You really have a screw loose, man. Nobody's going to go out there after that damn explosion. I've got six kids; I don't want to get blown to bits."

"Who's gotten blown to bits?" a voice inquired.

Clem didn't have to turn around; he knew who it was.

Meteor heard the voice too. He joyfully jumped up on Waldo Bronk, a reporter for the national Canadian Broadcasting Corporation in Inuvik. Waldo could make friends with any old dog; with people, not so easily. Barely twenty-six, he'd grown up in the warm Pacific Coast climate, but he wasn't about to be put off by the rigors of the Arctic.

When he'd landed the job three years earlier, people in Inuvik had given him one winter at most before he'd fly back to his Hugo Boss shops and golf courses.

Waldo disabused them of that thought. Clem had conceived a theory that Waldo would rather be a big fish in a little pond than a little fish in a big pond. At least for a few years.

"I've got nothing to say," Clem stated without waiting for the question.

The reporter, looking tall and lean despite his down jacket and beaver hat, gave a good-natured laugh.

"I've got news from the coroner's report," he bragged—in French so that Nuyaviaq couldn't understand.

Clem reacted quickly to his impoliteness. He turned toward Nuyaviaq.

"He's trying to foist a woman from Montreal on me again, this slyboots," he said, winking at Nuyaviaq, who simply shook his head.

"Watch out, that can be dangerous. We don't need more problems up here with women from Quebec."

"You're right," Clem said. "Meteor, come! We'd better hit the road."

He walked toward the back of the shed, knowing full well that the reporter would follow. Away from curious eyes and ears, Waldo made him an offer.

"I'll make you a deal, Clem. I'll tell you what the coroner found out, and you tell me what you know about the explosion. You must have kept a direct line to someone in Ottawa."

He took Clem's silence as a yes.

"There was no sign of violence. Just a bit of hash in her blood, but too little for a high. Cause of death was hypothermia."

Clem looked at him without a word. He entertained the thought that one day Waldo would go far, because that face, framed by his beaver hat, radiated nothing but amiable goodwill. Though he clearly had something up his sleeve.

The reporter kept at it. "But that doesn't answer two questions," he said. "Why was Helvin's truck there, and who took Gisèle there and left her to freeze to death?"

Clem remained silent. But Waldo was unfazed.

"Now then, the explosion. What can you tell me about that?"

Clem decided to give him an appetizer without saying there was no dinner to follow.

"In the Arctic, it's all about oil and gas and gold and diamonds and God knows what else. And about fish. Don't underestimate the last one, my friend. In a pinch people could live without money, but not without fish."

Waldo watched him intently.

Clem went on. "There's an important conference in a couple of weeks. To protect much of the international waters in the central Arctic from commercial fishing. Canada, the US, Russia, Denmark, and Norway have already signed a treaty. A masterpiece of quiet diplomacy, Waldo. Virtually ignored by the media but totally amazing nonetheless. Now they're trying to get other countries on board, like Japan, China, South Korea, and the European Union, too. My gut tells me that Canada does *not* want to risk a diplomatic incident involving another country before the expanded treaty is in the bag."

"So the whole thing will be declared a nonevent?"

"Unless you go out there, my good man, and investigate the hole in the ice yourself. You're probably too late, anyway. Just like the Aurora flying in from Yellowknife."

Waldo's boot groped around in the snow.

"Russia or China?"

"I know as much as you do, believe me."

Waldo suddenly seemed galvanized.

"Give me another clue, Clem. Just a tidbit."

Clem raised his eyebrows.

"Typical reporter. Give them an inch . . ."

He turned around, but Waldo didn't let go so quickly.

"You know that Helvin's turned up in Dawson?"

Clem was hooked.

"Who told you that?" he asked, spinning around.

"I'll tell you if you tell me why Helvin's meeting with some gold-mine owners. And they are rather sleazy characters at that. Decent people won't have anything to do with them."

Clem felt anger boiling up inside him, anger because this mere cub obviously knew more than he did. And anger because Helvin had put him into another tough situation.

He answered more aggressively than he intended. "I thought you dealt with facts and not rumors, or am I wrong?"

Waldo's youthful face turned red. Clem was pleased that he'd hit a sore spot.

His triumph was short-lived, though. Waldo was ready for the grand finale.

"I agree with you there, Clem. That's why it would be a good thing if your boss came back soon—to clear up some speculation. We've already got one dead woman on our hands; we don't need any more corpses."

The reporter turned on his heel, but not before scratching Meteor quickly behind the ears.

Clem stood there as if bludgeoned on the head again.

His mind was on Valerie Blaine, and he felt a twinge of panic.

CHAPTER 20

Their journey continued without any other unpleasant episodes, for the time being at least. They'd gone by the tall, sharply pointed peaks of the Tombstone Mountains, which seemed to impale the skies. A ptarmigan squatted in the middle of the highway without moving for a long time, to the group's delight; they advanced toward the bird, brandishing their cameras. When the people got too near for its liking, it flew off with a cackle, flashing its black tail feathers.

"Perfect camouflage," Glenn remarked; his mustache was a similar shade of black. "They're in the grouse family. Did everyone see those feathered feet and the red comb over its eye?"

This revelation, completely untypical of Glenn, astounded everybody, Paula above all, who wasn't so well versed in the fauna department. Valerie always enjoyed the knowledge her customers brought with them. She could have kissed the ptarmigan for its performance.

A little later a snowshoe hare hopped across the road. Faye braked much too slowly for the group's liking.

"Hey, people, the road's icy," she shouted to the rear. "You don't want a broken neck!"

As if in response, after the next curve, a car appeared, stuck in the snow on the shoulder of the road. Faye stopped, but nobody was in the vehicle.

On the North Fork Pass, a bare plateau opened up that stimulated a sense of vastness and forlorn fascination. There was nothing but snow and frost-covered bushes before the distant, mighty mountain ranges. Valerie could empathize with someone wanting to temporarily get lost in this silent, overpowering landscape for a while. The fog had dissipated, and the white light was as blinding as floodlights. As they neared the sixty-mile marker, marine-blue streaks appeared in the crumbling, overcast sky.

Valerie noticed tracks in the snowbanks on the roadside.

"Moose!" she shouted. It sounded like a battle cry.

Faye drove back to the tracks, and a lively buzz immediately came from the seats behind her. There was the moose, in the flesh, not a hundred yards away, bearing a giant set of antlers—fourteen points, Valerie counted through her binoculars. Everyone, even Anika, scrambled out of the bus amazingly fast so they wouldn't miss the sight.

"Don't scare him off!" Valerie called. She was thrilled by the sighting. And it was particularly fitting that they were near Two Moose Lake of all places, a lake she had just been describing to her group.

"The moose come here in summer to eat the grass in the lake because it's high in calcium," she commented, but nobody was listening. The tourists were gawking through their zoom lenses. She was too.

As the moose ambled off, a few of the spectators complained that their feet were cold.

"Shove some warmers into your boots," Valerie advised when they were back in the bus. "That's why they were invented."

"Where are we?" Trish asked, a map on her knees. She looked relaxed once again.

"In the Blackstone Uplands," Paula responded with rocketlike speed, "and now we're coming to the northern part of the Ogilvie Mountains." She'd regained her status as the Omniscient One.

Glenn spoke up more loudly than usual: "We're not in the taiga anymore because there are no trees. Only bushes can grow in the tundra."

Valerie was only half listening. She knew that the Dempster crossed the path of the Dawson–Fort McPherson police patrol at milestone seventy-two. Her parents were supposed to cross here on their snowmobiles, but they never got this far.

She never told her brothers that, just a couple of months earlier, she'd found out about some government documents concerning her parents' tragedy. But her request for their release was denied. She was told they were classified as "Secret." She had no idea why. Military secrets, perhaps?

Whitewashed mountains rose straight up from the plain to the sky. Valerie knew that there were many hiking trails here to mountain valleys and small lakes. Hikers must come upon a strange, fantastic world opening up before them at those heights. Would she ever see it? Would her brief life be long enough for all her dreams?

They took a quick lunch break at the Engineer Creek campground. After they started up again, Paula announced that they were crossing the Ogilvie Pass. At mile 160, Valerie had the Chevy stop to see Curt's cabin, an old, rustic structure owned by a local trapper she'd met a couple of years ago.

She led the group down a narrow path, where they found the cabin unlocked. Curt had given her permission to tour the place even when he wasn't there, so they let themselves inside to looked around. Two places to sleep, on two old mattresses that took up nearly half the small room. Cans lined a wooden shelf on the wall: condensed milk, soup, beans. A rusty saw hung beside the shelf on a thick nail, as did an ax. A bent fork lay on a wobbly table. Carol read out a note above the woodstove: "'There is more kindling and firewood in front of the cabin. Get ice from the river for water.'" She lifted the lid on a roasting pot on the stove and, to general merriment, found hard biscuits in it.

"I'm going to pop back and get my camera," Faye said. Valerie nodded. She took the opportunity to tell the group the story of the "Mad Trapper of Rat River," one Albert Johnson. He had a habit of raiding the traps the local Indians set in the Mackenzie River valley, which had earned him a visit from the police in 1932. Johnson shot and wounded one of the policemen, then barricaded himself in his rough-hewn cabin. In spite of a police attack that included a dynamite blast, the Mad Trapper managed to escape. Following a hazardous pursuit in a snowstorm, the policemen found his camp. In the subsequent exchange of gunfire, one of the cops was killed. Afterward, the pursuers regrouped and were reinforced by a helpful bush pilot. After several days they finally found their fugitive again, but he got away once more, fleeing until his tracks were discovered and a bullet finally ended his life.

"It took forty-eight days to catch him," Valerie continued. "The trapper and his pursuers put one hundred and sixty miles behind them during that time, in ice-cold Arctic temperatures. In spite of everything, the stamina and powerful resistance of this man . . ."

She stopped. Was that the sound of a motor? What was Faye doing?

"Just a minute," Valerie said. "I'll be right back."

Breaking one of her own rules—never leave a group of clients in an unfamiliar place—she hurried back up the path they'd taken. When she got near the edge of the brush, within sight of the road, her heart nearly stopped.

Another vehicle was parked behind their bus. A dark SUV. Two people stood beside it in black down jackets and fur hats with earflaps. Faye was talking to them; Valerie could see her gesticulating. At one point she turned to look toward the path, and Valerie could clearly make out the worry on her face.

Valerie quickly stepped back into the brush. Her heart was beating wildly now. Were those the men who tried to take away her cell phone? If so, she'd better not show her face.

She heard muted voices and a door slam. Then the SUV drove off in the direction of Eagle Plains, the same direction they were heading. Footsteps approached, then Faye appeared.

Valerie stepped out of her hiding place, causing Faye to stagger backward.

"For God's sake, Val! You scared the living daylights out of me!"

Valerie ignored her complaint.

"What was that about? What did they want from you?"

Faye just shook her head.

"Faye, those guys are mixed up with Helvin West!"

"Who?"

"Helvin West! Clem's boss. You know—he's been missing for several days." Valerie's voice sounded loud and impatient.

Faye raised a finger to her lips. "Psst! They're coming."

Valerie wheeled around. Carol and Trish were working their way up the path, their tightly locked arms leaving no space between their heavily clothed bodies.

"I'll explain later," Faye whispered. "You don't need to worry."

Valerie wasn't convinced.

She reduced her voice to a frantic whisper. "You don't get it, Faye—they could be dangerous. You . . ."

Faye whispered back. "Those aren't the guys you—"

"Hello!" A voice rang out behind them. "We thought you were never coming back."

Valerie gave a reassuring wave and smile in Trish and Carol's direction before turning back to Faye.

"I've got to know what—"

Faye interrupted her once again. "Valerie, trust me, I'll explain everything. You just have to trust me, OK?"

Then Faye shouted to the two sisters, "C'mon, girls, I'll open the bus for you. You look frozen through and through."

Valerie was rooted to the spot for several seconds. She felt anger welling up in her. Who was really responsible here? These were precisely the sorts of situations she'd dreaded. Should she insist on squeezing an answer out of Faye? If there was a screwup, then Faye wouldn't be accountable, but *she* would, as tour guide.

She watched as the rest of the group began to emerge from the brush, then went back to the cabin to make sure everything was in its proper place. As she headed back up the path toward the road, she fell in behind Glenn and Jordan, who were helping Anika through the snow. Over the next couple of hours, the landscape flew by Valerie like a blurry movie. She tried not to make her inner unrest obvious as they left the Ogilvie River behind and began their climb up to almost three thousand feet and the Continental Divide.

"Fasten your seatbelts, we're taking off!" Faye yelled to everyone's delight.

The highway cut across the high plateau of Eagle Plains, and Faye drove along it a little faster than Valerie liked; the only way to spot an oncoming vehicle was by the whirling, white cloud of snow it kicked up. Loud cries for photo ops increased. The sight of the bare Richardson Mountains—like sprinkled sugar loaves marching along the horizon— would make any amateur photographer's pulse start hammering. The sky above was a hazy, saccharine-bright blue. Now a cascade of photo stops began as the sun grew weaker and weaker.

All of a sudden, at mile 220, a red Silverado pickup ahead of them nearly blocked the entire roadway, but Faye braked so magnificently that the bus barely swerved as it came to a stop well behind the truck. That's when they saw a dark SUV stuck in a snowdrift by the side of the road. A rope hung like an umbilical cord between the two vehicles, and a man beside the road signaled for them to wait.

"Photo op!" Valerie shouted.

A few seconds later the bus was empty, and more than a half-dozen cameras—including hers—captured the truck's rescue of the SUV trapped in the snow. Valerie was hoping to get a good look at the occupants, but no such luck. Fortunately for the stranded SUV, there were two technicians in the truck who happened to be working on a nearby communication tower and had a strong towrope.

Once the vehicle was freed, the tour continued on its way, but the incident was hotly debated. How did the SUV end up like that? What would have happened if that telecommunications truck hadn't come along? Valerie listened in silence. Stories like this were legion. The snow on the roadside was soft, and if a car ended up in it, the wheels could easily sink in so that it couldn't get out without help.

Sometime after eight in the evening, they arrived at their hotel in Eagle Plains. After such a long day of travel, the long, flat-roofed brown building next door to a gas station was as welcome a sight as any luxury hotel. Valerie distributed room keys at the reception desk and let the group know that, because of the late hour, the kitchen was only offering lasagna. She was also able to announce that luckily it was a good night for the northern lights.

"The best time is probably between midnight and one," the receptionist added. "I can wake up anybody who wants to go out when it's almost time."

That generated shouts of enthusiasm.

Faye came inside after parking the bus.

"We need to talk," Valerie said.

"In your room or the bar?"

Valerie nodded toward the bar. As she turned to walk that way, her expression abruptly changed.

Three men were coming out. Two in uniform—and one in civvies.

Clem Hardeven. Once he saw her, he didn't take his eyes off her, and she could see the relief in his face. But why was he here?

She heard Faye's words as if through a fog: "I think you're going to want to hear this from me first: they've located Sedna."

CHAPTER 21

Three pairs of eyes were trained on her.

Two policemen were seated opposite her at a table in the Eagle Plains Hotel's modest dining room. Clem was off to one side behind them, leaning against the wall, his arms crossed. One of the policemen introduced himself as John Palmer and folded his hands on the green-and-white-checked plastic tablecloth. He looked about her age, no older. Palmer was stationed with the RCMP in Inuvik. The other Mountie was from Yellowknife; a stocky, brawny man maybe in his midforties, his last name was Edwards, but she'd forgotten his first name. He appeared to be an Inuk who'd climbed the ladder in the Northwest Territories' police. If she were still a journalist, she'd have loved to get his story. Edwards let Palmer do the talking, but he watched her closely, his stare penetrating and intimidating. Valerie imagined that he could effortlessly see right through a felon during an interrogation.

She heard voices and music from the bar in the next room. Occasionally, she looked away from the three men facing her to the pictures on the wall. Pictures of Jack Dempster and his rescue expedition.

"Sedna Mahrer contacted our office from Aklavik, because she'd heard that someone was asking about her in Dawson City," Palmer said.

Valerie frowned.

"Aklavik? What's she doing there?"

"That's none of our business. In our view, she's a tourist."

"But," she stammered, turning toward Clem, "that phone call—she begged me to help her because she feared for her life."

"Ms. Mahrer denied that," Palmer replied. "She knew nothing about the call you described to Mr. Hardeven."

Valerie shook her head, unnerved.

"How do you even know it was Sedna who called from Aklavik? I mean, anyone could have called your station."

Edwards cleared his throat.

"She'd called her brother first, and he advised her to inform us."

"I . . . the reason I'm skeptical is . . . when I was in the Beringia Museum in Whitehorse, Ken Gries, the director, told me a woman by the name of Phyllis Crombe had passed herself off as a friend of mine. I don't know anyone by that name."

She could see out of the corner of her eye that Clem was shifting his stance.

"I e-mailed Mr. Gries a picture of Sedna," she continued, "and it was obviously not her." But the police didn't seem interested. And Valerie couldn't tell them that Sedna had cleaned out Faye's bank account. Faye didn't want that to be public knowledge. Not yet.

"That's all we can do for the moment," Palmer explained. "Ms. Mahrer is free to make her own decisions. We can't simply order her to come to the station. I'm sure you understand."

It suddenly dawned on Valerie. "You're not here because of Sedna at all, are you?"

Edwards nodded. "No. Clem told us that you'd be here. We thought we'd take the opportunity to tell you about Ms. Mahrer's contact with us."

Clem spoke up. "I told them about the package with the gold nugget, Val. I think we'd better give it to them."

The package. How could she forget?

She was overcome by a feeling of confusion—so much happening and so much information that she couldn't process.

An hour later she was alone with Clem in her hotel room. The tour group was amusing themselves in the bar. At dinner they'd all stood in a corner of the dining room in front of a stuffed caribou decorated with a garland of artificial plants.

"I've got to get this picture, or nobody will believe me," Paula crowed, all pumped up on only one whiskey.

"Let me keep an eye on them," Faye had offered when Val appeared with Clem in the bar's doorway.

Now he sat in the chair in front of the window, while Valerie sat on one of the two beds, her back to the wall. Doors slammed in the corridor; hasty footsteps faded away.

Clem turned the shaman's rattle over in his hands, the one that Trish had found when she'd gotten lost on her way back from the outhouse. Valerie looked at him with an impulsive, warm feeling: his face in deep concentration, his strong hands turning the object, his dark brown hair—shorter than she'd remembered—his long arms propped on the arms of the chair, his feet firmly planted on the floor. She noticed the powerful appeal of his upper body clad in a wine-colored T-shirt under his fleece jacket.

He raised his head. "It's extraordinary that something like this was found in a place like that."

She was struck by the dark creases on the right side of his face. Of course: the assault. His head injury.

Clem's expression was as intent as ever. She'd once told Sedna jokingly, "Anybody with blue eyes like that will know it, and that spoils the effect."

Sedna feigned outrage by shaking her head. "That's sexist. What if somebody said that about your eyes?"

"My eyes aren't blue, my dear."

"But they are strikingly pretty, and you know it. So leave the guy alone."

Leave the guy alone.

Valerie had thought she was doing exactly that, unlike Sedna, who flirted with him.

He stroked his tanned face, which showed signs of strain.

"So you think Sedna left it there?" he asked as he gently set the rattle on the table beside him.

Valerie looked him in the eye and then at her backpack in the corner.

"I know it sounds . . . a little farfetched . . ."

Could she trust him? She needed an ally, and Clem hadn't disappointed her so far.

She hadn't told him that she was secretly prejudiced against people who tried their luck in the Far North. Basically, she thought like Alana Reevely. Or like the British nurse who'd given her a tetanus shot in Inuvik because Valerie had gotten too close to the teeth of a dog on the loose. The Englishwoman had casually announced, "There are three reasons why men come to the North: first, money; second, they're running away from something; or third, they're looking for something."

Valerie had laughed—she'd felt like a conspirator.

She took a deep breath and said, "For some reason, Sedna's retracing my parents' trip."

She paused for a few seconds before forging ahead.

"My father was Peter Hurdy-Blaine, and my mother was Mary-Ann Strong."

Clem leaned forward, his hands on his thighs.

"The hockey player?"

"Yes. Precisely."

Clem stretched his full body.

"I've heard their story. That he had to break off the Dempster Memorial Trek. His wife was killed in an accident."

"Is that all you heard?"

"Not exactly. I also heard that he never went back to the Arctic after that."

He regarded her with curiosity.

"Of course. Your name. Blaine. Never made the connection. It was such a long time ago."

"Thirty years. I was just a child when it happened."

"So what's Sedna got to do with your parents?"

"She wanted to take a helicopter to the place where my parents . . . where they last camped. I found that out in Dawson. She . . . she met my ex before leaving Vancouver and grilled him about me and my family. Or at least tried to."

She paused because she suddenly heard herself speaking. How odd this information must sound to an outsider.

Clem seemed to be absorbing it all attentively. "Really."

He leaned back in his chair.

Valerie brushed away some long strands of hair behind her ears with her fingertips, but they fell back in her face. Better to tie it in a ponytail, but her loose hair did keep her head warm.

"Then she called me one night and said somebody was threatening to kill her. As you can imagine, that caused a lot of anxiety—that's really an understatement. And now she's in Aklavik claiming she never called me to say that her life was in danger."

Clem nodded slowly. "I heard something else interesting. She latched onto a gold-mine owner and pumped him for information about mines and how to launder money with gold and pay for goods with it."

"Did she?"

"Yes, and in Tuktoyaktuk she asked about a man whose name was Siqiniq Anaqiina."

"What?" Valerie pulled herself up so fast that she almost slipped off the bed. "Siqiniq Anaqiina? That's the Inuit boy who was with my parents!"

"When?"

"On their last expedition when . . . when my mother died."

Clem cleared his throat. "How old were you when it happened?"

"Four. My twin brothers, Kosta and James, were about ten."

"That must have been hard on all of you." Clem's voice had a fragile note to it, a sensitivity that surprised her.

She turned his words over in her mind. No, *hard* wasn't the right word. *Confusing* maybe. What was hard was their father's sudden reticence, his abnormal distance. He became a stranger. Then Bella Wakefield came into their lives, and everything brightened up. Their stepmother never took trips; she was a stay-at-home mom. She was always there when the kids needed her. Their situation was stable. She continued to be an anchor after their father died. Until Bella fell ill—and questions cropped up.

"To this day, I don't know the precise circumstances around my mother's death. My father never uttered a word about it.

"I tried some time ago to find out some information from the government. They replied that the documents were classified. They couldn't or wouldn't tell me the reason why. I thought that was very peculiar. Kosta . . ."

A large truck stopped in front of the window, its motor left running. She spoke through the racket. "Kosta thinks there's nothing to be gained by messing around with the past."

Clem moved his chair nearer, away from the window and the noise. "Is that your opinion as well?"

"I'm not so sure. I think . . . certain people would probably find it fun to knock a national idol off his pedestal. I used to be a journalist. The media would definitely have a field day."

"Did you ever mention your parents to Sedna?"

"No, never. And only once did I ever talk about my ex in her presence. That was a mistake."

She moved forward and sat on the edge of the bed, her feet braced against the other bed.

"I thought we were friends. But we weren't really. I sensed it last summer when she took off from Inuvik."

"Val," Clem began to say, "I . . . there's something—"

She interrupted him. "Sorry, we've just been talking about me, but something awful happened to you. How are you doing? Aren't you supposed to be lying down and resting?"

He gave a laugh.

"Sure, under ideal conditions. But I wanted to make sure you got rid of that package fast."

"Why? Who'd send you something like that?"

He shrugged.

She didn't let go.

"Does it have something to do with Helvin?"

"Possibly. There's only speculation for now, though. But the Mafia is known to send nuggets to people as a warning not to mess with their business."

"Why would the Mafia target you of all people?" Valerie asked incredulously.

"I suspect they aren't targeting me; it could be more about Helvin."

"Have they tracked him down? Have you heard anything about him?"

He rubbed his palms together.

"Toria sent me a text message that he'd sent her an e-mail announcing his glorious return. Seems like there's a lot of that going around." His tone had become sarcastic.

"What do you mean?"

"People disappearing without a trace, then suddenly turning up again. First Sedna, then Helvin."

"Do you think . . ."

She gave him an inquiring look.

"That they've met? I'll bet you the most expensive snowmobile money can buy that the cops aren't counting that out."

"And Gisèle? Who—"

A knock at the door interrupted her.

Faye. Valerie stepped out of the room to talk, closing the door behind her.

"Everything cleared up?" Faye asked.

"You look like you've just showered, not me, so no," Valerie said.

Faye made a face.

"He won't let you?"

"Where are the others?"

"Still in the bar."

"I'll be right there. Thanks for keeping an eye on them."

Faye turned to go to her room.

Before Valerie closed the door behind her, she heard Faye say, "They're all adults, you know. You don't need to worry about them so much. They're doing OK."

Back inside the room, Clem was standing at the window, his broad back toward her. He turned around and asked, "Can I have a quick shower here before I beat it? There's no shower where I'm staying."

"Of course. I'm just going to check on my group in the bar."

She didn't dare ask where he was sleeping. She'd heard that the hotel was booked up, and there was no way she could invite him to spend the night in her room. She clutched her laptop under her arm as she walked out.

"I'll be back in an hour."

To her surprise, she found Paula in the bar sitting next to a roughneck, some tarot cards laid out on the table before them.

"So I don't get out of practice," she explained in reaction to Valerie's amused look.

The guy beside her laughed, showing some gaps in his teeth.

"The lady knows I only want to hear good news. Otherwise, she'll get a slap on her rear end."

"Hey, hey, hey!" Paula warned.

Valerie couldn't find Anika anywhere. Carol and Trish were sitting at the bar with Glenn and Jordan, talking to the woman serving drinks. Three men sat around a table drinking beer. One of them looked like the telecommunications worker who'd helped to haul the dark SUV out of the snowdrift.

Valerie treated herself to a sherry. A stuffed moose head on the wall watched her drink it. Afterward, she took her laptop out to the lobby, where the Internet connection was best, and ran through her e-mails. A message from Kosta made her heart skip a beat.

"I heard your friend Sedna has resurfaced. If you two meet up, please don't say anything to her about our family, and nothing about your plans. Even better, stay as far away from her as possible. Call me from Inuvik, I'll explain it all then. Hope all's going well."

Valerie read the message over and over again. How did Kosta know that Sedna had resurfaced and called the police? Did he have an in with the Inuvik RCMP? And why the warning? She'd only written him briefly about Sedna's interest in their parents. Did he know something she'd missed?

And why didn't he simply tell her everything in the e-mail instead of torturing her by making her wait?

She clicked in frustration on another e-mail she hadn't expected. From Ken Gries, the museum director in Whitehorse.

"I discovered something about your mother. Mary-Ann Strong was apparently a person of interest to the Canadian Secret Intelligence Service, CSIS. An old colleague told me that he was quizzed about her by a man he met at an academic conference. He found out later by chance that the man worked for CSIS. When I conveyed that to another former colleague, it turned out that the same agent had pestered her about your mother. I honestly cannot imagine why Mary-Ann Strong could have attracted the attention of CSIS back then. Perhaps you have some idea? You can reach me anytime; I have some more old pictures of your parents."

Valerie's head suddenly felt hot; her thoughts were spinning like a merry-go-round. She forwarded the e-mail to Kosta, asking him to look into it. Then she closed her laptop; that was all she could manage for one day. She slowly walked back to her hotel room, knocked softly, and, when she didn't get a response, opened the door.

In the light of the night table lamp, she saw Clem lying on the second bed. He was completely dressed and dead to the world.

She hesitated. Should she wake him up?

He must be exhausted. The violent attack. Helvin's disappearance. Gisèle's death. The Ice Road. And—she now realized—his concern for her and her tour group. Why else would he have hitched a ride on a truck to Eagle Plains?

She watched him sleeping there with a slight feeling of guilt, as if it were forbidden. As if she were crossing a line. With his rugged facial features, dark hair, and tanned skin, he looked dashing even in his sleep. A man of the North.

She quietly put away her computer, fished clean clothes out of her backpack, and made for Faye's room.

To her astonishment, Anika opened the door.

"I've just given Faye a reflexology foot massage. You can have one, too, but not tonight. Time for me to go to bed. Good night."

She was barely out the door before Valerie announced the reason for her visit.

"Can I spend the night here with you? Clem is in my room, sleeping like a baby."

Faye shook her head.

"I don't think it's a great idea. I snore like crazy, and I'm feeling a little stuffed up, which always makes it worse. I'd keep you awake all night."

"But—"

"Don't you trust him? He seems like a perfect gentleman to me, Val. I don't think you need to worry; he won't lay a finger on you. He'll probably never even know you're there, if he's that tired."

"You can talk, you—"

"Am *I* going to sleep in a room with him? Am I?"

Valerie sighed.

"Can I at least shower here?"

Faye laughed.

"Sure, go ahead. I'll go to the bar for a while."

Valerie didn't move. Faye still owed her an answer.

"Will you finally please tell me now, who were those two men in the SUV today?"

"Not two men, a man and a woman. They wanted to take pictures of the caribou herd and asked me if we'd seen it."

"And who told you that Sedna had turned up?"

"The two cops. We chatted for a bit outside after I parked the bus. Can I go now?"

And off she went.

Valerie was in the shower inside of a minute, washing away the tension and stress of the day with the pleasantly warm water.

There was one question she couldn't shake off: If those two in the SUV were as harmless as Faye said, why all the secrecy? Why couldn't she have said that right away?

"I'll give that smart-ass a talking-to sometime soon," she muttered to herself.

CHAPTER 22

"So this is where it's buried."

Her remark sounded borderline cheerful. Maybe she should dampen her enthusiasm a bit, make it more appropriate for the situation. After all, she didn't want to jinx things now.

Her qualms evaporated when he responded in the same tone of voice. "Yes, it's a good place to hide something."

He looked around, scanning their surroundings with a keen eye before unlocking the door of the little shed. She followed his gaze across the empty, snow-covered plain stretching before them. The Arctic Ocean began somewhere around here, but for somebody unfamiliar with the area, it was impossible to tell where the land ended and the ocean began. Water and earth blended into a single icy wasteland, a frozen landscape, its borders obscured by the milky, dim light of a cold day.

She was glad he'd been as careful as she was to keep their intentions a secret. She didn't want her mission to be thwarted at the last minute. By anybody.

This was the perfect day. The whole village was celebrating a wedding in the community hall. Everybody was invited. The opulent feast and the gifts had been the prime topic of conversation for days.

"I've always wanted to come here," she said as she looked through the open door into a cramped square area. Trampled snow surrounded a wooden hatch.

"Anybody coming here must have seen this."

He didn't answer; he was busy unrolling a stiff, coiled rope in the corner.

Normally, she wasn't such a talker, but she was so excited that the words just kept coming.

"How can something stay hidden here when people are always using this shack?"

He smiled.

"Nobody would think of looking here, precisely because it's such a popular spot."

She looked at him quizzically.

"There's a labyrinth down there," he explained patiently, "and not all the chambers are accessible to everybody."

He heaved the hatch lid up and let it rest against the wooden wall. Inside, she could see the upper part of a narrow shaft, its sides covered with a thick layer of shimmering ice crystals. She took a step closer to the dark, yawning hole and saw the iced-over ladder leading downward.

For the first time, she felt something like tightness in her chest.

"So that's what it looks like," she said. "Pretty steep. And deep. Good God!"

She was momentarily blinded by a beam of light; he'd put on a headlamp. The ice on the rungs flashed.

"And as smooth as glass," she added.

"This rope here will secure you," he explained. "I'll tie it to the post over there and hold it tight so nothing can happen to you."

She nodded but just stood there.

"Should I take off my gloves? They're too thick for me to grip the rungs."

"Better not. It's cold as ice down there."

"I can just toss them in and put them on again down there."

He wasn't persuaded.

"The rungs are frozen."

She relented. "I'll try it out with my thinner driving gloves." She took a pair of full-fingered gloves out of her jacket pocket.

He helped her slide the rope around her upper body and shoulders as if she were a sled dog. Then he tied the other end with a triple knot around the post. She turned her back to the hole and prepared to start down the ladder, her hiking boot groping for footing in the abyss, her hands on the rungs.

"Just a little lower and you'll feel the first rung," he coached her. "That's it."

She felt the rung beneath her foot, then moved her other one down.

"Now it's just one step after the other," he said encouragingly.

She carefully climbed down, glad to have the rope under her armpits.

The descent felt like it was taking forever. Somebody had told her it was thirty-three feet. She had no idea how far she'd gone and didn't want to look down. The light from his headlamp blinded her.

"Damn! I left my flashlight in my backpack," she shouted. "It's in the pickup."

His voice echoed down to her.

"No problem. I'll go get it."

"My camera is in there, too."

How could she be so careless? Perhaps it was because she'd been so excited.

"OK."

"How much farther?"

"Just a few more steps."

Suddenly, she sensed a larger gap between the rungs and grabbed the ladder firmly.

"You did it! That's the floor," he said from above.

She felt solid ground beneath her boots. And a simultaneous crippling cold that made breathing difficult.

Of course. What did she expect? This cellar was supposed to be just like a freezer.

If a cold hell exists, then it would have to be here, *she thought, with a shudder. A labyrinth of dread. It wouldn't be out of place in a thriller.*

Best for them to get the job done quickly.

"I'm going to untie myself from the rope," she shouted. "Please don't forget my backpack."

She heard him tramping around above her. The rope flew upward, and its grating sounds died away. A light still shone from above. He must have placed his headlamp on the edge of the opening.

She ventured a couple of steps toward the main corridor, which was sugared over with ice crystals.

It crossed her mind that her cell phone was also in the backpack. How stupid of her. He definitely would not steal it, she thought. She felt for the two chocolate bars in her jacket pocket, one for herself and one for him, and found the warming pads as well.

She thought she heard his voice in the distance. Then crunching and tramping once again.

"Hello?" she yelled.

At that instant the hatch lid above her slammed shut. With a single stroke, it became dark all around her.

She waited a few seconds for the lid to be opened up again. For him to say he was sorry about the slipup.

"Hello! Hello!" she repeated.

She heard a dull thud as if somebody had slammed a door shut. Then absolute silence.

She shouted his name. Over and over. In growing desperation.

She tried to find the ladder in the dark. But her hands only felt the little pointed teeth on the wall of the icy grave.

The ladder must be here, right here!

The farther she fumbled her way along, the less she knew where she was.

CHAPTER 23

"Well, this calls for a celebration!"

Carol hoisted a large bottle of Baileys up in the air. They'd crossed the Arctic Circle. The group applauded enthusiastically and stood for photographs beside the marker indicating the sixty-sixth parallel. Valerie had been on this wooden platform with Sedna last summer and snapped the mountains that the snow changed so radically now in April.

While they were clinking glasses, a dark SUV turned into the parking area. The little group stared at the bundled-up occupants as they got out.

"Have you seen any caribou?" Faye shouted at them.

"Sorry, not yet, but we're still hoping!" A woman's voice.

Valerie pushed everybody to get a move on.

"At your service, madam," Faye said, as Valerie shepherded the group into the Chevy. It was meant to be funny, but she gave Faye a dirty look.

When they were in their seats, Valerie thought to remind the group that they'd be crossing the border between the Yukon and the Northwest Territories in about an hour. "Don't forget that it's illegal to bring alcohol into the Territories, so be sure you don't have any on you then."

They drove into Richardson Mountains territory; the range extended almost to the Arctic Ocean. The winds could be brutal here, strong enough to blow a truck off the road. Truckers actually called it Hurricane Alley. Only on the lee side of the valleys did trees have any chance of growing. And nothing grew on the mountainsides, with their menacing, rocky, snow-covered tentacles that stretched down to the highway.

A stark moon landscape, that's how Valerie saw it—a bulky white mass against a delicately painted sky-blue. In her view, the surrounding landscape seemed like a high mountain region, although the bus's altimeter read only 2,790 feet above sea level. Sometimes the rocky giants loomed so close that she compared them to sleeping polar bears suddenly stretching up to their full height.

Trish spoke up from the back seat. "Do you people know what this reminds me of?" she exclaimed in her enthusiasm. "Those boulders on the white slopes look like silver decorations on the frosting of a white cake."

"You hit the nail on the head," Faye responded. Valerie noticed she was in very high spirits.

Valerie hadn't told Faye about her night with Clem, because there was nothing exciting to report. Maybe that's why she was feeling impatient and a bit irritated today.

The fantastic one a.m. northern lights display had been the major topic of conversation among the group at breakfast that morning. But Valerie had missed the lights, as well as the morning meal. The physical proximity of Clem Hardeven in her room had kept her awake much of the night, and when morning finally arrived, she simply overslept. When she did wake up, his bed was empty. Just a little note: "See you in Inuvik." She had tucked the piece of paper into her notebook.

As they drove on, Paula was holding forth, as predictable as the evening news.

"There's the tundra again. If we have any luck, we'll see Dall sheep and grizzlies."

"Grizzlies? Not in winter, my dear," Anika interjected. "They're hibernating."

"But there are gyrfalcons to make up for it," Jordan chimed in.

Just then, Glenn shouted, "Photo op!"

He had spotted a caribou by the side of the road, torn to shreds. When they got out, they found wolf tracks in the snow. A few in the group took pictures of the scene.

It was too cold and windy to stand outside for long, so they soon piled back in the Chevy and continued on their trip. They were getting near the Rock River campground, which was sheltered from the wind. Valerie had just turned around to announce a coffee break when Faye slammed on the brakes.

"Holy . . . !" she yelled.

They stared spellbound at something a hundred yards down the road. A stream of white-brown, thin-legged bodies pouring across the road.

Caribou. Thousands of them.

Valerie sat there as if turned to stone. She couldn't believe it. Every year she'd hoped to see migrating caribou. And now, when she'd least expected it, her dream was coming true.

Anika was the first to find her voice again. "OmiGod! OmiGod! OmiGod!"

Soon the whole minibus was buzzing with chaotic excitement.

Valerie silenced them all with a hand motion.

"Please, no noise, especially when you go outside. This is the chance of a lifetime, so we don't want to scare them!"

In the next half hour, the tour group split up and, one by one, moved along the road, in slow motion and almost total silence. They behaved like tardy churchgoers tiptoeing into the chapel. The only sound in the air was the thud of hooves and an occasional plaintive murmur. Mothers gave muted bleats to keep the young by their side. The shape of this vast sea of animals—a heaving, vibrating parade of slim, forward-moving bodies—constantly morphed, like a river that spread out and then narrowed. Valerie was completely transfixed. She'd stopped taking pictures; she just wanted to look.

This must be the Porcupine herd Clem had told her about. The caribou were en route from their winter feeding grounds to open tundra. Their antlers pierced the air like thin little arms, stretched up to heaven as if the animals were pleading for something from above. Perhaps a safe pilgrimage to the plains where they hoped food was abundant.

Suddenly, Valerie recalled something Pihuk Bart had said to her two winters ago. He'd shared with her a prophecy: "In the year that you witness the caribou migrating, the secret of an involuntary death will be revealed to you. It will be a year of terror and beauty. The caribou will carry the souls of your descendants between their warm flanks."

She gave a start. Somebody had stepped up beside her.

"I'll never forget this moment as long as I live," Faye whispered.

She'd stopped snapping pictures too. Some living, breathing images had to be taken in and burned into one's memory forever.

The tail end of the herd increasingly thinned out.

"Where are your friends, the caribou aficionados?" Valerie whispered back.

"They're not my friends. You and me are friends."

She turned around and saw the dark SUV several feet behind the Chevy. The couple was standing on the hood. In her surprise, she waved at the two of them, and they gave her a thumbs-up sign.

When they got back on the road, Carol distributed the remainder of the Baileys.

The SUV followed them over the Mount Richardson Pass, which opened up onto a view of the Peel River and the Mackenzie Delta. Valerie decided they'd stop at Fort McPherson later, on the way back, to look for the graves of the Lost Patrol. They drove on instead to Tsiigehtchic, a Gwich'in village also called Arctic Red River. They made a brief stop at the post office and at the trapper store with a sign depicting a dogsled above its door. A lone husky, tied up on a short chain, watched Valerie. She had to look away; she couldn't get used to the fact that many sled dogs led a miserable life. She'd heard about one in Inuvik two years ago whose body had literally frozen to the floor of its hut. When it was discovered, it was barely alive.

They crossed the frozen Mackenzie and stopped at the spot where the road aimed straight as an arrow toward the horizon for twenty miles. Valerie had calculated the distance after a customer on her first tour wanted to know. They then crossed the taiga with its tree growth, unlike the tundra. The landscape along the highway grew less dramatic, and Valerie saw that almost everybody was snoozing. A string of trucks came toward them.

Without warning Faye called out, "We've got to stop. Police."

Valerie saw the patrol car behind them. When they'd come to a full stop, an officer stepped out and came over to them. He poked his head through Faye's open window.

"Where are you going?" he asked.

Valerie didn't know him. He must be one of the RCMP posted to the area.

"To Inuvik. We're a tour group."

The officer nodded and scanned the bus's passengers.

"Could you open up the back please?"

Valerie got out and went to the rear of the Chevy with the policeman. She helped him unload the baggage. He opened some of it and searched through a backpack. She hoped everyone had heeded her warning and no one was hiding any alcohol. After several anxious minutes, the officer heaved the baggage back into the vehicle and closed the door.

"Are you going to Tuktoyaktuk?" he asked.

Valerie nodded. "We're going to see the ice cellar, or the ice house, as they call it there."

"There was an incident in the community. A man was beaten up. I'm sure you'll hear all about it when you get there. But we arrested the perp, so nothing to worry about. Have a good trip!"

"Thank you," Valerie replied, perplexed, as she watched him get in the patrol car.

Her head began to spin. A man beaten up. In Tuktoyaktuk. There was always a row whenever alcohol was involved. But so much had happened in the past few weeks already. Gisèle's death. The attack on Clem. Sedna's disappearance and mysterious reappearance. The gold nugget. The police in Eagle Plains. Valerie blinked at the blinding setting sun. She felt a bit dizzy.

Glenn Bliss was standing outside, shaking with cold and trying to smile. His mustache trembled.

"Gotta go," he said.

Valerie nodded. "I'll tell the others."

She climbed into the Chevy and asked Jordan to go with Glenn. She said to Faye, "I think Glenn's got motion sickness. He's pale as a sheet."

Faye's expression was inscrutable.

"Well, well," was all she uttered.

CHAPTER 24

Clem stumbled into the bar of the Great Polar Hotel. He'd spent the whole ride from Eagle Plains to Inuvik in the bunk behind the driver's seat in Reg Mason's eighteen-wheeler. Reg brought vegetables and fruit from British Columbia to Inuvik every three weeks; people bought them off the shelf in his truck. Clem's head felt like an overripe plum ready to burst. Reg had listened to a trucker's program the whole way, "Trucker Tunes," at a volume that made restful slumber impossible. But it would have been a far greater torture for Clem to drive the 225 miles himself.

"At last," Phil Niditichie shouted. "Where the hell were you? Doing a disappearing act like Helvin?"

"You guys could booze it up enough without me," Clem grumbled as he ordered a White Russian.

"Jesus! You look like your grandmother peeled you and threw you on the barbecue," Johnny Redbeard Wills needled him.

"Leave him alone," Poppy Dixon shouted. "If somebody had bashed *your* head in, you wouldn't exactly look like Miss Universe."

Johnny didn't let go.

"Compared to Roy, this guy here got off real light."

Clem suddenly felt that all eyes were on him.

"What? What are you guys gawking at?"

Nobody said anything for a few seconds. Then Poppy burst out, almost in a stutter, "You *have* heard about Roy Stevens, the ranger out of Tuktoyaktuk?"

"What am I supposed to have heard?"

One of the men whistled softly through his teeth.

"He's in the hospital. Somebody bashed his skull in," Poppy said.

Clem stared at Poppy in disbelief.

"You're kidding, Poppy, aren't you?"

But the men's faces told him that it was true.

Johnny piped up again.

"For crying out loud, Clem, that's what happens when you leave your cell phone off."

Clem felt a surge of anger.

"Isn't anybody gonna tell me what happened, or are you all gonna just sit there like bumps on a log?"

"They found Roy today bleeding from a head wound," Phil said, "in Tuk, in front of the ice house. Couldn't even talk. He's in the ICU, in an induced coma."

Clem's hands quickly turned clammy.

"Which hospital?"

"First here. Then they stabilized him and flew him to Yellowknife. Then they shipped him to Edmonton."

"Why . . . Who . . . ?"

"Wouldn't we all like to know. First you, then our ranger. This monster's got to be taken out of circulation fast. What are the police doing anyway?"

Now they all talked at once.

Clem's voice cut through the babble like a drill through ice.

"John Palmer was in Eagle Plains with the RCMP guy from Yellowknife."

"Right, because of drugs." Poppy shoved his beer glass dangerously near the edge of the bar.

"Drugs?"

"The girl from Dawson . . ."

"That Gisèle woman?"

"Yeah, she wanted to sell stuff to some people in Eagle Plains."

Phil slammed his fist down on the table.

"The perp sure as hell didn't go from Eagle Plains to Inuvik. They should be looking for him right here instead. Maybe Roy knew something and now . . . ?"

His hand slid like a knife across his throat.

Clem was about to shake his head but caught himself in time. No quick head moves with his concussion.

"I bet the RCMP knows more than they're telling," he said.

"Well, now, doesn't that make us feel a whole lot better," Poppy sneered. "The Yellowknife guy is supposed to be an expert."

Clem pulled his hat down over his ears.

"We should all be scared if they have to fly in somebody like that."

Not waiting for the crowd's reaction, he made for the door.

The sun was still shining. It seemed an illusion considering the dark events of the preceding days. He thought of Valerie as he got back to driving his truck, against doctor's orders. She couldn't have wished for better weather after the winter storms they'd had. But would the awful assault on the ranger have an impact on her tour? Would she cancel her trip if she found out? The thought bugged him more than he liked.

A mental image took shape: her body's silhouette under the bedcovers, her long brown hair like tendrils on the white pillow, her hand pressed against her chin. He wished he could have stayed in Eagle Plains longer. Maybe the quiet peace of the morning hour would have led to something sexier. He wallowed in the scenario of her expected response. His erotic fantasy was quickly supplanted by the thought of Roy and his bleeding head on the snow. Was it the same guy who had attacked Clem?

He drove south down the highway where Valerie's minibus would be heading for Inuvik in a matter of hours. No hurry; the sun wouldn't go down until ten.

Half a mile after Inuvik, he turned down a wide, snow-covered road. The bush ended after a few hundred yards as Alana and Duncan's house and dog pens came into view. He had to avoid an oncoming red SUV, which he recognized at once; he waved to the driver. To his surprise Toria West's car didn't stop but went past him and out of sight behind the bushes.

"What the hell . . ." Clem was irritated.

In the mudroom attached to the house, he found Duncan preparing the dogs' food.

"Back from Eagle Plains?"

"Yep. Did Meteor behave himself?"

"I'm sure he did. Alana took him along with some tourists to Fowler Lake."

"When'll she be back?"

"Two hours maybe. She can drop Meteor off at your place this evening."

Duncan distributed fresh meat among the dogs' bowls.

"For Bolter's team. The dogs really worked hard today."

Clem chose not to beat around the bush.

"I saw Toria's car. What was she doing out here?"

"Toria? She's thinking about getting a puppy for her kids."

"What? You've got puppies?"

Duncan put the bowls on the ledge of a little window.

"No. And that's what I told her, too."

"Did she mention anything else? Helvin?"

"Naw. I didn't ask either. Sorry, I gotta put more wood in the stove. You want to come in for a while?"

Clem declined. "Gotta go back. Did you hear about Roy Stevens?"

"Yeah. Ugly business. I hope the snowmobile race won't be canceled, since he's the one who organized it. Take care. I'll see you later."

Duncan closed the door to the living quarters behind him.

The Muskrat Jamboree. So many things were casting their shadows over the spring festival. Over the festival and the inhabitants of Inuvik and Tuktoyaktuk, for that matter, and over tourism and the Ice Road. And coexistence in the Arctic, Clem mused, because the mysterious explosion on the ice now haunted him even in his dreams.

He stared at the dog bowls. It occurred to him how easy it would be to mix poison with the dogs' food. He was astounded that Duncan wasn't more wary after Booster had died. Didn't Alana tell Clem in confidence that Duncan believed that Booster had been poisoned? Maybe he'd left the food on the window ledge that day, as he'd done just now, to run upstairs for a few minutes, and somebody had slipped into the mudroom during that time.

Clem thought of Meteor as he drove home. The sooner he had his dog back in the house, the better.

Something else struck him as peculiar. If Toria was really interested in a puppy, why didn't she simply phone Duncan beforehand instead of driving out there? Alana and Toria didn't like each other—that was common knowledge. But Duncan was everybody's friend.

Clem parked in front of his house and looked around carefully before going in. No way he'd let that thug hit him twice. He'd come away with just a scare, but maybe his attacker hadn't finished the job. Like with Ranger Stevens, poor bastard.

The kitchen was warm because the oil heat was on. He'd barely put the teakettle on the stove when the phone rang.

"Are you alone?" Lazarusie's voice was muted.

"What's up?"

"Danny saw it all happen."

"What are you talking about?"

"The thing with Roy."

CHAPTER 25

Helvin West orbited his new snowmobile, patting it tenderly like a thoroughbred stallion. Clem had recently bought a new snowmobile, and his boss evidently wasn't about to play second fiddle.

"I'm gonna win this race," he said over and over.

They'd met at the Suntuk Logistics building. The sky was gray, but the forecast was holding steady. Almost no wind, and no snow expected. Helvin was in an excellent mood, making Clem all the madder, but his boss didn't seem to pick up on that.

Clem folded his arms across his chest and planted his legs apart.

"Maybe you didn't hear the news that somebody knocked Roy Stevens over the head, and he's out of the race?" he inquired. Even Helvin wouldn't be able to ignore a question so drenched with sarcasm, he thought.

Wrong. His boss had very different priorities. At that moment, his attention was entirely focused on the snowmobile race.

"With you and Roy out, I'm going to be the one to win this race," Helvin said. He leaned over the machine and kept on talking.

"I'm sorry for you two, Clem, but this little beast will save your honor. We'll show those greenhorns from Paulie Umik's team that we're still top dogs."

Clem watched Meteor marking his territory around the parked snowplows. At least somebody can piss on Helvin's leg.

"They've taken Laz's daughter Tanya in for questioning."

Helvin made a face.

"Always thought Tanya would go off the deep end sometime, with all the drugs she's doing."

Clem went on the offensive. "Helv, I have a letter in my pocket—my resignation. Unless you come with me to the office right now and explain in minute detail what you've been up to the last few days, I'm laying it on your desk."

His boss straightened up.

"What? Resignation? You're off your rocker! You're still not right in the head!"

Minutes later, they were sitting in the overheated company office, where Helvin's snowmobile trophies were lined up on a shelf behind him. Clem's threat hanging in the air had loosened his tongue.

"Hey, man, I shouldn't be telling you anything, really. But three years ago Richard talked me into putting some money into a mine. He said gold was the best investment you can make."

"Richard Melville," Clem said with derision.

"I had to do something, Clem. Nothing's going to happen here without the gas pipeline. We can flush all our plans for the future down the toilet. How many people can we fire? There's no more flesh on our bones. You *must* see that, too."

Clem was silent. He envisioned a headline in a big Canadian newspaper: "Mackenzie Pipeline Dead and Buried."

Helvin drummed his fingers on the table.

"I made good money in gold for three years. That helped us all. And paid everybody's wages. We've just got to hang in there until gold goes back up."

Clem looked him straight in the eye.

"You still haven't answered my question. Why did you suddenly up and leave for Dawson?"

"We needed cash. And now we've got some investors."

Helvin looked out the window. So did Clem. He could see the new snowmobile from there.

"The Chinese are snapping everything up. Richard doesn't like it. He also doesn't want to have the Mafia around his neck. You know what they did to Stew Grant? He couldn't repay them so they destroyed his face. He needed a plastic surgeon so he could look more or less human again."

Clem had indeed heard about it. Not about Stew Grant, but about other victims. They'd borrowed from organized crime gangs to keep their mines afloat. When gold tanked, they didn't have the revenue to pay the Mafia the horrendous interest they charged. So the mob asked for gold instead. Perfect money-laundering scheme.

Clem leaned forward.

"You were seen getting into an SUV in Dawson with a couple of guys. Who were those characters?"

Helvin was startled but quickly recovered.

"TV guys. From San Diego."

Clem waited.

Helvin rolled his chair back and forth.

"This has got to stay between us, you hear? They're planning a reality show for the summer."

"I thought you'd had your fill of that with *Ice Road Truckers*."

"It's not about the Ice Road, it's about gold mining in the Yukon. We're in on it."

"If your mine's still around next summer."

"It won't go broke, old man, not that one. We've found the money. A very tidy sum."

Clem jumped out of his chair.

"And why, my good man, why did those TV guys run away when the police showed up?"

"Police? Where?"

"Somebody tried to photograph their license plate in Dawson, and they got aggressive. And when the fuzz turned up—whoosh—they were off!"

"I know nothing about that. But you know what the Americans are like. Paranoid. Especially in wicked foreign countries. And I'd get a little worked up, too, if somebody was photographing my license plate. Who was it, by the way?"

Clem ignored the question. He'd never betray Valerie. But Helvin put two and two together.

"Pretty little Valerie has a bit too much imagination for my taste. You obviously like imagination," he said with a leer.

Clem gripped the back of his chair with both hands and held it in front of him like a bulwark.

"Somebody tried to send a package from Dawson to Inuvik for me. With gold in it. A big, fat, shiny nugget."

Helvin flinched noticeably. Clem fired off another salvo.

"And another gold nugget was found near Gisèle's body. Is there a Santa Claus going around and tossing gold away like confetti? Helv, who is playing what game here?"

His boss started drumming the desktop again with his right hand. He shut his eyes.

Playing for time, Clem guessed.

"That nugget, she wanted to give it to me." Helvin's voice had softened.

"Who?"

"Gisèle. She brought me a small package."

Clem let go of the back of the chair so forcefully that it almost tipped over.

"So you *did* meet her? But you've always denied it."

"She met *me*, goddammit. She climbed into my truck when I was leaving Bernie's Hardware Store. She said she had a message from Richard. And she gave me the package. I opened it. What a goddamn joke. Wasn't hard to see it wasn't from Richard. She swore up and down that it was."

Helvin was so agitated that he was red in the face.

"Clem, in Dawson you get nuggets from gangsters. As bait. As a reminder that they'd love to lend you money—and get you in their clutches forever. I gave her back the nugget and threw her out of the truck."

"Jesus, Helv! Do the cops know?"

"No, not yet. But I'll come clean. As soon as the race is over."

Clem couldn't believe his ears.

"Holy shit, Helv! You withheld information from the police, and now you've made me an accomplice!"

"Oh, don't be such a wimp. C'mon. You've got more dope on the people here than you can stuff into a sealskin. Are you really going to lose sleep over this? In just a few hours, they'll hear the whole story. It's not a catastrophe."

Clem was speechless in the face of Helv's cockiness. His boss took that silence as acquiescence.

"I had nothing to do with her death, Clem. Absolutely nothing. I threw her out, but she must have followed me here, God knows how. I was just stopping by the office for a minute, so I left the motor running. But I got held up by some phone calls. She must have climbed in and taken off. That's how it must have happened."

Clem slammed his hand on the table.

"What a load of bullshit!"

He stared at Helvin. Maybe that actually did happen. She took the truck—or somebody stole it for her.

But why did Helvin disappear right afterward? Was he lying about other things as well? Before Clem could ask that question, the door opened and Meteor came running in, followed by Helvin's secretary, Laura Minetti.

"That dog's driving everybody crazy out there," she announced.

Clem got ahold of Meteor; the dog wagged its tail furiously.

He turned toward Helvin again. "Does Toria know all this? She was at Duncan's yesterday, wondering about buying a puppy for your kids."

Helvin shook his head.

"Somebody's pulling your leg. Alana, I'll bet."

"No, it came from Duncan. Alana wasn't there. Toria's car was leaving just as I was driving up to their house. She didn't even stop. No time for the man running her husband's business in his absence, I suppose."

"Duncan? He should keep his big mouth shut. Phil's coming, gotta run."

Helvin got up and pulled his winter jacket on over his snowmobile suit, then grabbed his gloves and gave Clem a hearty slap on the back.

"That Valerie has really got you hooked. I hear you even went to Eagle Plains to see her, eh?"

Clem said nothing.

He didn't let loose until he was in his pickup. Meteor clearly didn't know what end was up and stared at his owner in confusion until Clem took pity on him and stopped shouting.

He parked above the bank of the Mackenzie and walked down onto the frozen river, where the festival games were in full swing. A man in a cowboy vest and a cap lined with braids threw his harpoon with tremendous arm strength. Pihuk was all dolled up for the big event. Clem had to admit he was a good harpooner.

Farther back, near the temporary wooden shacks for the organizers, a tea party of elderly Inuvialuit women was sitting on folding chairs, wearing their traditional Mother Hubbard parkas, their fabric patterned with flowers or garish colors, their hoods lined with fur that framed their faces like a lion's mane. The women were watching closely as a dozen people spread their legs on two parallel boards and fastened them with loops. The boards looked like super-long skis.

A large circle of spectators surrounded the board runners, amused by their awkward contortions. The old women on the chairs giggled and chatted noisily. Among the chatter, Clem heard a familiar voice. He looked closely at the group and saw that one of the faces, partly hidden behind sunglasses and a turtleneck sweater pulled up to the chin, was younger than the others.

"Valerie?"

The woman pushed her sunglasses up.

"Clem!"

She stood up and spun around to face him.

"Look what I've got!"

He never would have expected to see her wearing a proper Mother Hubbard parka, lined with caribou hide and richly decorated on the outside. Until now, she hadn't acquired a taste for the colorful embroidery and ruffles along the hem. She looked good in turquoise. Clem thought she looked radiant. She stroked her pelt gloves over the fur on her hood.

"Look. Wolf and coyote. Very warm and light!"

Her olive-green eyes sparkled in her half-covered face. Clem felt butterflies in his stomach.

"And where are your little lambs?"

"Some are in the dining tent trying muskrat meat. Faye's over there with Anika having hot soup. And the rest of them . . . ah, yes, there they are."

She pointed to a stand where two girls poured hot maple syrup over crushed ice and rolled the mixture onto wooden sticks.

Valerie raised the paper cup in her hand.

"I'm sticking with hot tea. We just watched the muskrat-skinning."

"Who won this time?"

"An old woman from Aklavik in one minute and sixteen seconds."

Clem laughed. "Of course, another woman. I thought so."

Loud shouts and laughter interrupted their conversation. The board race had started. Two teams tried to coordinate their leg movements to hit the finish line first.

"Come over here." Clem took Valerie behind the shed where it was quieter.

"I'm leaving tomorrow for Tuktoyaktuk to see what's going on. I basically don't foresee any problems for you and your tour. Weather's supposed to be good tomorrow."

She nodded. "Heard anything else about Sedna?"

"Not yet."

"It would be so . . . unlike her to miss this festival. She'd have enjoyed it immensely."

The smile had vanished from Valerie's lips.

"Maybe she'll still show up; the festival goes for several days yet."

"I wonder why she's so hell-bent on my family. Why . . ."

She stopped there and looked out over the frozen river.

Clem cleared his throat.

"Val, there's something I'd like to tell you."

She looked at him expectantly.

"When you two were here last summer, you and Sedna, she . . . she paid me a visit that second night. I think you were with Marjorie Tama and her workshop for the tourists. She brought a bottle of vodka with her, and we kinda started talking."

Valerie's eyes were riveted on Clem.

"She told me you were in a new relationship and showed me a picture of you and a man, a good-looking guy."

"What?" A crease materialized between her eyebrows. "What guy? What did he look like?"

"Blond, thin, tall."

She thought for a moment and exclaimed, "Sean! That must be Sean."

She laughed but didn't seem amused.

"Sean is gay and has a partner. We're all in the neighborhood watch—or were—Sedna, me, and Sean. We patrolled the streets, for security. You probably don't have anything like that in Inuvik."

He avoided looking at her as he continued speaking.

"We put away a lot of booze, and . . . then I slept with her. It was a huge mistake, I knew that instantly. The next day I flew with you and Fritz, that German pilot, to Banks Island. She wanted to come along to see musk oxen but . . . I didn't want to have her with us. I'd been looking forward for months to spending that day with you. I wanted to be alone with you."

When he looked at her again, Valerie was staring somewhere out into space. Now he had to let it all out; that, he knew.

"I told Sedna there wasn't room in the chopper, that the pilot was waiting for somebody else. She smelled a rat, naturally, and was furious. She . . . she said, 'Why does Val get everything? Everything falls into her lap! She's a parasite, always living off other people.' Then she disappeared for a few days, and you were beside yourself because you didn't know whether or not something had happened to her."

Val stayed quiet for a while, far too long for Clem's liking.

"I hope . . . I wanted to tell you this for a long time, but . . ."

She laid a hand on his arm.

"Thank you, Clem. Thanks for telling me what you've just said."

Her expression was still serious.

"I've got to process this. So much has happened. I've got to . . . ," she said, pointing in the direction of the festival area. "I've got to settle a few things."

Then she looked into his eyes.

"Please call me when you're back from Tuktoyaktuk."

She turned around, and Clem watched her walk away in her new parka. The sleeves and attached gloves embroidered with pearls swung back and forth.

CHAPTER 26

A loud noise jerked Valerie out of her sleep. Somebody was pulling open the minibus door. She blinked, in a fog, as someone climbed into the passenger seat.

"You're sleeping through our festival."

"Marjorie! You scared the living daylights out of me!"

"What are you doing here? You're missing the best part! Two people from your tour are filming the snowmobile race."

Valerie had decided to take a brief nap in the driver's seat. She clicked it back upright, then the two women hugged as well as they could, given the constraints of the small space. Valerie smoothed back her long hair.

"I relieved my driver so she could get out for a bit. We keep the bus running so my guys can come back anytime and get warm."

"Yeah, easy to freeze if you don't watch out. I see you've got a new parka; that'll keep you warm."

"Marj, how could something so awful happen to Gisèle? It's horrible to die that way. So young."

Marjorie took off her gloves and put them in her lap.

"These young women . . . They come to Dawson for adventure. They haven't a clue what people do to survive here. Most of them go home come winter, thank God."

Valerie sighed.

"Her parents must be desperate. And they still don't know exactly what happened?"

"Somebody knows something. It'll come to light sooner or later."

Valerie strained to hear her. The bus's motor was running, and the snowmobiles were howling outside. The women smiled for a moment, overjoyed at seeing each other again. Valerie was grateful to Marjorie for her friendship. Inuvialuit women could be standoffish toward female tourists or women who moved there. Valerie could relate to their reserve. Many women traveling to Inuvik couldn't be bothered about indigenous customs and relationships.

Marjorie pushed back her hood.

"Your friend is talking to people about your parents."

"What?"

Valerie whipped forward against the steering wheel.

"Peter Hurdy-Blaine was your father, wasn't he?"

Valerie nodded.

"I don't noise it about. It's not easy having a father everybody knows."

Marjorie took Valerie's hand for a moment.

"My father chased polar bears, your father chased pucks."

She laughed. Valerie didn't always understand indigenous humor, but sometimes it dispelled anxiety. Not that day, though.

"My . . . friend, who you mentioned, who's she telling about my parents?"

"A couple of people here and in Tuk. She wants to find out exactly what happened when your parents followed the route of the Lost Patrol."

"Do you know where she is right now?"

"She turned up in Tuk a few days ago."

In Tuktoyaktuk! Valerie had to let Clem know.

Clem. Who'd slept with Sedna.

It was a big mistake.

"She was asking about a boy who was supposed to have gone on the trek with your parents."

"Did she talk to you? Was there anything you could tell her?"

"She did. And no. I don't know what she's after."

"Me neither, Marj. What's motivating her? It's as if she wants to . . . torture me."

"Your poor mother. It was an accident, that's the word around here. A hunting accident."

An accident. Apparently, no one here suspected suicide. Clem had already told her that.

Valerie didn't dare interrupt Marjorie.

"Two local families moved to Yellowknife afterward. I don't know how or why. They certainly didn't have the money to fly, but they did."

Valerie felt her heart tightening.

"Marj, do you mean to say somebody gave them money?" Hush money.

"It might just be a coincidence," she heard Marjorie say. "The money might have come from a government program in Ottawa. For educating the kids. I dunno."

Valerie stared straight ahead through the dirty windshield. A circle of warmly dressed people stood around several pyramids of piled twigs and branches, and flames were flickering up. Teakettles would be put on the fire in a few minutes, and whoever got the snow to melt and boil first would win the teakettle contest. She spied two familiar faces among the interested onlookers, a man and a woman: the caribou photographers.

Once again, Marjorie's fingers grasped Valerie's hand.

"You know it was your mother's spirit that guided you here, don't you? You do know that? Her body was flown to Vancouver or wherever, but her soul is still here. Talk to her, Valerie. She'll give you counsel and guide you."

Valerie had to hold back tears with all her might.

I have one mother who has Alzheimer's and another who's been dead for thirty years. I can't talk to either one.

Marjorie didn't let up.

"Maybe conjuring up her spirit will help."

"You mean with a shaman?"

"With a good shaman. Why not?"

Valerie thought of Pihuk Bart. And his prophecy.

"We saw the caribou herd near Rock River. A sea of caribou. Pihuk prophesized to me two winters ago that when I saw the caribou migrating, I'd learn the secret of an involuntary death that same year. That it would be a beautiful and terrible year. And he said the caribou carry the souls of my descendants with them."

Marjorie Tama's face brightened.

"Yes, Pihuk knows a lot. Maybe too much. He—"

The rear door opened quickly, and Jordan Walker heaved his tall body up inside the bus.

"The snowmobile race hasn't even started, and there's already an argument," he announced breathlessly. "Because the course was modified, if I understood rightly. I'm going back in a minute, but I've gotta warm up a bit first."

"There—the kettles are steaming!" Marjorie shouted. "Is that hot enough for you?"

She broke into her irresistible laugh and got out of the car.

"See you soon, Valerie!"

Faye knocked on the driver's side window. In her fur hat, she looked like the detective Marge Gunderson from the movie *Fargo*.

"Changing of the guard!"

The white steam from her mouth turned the window into frosted glass for a brief moment. Valerie felt a mounting wave of affection. Faye would never take off from Inuvik the way Sedna had last summer.

And she wouldn't come on to men Valerie knew. Maybe it wasn't her fault that things had gone wrong with Sedna.

Valerie whipped out her cell phone and sent Clem a text message: "Sedna is apparently in Tuk. Can you find out anything?"

She looked at Faye.

"Sedna's in Tuktoyaktuk, or so I've heard."

Faye's jaw dropped.

"I was just about to tell you. Some guy told me he'd seen her *here*. About an hour ago."

CHAPTER 27

Frenetic barking drowned out all other sounds. Alana Reevely's sled was at the ready, her dogs all hitched up. Clem watched her going from dog to dog, checking the straps. It was the dress rehearsal for Sunday's race. Alana's assistants—young people from Inuvik—restrained the excited animals; bitten by race fever, they would have otherwise shot off immediately. Clem couldn't see Duncan anywhere, not even behind the pickup he'd brought the dogs in. The cage hatches on the tailgate were open. He caught sight of Pihuk among the spectators; both he and Alana spotted Clem and came over.

"Where's Duncan?" Clem roared.

Alana screwed up her pretty face.

"Forgot something at the house. He's been so absentminded lately." Then she smiled.

"I heard Valerie's here. That's fantastic! I was afraid she wouldn't come because of Gisèle and Roy. Have you seen her yet?"

Clem nodded. So now Alana was onto his weakness for Valerie. His sortie to Eagle Plains had probably made the rounds here too.

"Yeah, I've seen her. She's got six people with her. They're going to Tuk tomorrow."

"Is Tanya still locked up? Do you think she might have had something to do with Roy's getting beaten up?"

Clem blew a puff of white air upward.

"I dunno. I'm going to Tuk to ask around. Say, has Meteor serviced Leila yet?"

Alana reacted with surprise.

"Not that I know of. Why?"

"Toria was at your place. Duncan said she wanted a puppy."

Her face grew dark.

"Well, she damn well won't get a puppy from me. The way those people treated their last dog. It almost froze to death, chained up at minus twenty-five. No thank you. When was she at our place?"

"Yesterday. When I wanted to pick up Meteor. You were out with him."

Alana turned toward the dog team again.

Pihuk butted in.

"I think Toria was snooping around your dogs, Alana. I see her red car at your place almost every week. I wouldn't be surprised if Helvin shows up with his own team."

He laughed as if he'd told the funniest joke in his life.

But Alana didn't join in. Sharp creases appeared around her well-formed lips.

"I don't give a damn about whatever Helvin and Toria are up to."

Clem attempted to defuse the situation.

"In any case, I'll be rooting for you on Sunday," he promised.

Alana raised an arm and would definitely have made a *V* for Victory sign if she hadn't had thick gloves on.

When Clem was sure that Alana was out of earshot, he asked Pihuk, "How come you keep seeing Toria's SUV at Alana and Duncan's place?"

"I take my snowmobile past there on the way to my hunting cabin. Why?"

"Just asking."

Clem escaped to his pickup before Pihuk could draw him into a longer conversation. Driving along the Ice Road, he saw Alana's dog team bounding ahead. He kept the car even with the dogs and checked the speedometer: twenty miles an hour. Pretty good for dogs that young.

The road curved gently away from the racecourse at the spot where Gisèle had died in the cold—the fluttering, black-and-yellow police tape was still up. No candles, no plastic flowers, no cross. Was Tanya Uvvayuaq involved in Gisèle's death? And what might the ranger, Roy Stevens, have known that Tanya would want to keep him quiet? Whoever the perp was had certainly succeeded in that; Roy was still in an Edmonton ICU, unresponsive.

Clem picked up speed. He couldn't remember how often he'd driven across the Mackenzie ice to Tuktoyaktuk. At times in snowstorms and whiteouts that had caught up with him faster than he expected. Still, he couldn't recall a greater feeling of tension than now. He feared for his friend Lazarusie and his family; he feared the worst.

Everything seemed normal on the Ice Road: half a dozen oncoming trucks, drivers waving at him. The traction on the ice was amazingly good; his boys on the graders had done good work. Temperatures were rising, but the road would be passable for about two more weeks. He saw an occasional long crack in the ice—nothing to worry about as long as its thickness was checked regularly.

He reached Tuktoyaktuk two and a half hours later. There were four snowmobiles in front of Lazarusie's place. Electric cables hung like garlands from the poles lining the road and crept over the board front of the house. Clem mounted the snow-covered steps and noticed blood on them. He hammered on the door. Lazarusie opened it, holding a sharp knife in his blood-smeared fingers.

"What the hell . . ." Clem gasped.

Then he saw the gutted caribou on the kitchen linoleum.

Lazarusie's wife knelt beside it, cutting up pieces of meat that landed in plastic buckets. Every so often she popped a piece into her mouth.

"Give some to our friend here," Lazarusie shouted at her.

"Tea wouldn't be a bad idea," Clem said, trying to circumvent the rules of hospitality without disrespecting them. They exchanged a few banalities about the postponed snowmobile race and last year's winners at the Muskrat Jamboree before Clem got around to significant matters.

"Where'd they take Tanya?"

Lazarusie wiped his brown face with the back of his hand.

"Inuvik. To a cell in the RCMP jail."

"For how long?"

"Dunno. I've got no money to get her out. A ranger . . . it's real serious. But she didn't do it."

"Did Tanya—"

"Damn right she did it."

A boy's voice interrupted him. Only then did Clem see Danny standing at the door to the hall leading to the bedrooms.

"I saw her," Danny went on. "She hit Roy."

Danny had on a green hooded sweatshirt bearing the words "The True North Strong and Free," a line from the national anthem. The left side of his head was shaved bare; on the right side, his straight black hair fell over his face.

Lazarusie didn't look at his son when he said, "Danny's glad that Tanya's in jail because there's peace and quiet in the house now. But she—"

"What crap, Dad! I. Saw. Everything. She was ready to grab the backpack and Roy came out and—"

This time Clem interrupted the boy.

"Came out of where?"

"The ice house. Roy tried to snatch the backpack back, and Tanya flattened him with her mace."

"Mace? She has a mace?" Clem looked at him, thunderstruck.

He shrugged.

"Yeah, she gets stuff like that on the Internet. I told you already, Dad, but you don't believe me." He pushed at the sides of the doorframe with outstretched hands. "Something funny's going on with Tanya, Clem. You know she's Abel and Resa's kid? She's adopted. That girl was creepy before she could even walk."

Lazarusie muttered something, but Clem was thinking ahead.

"Where's the backpack now?"

"Dunno. She hid it."

Danny's father shook his head.

"Boy, something's not right. Since when does Roy go around with a backpack?"

"It wasn't Roy's—it was way too small. I have no clue whose it was."

Clem got up and stood face-to-face with Danny.

"Did you tell the police about the backpack?"

Danny bit his lower lip.

"No. Like I said, I dunno where she stashed it."

Clem turned to Lazarusie.

"I'm going to the ice house. You've got a key, eh? Come with me— I'll need you."

Danny stepped into the kitchen.

"I'm going too."

"You stay here!" His mother hadn't uttered a peep—until now.

As they were leaving, Clem heard Danny's loud complaints.

"He's a good kid," Lazarusie said as they drove through the village. A snowmobile came toward them with four people on it—young parents and two little kids. Lazarusie was visibly upset and talking a blue streak.

"He's a good kid," he repeated. "I know that. He doesn't want to be a shaman, but he's a good kid anyway. He wants to protect his mom—she's scared of Tanya sometimes. That's why he called the cops and gave them the dirt on her. She's got the wrong friends. They come from Dawson and give her drugs. She listens to loud music and drinks."

To their right a white emptiness stretched out to the horizon: the frozen Arctic Ocean, known thereabouts as the Beaufort Sea. To their left, under a gray, impervious sky, they saw the little white church and its unoccupied manse.

Clem pulled off the road when the plowed section ended and parked, leaving the motor running to avoid any trouble restarting. He stuffed a flashlight under his down jacket. They went the rest of the way on foot. A little wooden shack was built over the ice house entrance, and around it there were numerous footprints in the snow. Lazarusie turned the key in the lock, and it opened readily.

"It wasn't locked," he said.

The wooden lid lay as usual over the narrow square opening.

"The rope." Clem pointed to it.

It lay unrolled and twisted up on the floor. Someone hadn't put it back properly.

"What was Roy doing here?" he asked. "Does he have a cold-storage chamber?"

"Dunno," Lazarusie murmured.

Clem took a step to the side.

"I'll help you with the lid."

"Let me—wait, what's that?" Lazarusie's face tensed up.

Now Clem heard it too. A faint cry some distance away. It cut through him like a hot knife through butter.

"Quick, the lid!"

It banged against the wall after they lifted it up.

They stared into the pit below.

"Hello?" they shouted simultaneously.

They heard a whimper in reply. A human voice. A woman's voice.

Clem directed the flashlight beam downward.

He saw a shadow at the bottom of the ladder. Then he heard the voice again. Weak, plaintive.

"I'm going down. Give me some light," he said, handing the flashlight to Laz.

Clem held firmly on to the edge of the opening and slid down into the darkness until his feet felt the rungs.

Lazarusie pointed the flashlight below.

That's when Clem saw her. First her upward-turned face, with glittering ice crystals on her eyelids and eyebrows. Her skin was white, and there were more crystals on the scarf over her mouth.

He could make out some words. A desperate plea.

"Please, please."

"Good God!" The words slipped out of his mouth. He turned back toward Lazarusie. "The rope. Throw me the rope!"

He looked down and shouted, "We'll save you. You'll be safe in a minute. We'll get you out of there."

He tied the rope around his waist and climbed down the icy ladder rung by rung.

As he reached the bottom, the eyes in the face—quite close now—blinked.

Now he was positive. The prisoner in the cellar was *not* Sedna.

So who was she?

CHAPTER 28

Valerie left the bar and went to the reception desk where Clem was waiting. His expression told her he'd been through some awful experience.

"Where to?" he asked.

"Not the bar. They're at it again. Phil claims Helvin tried to bump him off his snowmobile intentionally. That's why he came in second. They're looking at Glenn's film footage to see what actually happened."

"A rerun of last year's drama. Except Phil was the accused then. Good thing there's a video this time."

She thought for a few seconds before speaking up: "I think it's better if we go to my room."

When they got there, he took off his boots and jacket in front of the door. Then he sat down on one bed and she on the other.

Valerie couldn't contain her impatience.

"What happened?"

What he told her took her breath away.

"Oh my God! How long was she stuck in there?"

"Probably two days. Maybe Roy took her to the ice house. He probably had a key," Clem surmised.

She looked at him, horrified.

"The ranger locked her in?"

Clem rubbed his forehead.

"No, I don't think so. Why would he? It must have been a mistake. An accident. He certainly didn't want to put her at risk. Even if . . . let's assume . . . but no, that's absurd. He'd have to have known that somebody would find her alive. Your tour group, say. That would have fingered him."

He unzipped his snowmobile suit and took off the top half. The heat was on full blast.

"Tanya was always looking for money or to steal something so she could buy drugs. The poor woman must have become a target when Tanya heard about her being in Tuk and talking to people. Danny told us she stole the woman's backpack. It had probably been left in the pickup, and Roy was coming back to get it. Maybe her camera was in it. And Tanya swiped it off Roy."

His words came slowly, haltingly.

"Roy confronted her, and Tanya knocked him down. Then she probably spotted the open cellar door . . . Tanya didn't want the woman to sound the alarm. So she slammed down the lid and closed the door to the shack without locking it."

He looked around.

"I need a strong, hot coffee. How about it?"

He pointed to the coffeemaker.

Valerie nodded, still stunned.

"Sure thing."

He filled the pot with water.

"It took us about half an hour to get her up out of there. She'd slipped and sprained her ankle trying to go up the ladder in the dark. What a nightmare. Two days!"

"Will she pull through?"

"I think so. She had extreme hypothermia—her speech was pretty incoherent. We laid her down in my warm truck. We got instructions from the ambulance service not to move her again because of her ankle or worse. Fortunately, the helicopter came pretty quickly. The RCMP has taken over now."

He sniffed.

"They'll have some explaining to do. Apparently, nobody thought to check the ice house. Incredible."

"But how would they know Roy had somebody with him? The lid was down. The ice house door was shut. The woman's backpack was gone. And Roy couldn't talk."

The coffee machine gurgled loudly.

Valerie clasped her hands together.

"So it isn't Sedna; Faye told me someone saw her at the snowmobile race. So who could the woman be? Does anybody know if there's a woman traveling around here by herself?"

"I got your text message saying that Sedna had been spotted in Tuk. I thought it would be her."

Clem poured coffee into a white cup and handed it to Valerie before continuing.

"The police haven't made the woman's name public yet, so I'm not allowed to tell you. The immediate family has to be notified first. And she's not allowed visitors until she's stable."

Valerie's conversation with Marjorie Tama crossed her mind. "Your friend," Marj had called her, never referring to Sedna by name.

Her heart began to thump. Suddenly, she had a hunch.

"Do you remember I told you about that woman in the Whitehorse museum who pretended to know me? She said her name was Phyllis Crombe. I don't know any Phyllis Crombe. I found out that she was considerably older than Sedna." Her voice was nearly hoarse now. "The woman you found, is her name Christine? Christine Preston?"

The astonishment on his face said it all.

Valerie jumped up and paced back and forth between the door and the bed.

"She was a childhood friend of my mother's. She turned up at one of my presentations, introduced herself, and gave me an envelope with an old article about . . . about my parents' disaster. Here, you can read it for yourself."

She took the article out of her handbag and passed it to Clem.

"Why . . . why are these people showing up all of a sudden and asking questions about my parents? What's that woman doing here? First Sedna, now Christine Preston! Do I mess around in *their* family history? What took place back then was bad enough. They ought to leave us in peace! I . . . I . . ." She struggled to find the right words. Tears welled up in her eyes.

Clem put down his cup and went over to her. He first laid his hand on her arm, then he drew her to himself, and she offered no resistance. She leaned her head on his shoulder and felt his arms wrap around her back.

He pressed his warm face to hers, and she heard him whispering. Words she didn't catch, but they aroused a longing in her. She raised her head and looked at him.

"It'll make things more complicated," she said softly.

He smiled.

"No, it'll make things much simpler."

He held her tight, then he kissed her. His lips were rough from the cold, his movements gentle and searching.

Her body reacted at once, paying no heed to whatever mental reservations she might have had. Her hand wandered up to his face and over his hair and the back of his head. Suddenly, she couldn't get close enough to this man. His passion swept away her laboriously maintained reserve. She lost all awareness of time and place—until a cell phone melody broke the spell.

She let go of him and said breathlessly, "You have to take it."

He nodded and fished the phone out of his pants pocket.

The voice at the other end was so loud that Valerie could hear it.

"You tell Helv to give up first place, or I'll tell the police who I saw Gisèle with before they found her body."

"Phil, why—"

"He rammed me—it's all there on the video. Either he admits he's wrong, or I go to the cops!"

"What's gotten into you? I'll be right there." But the connection was already lost.

Clem checked the phone, put it away, and looked at Valerie. She didn't let on that she'd heard the whole conversation.

He took her hands in his.

"I have to go. It's urgent."

He slowly stroked her hair and tried to read the expression on her face.

"Let's not let this go. I've waited a long time for this moment."

His words were touching. She took his head in her two hands and briefly pressed her lips against his mouth.

"It can only get better."

She would want to erase that sentence from her memory afterward, born as it was out of confusion and wishful thinking.

Clem slipped out of the room. She sat down on the bed, her thoughts racing. Clem's kisses. Christine Preston. The Ice Road. Gisèle. That odd phone call.

She went to the bathroom and looked at herself in the mirror. Although she felt stressed, her face was beaming. She quickly splashed cold water on her burning skin and applied some lip balm.

A minute later, she was knocking at Faye's door.

"I thought you'd come by when you were finished with the ice master," Faye said as she let Valerie into her room.

"You really don't miss a trick."

Faye grinned.

"Come sit down. I walked past your door and heard voices. So tomorrow we're off to Tuktoyaktuk?"

Valerie realized that Faye hadn't heard anything about Christine.

"That's crazy," Faye whooped after Valerie's detailed report, from their first meeting up to Christine's rescue from the ice house.

"Can we still go down in the cellar after all that's happened?"

Valerie shrugged.

"I have no idea. I'll have to get that straightened out, I suppose."

She pressed her hands to her burning face. Faye sat down beside her and put an arm around her shoulder.

"I know you really don't want to hear this, but I've got to tell you. On Glenn's video—you know, of the snowmobile race—you can see Sedna for a brief moment. I'm absolutely certain. She was in the crowd at the starting line."

Valerie sat bolt upright, and Faye's arm slid down.

Faye carried on: "I discovered something else, too. Sedna bought supplies in Inuvik. She was interested in a camp stove, something with propane. She told the store owner she'd had problems with another gas stove."

"How'd you find all this out?"

Faye produced a good-natured laugh.

"I ask around, my dear. Isn't that why I came along? I do want to track Sedna down." She winked. "Sometimes it pays to hang out in the bar."

"I could use a drink right now. That must have been a nightmare for Christine. Unimaginable."

"What are gals like her thinking? This is the Arctic, for Pete's sake! Not a Vancouver beach."

But Valerie was already somewhere else in thought.

"So Sedna's in a place without electricity. What's she up to?"

"Wouldn't I like to know. And why does this Christine lady suddenly pop up here? That can't be a coincidence."

Valerie stood up.

"I have to get a few e-mails off. So tomorrow at seven? Thanks for everything."

She went back to her room and booted up her laptop.

A message from Kosta was in her in-box.

"My dearest darling sister,

I found out more about Mary-Ann Strong's alleged secret service contacts. I got help from a friend in the States. The US authorities lifted the ban on certain documents after thirty years. It looks as if Mary-Ann sent regular reports on the Arctic to the prestigious Institute for Nordic Studies in Boston. The Canadian intelligence agency got wind of it and considered her an informer for the Americans (typical overreaction), so it kept an eye on her activities. US secret service agents had apparently read her reports concerning events and people in the Arctic. It was all very routine. The documents also record her death by rifle bullet. The Canadians apparently contacted the Americans about this through diplomatic channels. In the end, it nonetheless emerged from the appraisal of her reports that Mary-Ann's records were harmless, and it was concluded that her death was unrelated to her activities.

I have discovered some other interesting facts; I'll tell you about them in more detail soon.

Any news about Sedna Mahrer?

Kosta"

Valerie began typing her reply and didn't stop until it was eleven.

CHAPTER 29

"The caribou photographers again? It's like they're following us or something."

Valerie caught sight of the dark SUV in the rearview mirror. They'd just turned onto the Ice Road, and the group immediately demanded a photo stop for the ferries and barges that had been drawn up on land.

Faye looked straight ahead.

"The Ice Road doesn't belong to us, my dear."

Valerie kept quiet. She didn't want to spoil everyone's good mood on this sunny day. The sky was a pristine blue, like an unwavering canvas. The previous year they'd crawled along the ice in a blizzard, a white wall of snow in front of the windshield. Nobody had wanted to step out into that ice-cold inferno to snap a few pictures then.

A little while later, Trish spotted the black-and-yellow police tape, marking the spot where Gisèle Chaume's body had been found. Faye braked so gradually that the Chevy came to a halt a couple of hundred feet past the tape. They got out and waddled like ducks over the slippery footing.

"What? No cross to mark it?" Anika shouted as she felt her way along the ice, holding on to Valerie's arm. Paula seconded her.

"They never even lit a candle for poor Gisèle."

"We've got emergency candles in our luggage," Jordan remarked helpfully as he set up his tripod.

"Good idea!" Trish shouted.

Valerie had no choice but to part with two of their emergency candles. Not much of a risk given the beautiful weather. The dark SUV drove past them and was soon out of sight. Paula walked carefully, ministep after ministep, in the direction of Inuvik and climbed the wall of snow the plow had piled up by the roadside. Too much coffee for breakfast, Valerie surmised. Anika, who turned out to be a fan of true-crime cases, inundated her with questions.

"Where exactly was the body lying? Couldn't Gisèle have made it to Inuvik on foot? Was it bright enough yet? Is there cell phone reception out here?"

Carol shook her head.

"Why do you think we have a satellite phone in the car?"

Paula was the last to get back to the bus.

"Look what I found." She held out her hand to Valerie as she was getting in.

A blue cigarette lighter. Plastic—a dime a dozen. Except for an inscription: "Booster Adventures."

Valerie looked at the lighter and deliberated.

"May I keep it?"

"Sure. My gift to you," Paula said with a laugh before she turned her focus to the group. "Are you all aware that we're traveling over water?"

Everyone in the back seats began to chatter, but Valerie was lost in thought. Faye was also quiet now, concentrating on seeing cracks in the ice. Her speedometer needle never passed forty.

Valerie didn't exactly know what to expect in Tuktoyaktuk. She'd called the police station to ask if the ice house was accessible again, but they couldn't provide a real answer. So she decided to find out definitively once they got there.

The hills and the bony, fir-treed ridges on their left disappeared as the landscape flattened out to the horizon, as if someone had gone over it with a rolling pin. Valerie loved that white nothingness, the unobstructed, undisturbed vastness where your gaze could get lost.

Several trucks, a grader, and a plow came toward them, stirring up huge white clouds of snow. Later, when the road had grown to more than six hundred feet wide, they stopped again so the group could study the bare ice, which shimmered bluish, purple, and greenish, with black intervals, covered by a mesh of white lines—a frozen kaleidoscope.

Valerie saw an opportunity to organize the obligatory group photograph. Minus her and Faye, they formed a half circle on the ice. Valerie shot the same picture with eight different cameras. Then she took a shot of Faye standing in the middle of the Ice Road, raising her arms to heaven with her eyes closed. Would she send this picture to her relatives in Haiti? Valerie liked to think so.

A little while later they passed a wrecked vehicle, a white pickup emblazoned with the black lettering of a rental-car company in Inuvik. Valerie thought of Helvin West's truck near where Gisèle's body was found. The police hadn't deemed him a suspect. Did Gisèle really steal the pickup as Helvin claimed?

"What's that?" Carol shouted, pointing to peculiar large humps on the horizon.

"Pingos!" Paula and Valerie shouted at the same time.

"They look like ice volcanoes," Anika remarked.

Valerie yielded the floor to Paula.

"They are not volcanoes; they have a core of ice with a layer of earth on top."

"But they're white," Trish replied.

"Of course, because there's snow on the dirt."

"Massive lumps of ice and dirt," Glenn interjected.

"How high are those pingos?" Anika wanted to know.

"The highest in the area is over one hundred and sixty feet," Paula declared. "And pingo means 'little hill' in the indigenous language. Inuvialuktun, in case you're interested."

During their slow approach to Tuktoyaktuk, Valerie was thinking about the next sight on the horizon, the buildings of the DEW Line—the Distant Early Warning Line—and its anti-aircraft and radar installations. It had been built in 1957 to defend against Russia's nuclear force. Valerie had a little spiel prepared—her customers were always amazed at the sight of radar towers and a military base in the middle of an Arctic landscape. Faye saw them first.

"Are they drilling for oil over there?" she asked.

Before Valerie could answer, Glenn chimed in.

"This defense system was built during the Cold War and stretched from Alaska through Canada to Greenland. It was built in case the Russians sent bombers to North America over the North Pole. From 1954 to 1957, the Americans built forty-two stations in the Canadian Arctic. They also paid the full cost; the Canadians didn't contribute one red cent."

"Why not?" Carol asked.

"Because the Canadians were slackers. They probably didn't have the money for it."

Visibly pleased with himself, Glenn added a few statistics.

"More than four hundred and sixty thousand tons of material and equipment were transported into virtually uninhabited regions. All that sand and gravel could have built the Great Pyramid of Giza two times over."

Valerie was astonished. She recalled that Glenn was American. And the others were impressed—even Paula, who couldn't contribute anything to the topic.

"Were Americans stationed in Tuktoyaktuk?" Paula asked.

Glenn really got going then.

"Actually, the Canadians wanted to man the bases, but they didn't have the required specialists. So a lot of Americans worked here."

"Are the bases still operating?"

"Most of them are not. The entire system was modernized later, in 1985, I think. Since then, it's been called the North American Aerospace Defense Command. The Tuktoyaktuk base is still operated by remote control, or so I read somewhere."

The year Mary-Ann Strong died—1985. A young, adventurous woman whose travel reports from the Arctic had fallen into the no-man's-land between two neighbors who were officially allies but kept a sharp, steady eye on each other nonetheless. The government in Ottawa feared for Canadian sovereignty in their northernmost regions, which make up a fifth of Canada's landmass. Nothing's really changed there, Valerie thought. Except that the threats today were new ones. According to a newspaper report, somewhere out there on the vast ice now lying before her eyes, hunters had witnessed a giant explosion.

The bus passengers were talking about something else now. Their conversation focused on the first visible houses in Tuktoyaktuk, the stilts they stood on obscured by the snow.

Valerie and Faye dropped the group off at the one store in the village, then drove on to the schoolhouse to pick up the key to the ice house. A teacher referred them to Lazarusie and gave them directions.

When they arrived at Lazarusie's house, he was just leaving it, so Valerie hopped out of the minibus and waved him down.

"Laz!"

He turned around. His face brightened when he recognized her.

"You're lucky. I was just off to Inuvik to see Tanya."

"How's she doing?"

"Not too well. She talks too much. She's telling the RCMP just what they want to hear. That Gisèle sold drugs. That she wanted to meet Gisèle on the Ice Road that night to buy some hash, but she didn't make it. But she isn't telling them anything about Roy."

He rubbed his nose.

"Tanya was here the night Gisèle died. We were all here. She's got an alibi."

Valerie wanted to hug Lazarusie to comfort him. Instead she asked, "Has Tanya got a lawyer?"

Lazarusie shook his head.

"I'm going to Inuvik now to meet Clem. He knows a lot more about these things."

Valerie felt a slight twinge in her stomach at the mention of Clem's name. Whatever did she get herself into last night?

Lazarusie mounted his snowmobile.

"If you're here for the key to the ice house, you don't need it; the police are guarding the place."

He was right. A man in uniform came to meet Valerie and her group as they neared the ice house later that day. She recognized him at once—John Palmer, the RCMP officer she'd met in Eagle Plains.

"You've heard what's happened?" he asked by way of a greeting.

She nodded.

"May we still go in?"

Palmer pointed to an Inuvialuk standing beside the open ice house door.

"Yes, but we'll be supervising. Has everyone filled out the required form?"

She said they had and showed him the waivers where the tour members agreed to assume sole responsibility for any accidents in the ice house. Valerie was relieved that Anika had decided against the adventure. She was resting in the heated minibus.

Inside the little shack, a man Valerie knew from ice fishing the previous year—he called himself Gary, but she couldn't remember his Inuvialuit name—and his assistant helped Faye, the first in their group to put on the safety rope and disappear through the opening. Valerie stood alongside the others and watched.

Palmer gestured for her to step outside.

"I wanted to talk to you as well," he said. "Do you know a Christine Preston?"

It was obvious that he already knew the answer to that question. Who had told him? Clem? No, probably Christine herself. That must mean she's improving, Valerie thought.

"Yes, she came to one of my presentations. She said she was a childhood friend of my . . . my late mother. You know, she could easily have come with us. I'm surprised she didn't. Then this thing here"—she pointed through the doorway to the hole in the floor—"wouldn't have happened."

"Do you have any idea why she's here?"

"No, I'd love for her to tell me. Would it be possible for me to talk to her soon?"

"You'll have to call the hospital. She gave us a message on her way there: 'Tell Valerie not to blame Roy.' She insisted that we tell you that. Do you know what she meant?"

"Not a clue. Maybe that Roy didn't deliberately lock her in the cellar?"

"That's possible. Still . . . why was it so important to her for you to know?"

He eyed her attentively.

"Not a clue," she repeated. "Maybe she was simply . . . traumatized. After all that's happened. Excuse me, I really should catch up with my tour."

Inside the wooden shack, Valerie tipped Gary and his assistant before they secured the rope around her shoulders and waist and helped her put on a headlamp over her hat. Shouts and an occasional sharp cry rang out from below.

She placed a foot cautiously on the icy ladder but stopped when a sudden thought struck her.

"Does Roy have his own ice chamber down here?" she asked Gary.

"His father does."

"His father's from Tuktoyaktuk?"

Gary nodded.

"William Anaqiina. He moved away—to Yellowknife with his whole family."

Valerie clung to the ladder like glue. Anaqiina. As in Siqiniq Anaqiina. The boy who had been her parents' guide.

"Is one of his sons called Siqiniq?" she shouted above her.

Gary thought about it, then said something to the other man in his native language. The man answered in Siglitun.

"He thinks so."

Valerie pulled herself together and then descended one step at a time, her gloves seeking a grip on the upper rungs.

Somebody with a flashlight was at the bottom. Another policeman.

She nodded at him before she disappeared into the labyrinth of ice chambers like in a trance. In spite of Christine's terrible experience, she couldn't help but be moved by the magic of this underworld. Ice crystals covered the roof and the walls, ending at a gray-brown, marbled, frozen layer of dirt. Everything sparkled in the beams of their headlamps. Here, thirty-five feet under the earth's surface, the permafrost never thawed.

Valerie moved with extreme caution over the icy ground. Some wooden doors with dangling chains stood open; they led to twenty ice lockers belonging to local families.

Faye loomed up at the end of the corridor.

"Nobody with claustrophobia?" Valerie asked.

Faye shook her head.

"I have to admire Christine's grit. No light and not a sound down here. I would have gone crazy with fear."

Valerie shuddered.

As Christine was hoping and suffering down here, she thought about me. And about what she absolutely had to tell me.

CHAPTER 30

Clem was already in a lousy mood before he—yet again—went searching for Helvin. One of his men patrolling the Ice Road around noon had nabbed a trailer truck for speeding. Forty-five miles an hour instead of twenty. The truckers had it pounded into them over and over that going at that speed would make waves under the ice that couldn't find an exit so they would force open deep cracks. If that happened, then their only truck route would be destroyed. Clem couldn't fathom why those idiots tried to saw off the branch they were sitting on. He'd spent a lot of time talking with the driver and his boss. Once again, Helvin couldn't be reached by cell phone.

He didn't turn up until an hour later, just as Clem was futilely interrogating Laura Minetti about his whereabouts. Clem ran outside and swung himself up inside the sixty-tonner Helvin was driving.

"I can't talk. Gotta go," Helvin argued, seeing he was trapped.

"Phil called me yesterday ranting about the snowmobile race. He says he saw you with Gisèle before she died. Did you tell the RCMP everything?"

Helvin was outwardly unmoved.

"Phil couldn't have seen me. It was morning, and Phil teaches at the college in the morning."

"Phil said that if you don't surrender first place in the race, he'll tell the police that he saw you with her."

Helvin drummed his fingers on the wheel.

"Helv, that's—"

Clem was interrupted by an incoming text on his phone. A message from Valerie.

"He's welcome to first place," Helvin said. "I didn't bump him deliberately, but if that's what he wants to call it, let him."

Clem couldn't believe his ears. Helvin West would never forfeit a win so readily.

"You're not serious, Helv! Go to the police and just tell them everything before you make it worse."

"Nobody was there when I went to the station. They were all in Tuk, searching the ice house."

Clem looked at his boss skeptically. Another shabby excuse. A thought began to take shape in his head, quietly at first.

"Goddammit, Helv, who the hell asked Gisèle to give that nugget to you?"

More finger drumming.

"Richard Melville thinks it was Sedna Mahrer. He gave her two nuggets."

"What for?"

"She probably sweetened his days."

This is getting crazier than ever, Clem thought.

"So why, for Chrissake, did she send one to you and one to me?"

Helvin turned his head, and his lips tightened into a thin line.

"Maybe for revenge. So that we'd think the nuggets were from the Mafia. To scare us."

"Revenge? For what?"

"Because we both had a one-night stand with her and nothing more."

Clem was speechless for a few seconds. Then he jumped off the truck.

"You can ask Sedna if you find her," Helvin shouted at him.

"Talk to Phil. And you'd better talk to the RCMP," Clem retorted before slamming the door.

He'd barely gotten into his pickup when he opened Valerie's text.

"A woman in my tour group found this lighter near where Gisèle was found. Coincidence? What should I do with it?"

He'd hoped to read something about her feelings, words intimating how happy she was about the previous night. When he saw the picture she'd attached, his disappointment evaporated.

He knew immediately the person he had to talk to—right away.

But first he called Phil and informed him that Helvin had relinquished first prize. Phil was overjoyed. Clem didn't let him off the hook quite so easily.

"I want to know exactly what you saw, or I'll start talking about what you were up to in Whitehorse."

"What do you mean? I'm not gonna be blackmailed."

"Your wife certainly wouldn't be happy if she hears what I've got to say."

Clem had only heard rumors of Phil's visits to a certain lady in Whitehorse, but he gambled—and won.

His prompting got Phil to talk.

And with every bit of information Clem heard, another lightbulb was turned on, every one as bright as the North Star.

He drove back to Inuvik, turned onto Breynat Street, and parked in front of a huge building that looked like a hangar. The front was covered in glass and sheets of metal. Had it not been for the sign, INUVIK COMMUNITY GARDEN, you could have mistaken it for a hockey rink, which is what the building had once been. These days, the community garden was the pride of Inuvik. Even Clem, who didn't have a green thumb but liked his fresh vegetables, thought the idea of a greenhouse in the Arctic was great.

The glass roof let in a lot of light. Many people were walking around among wooden frames, vegetable beds, and blue barrels. Alana was loading a wheelbarrow with tools and pails at the back. Gardening was her second passion, common knowledge in Inuvik. Gardening and dogs.

The gates to the garden were officially opened in May, but impatient gardeners like Alana always found an excuse to start preparing as early as possible.

"Clem! *You're* here! I never would have expected this in a million years! We need volunteers." She winked at him.

Her cheerfulness dissipated when he took her aside to a quiet corner and showed her Valerie's photo on his phone.

"Where did you take this picture? I never distributed this lighter. I'm testing all sorts of versions. I'd like a bright purple with a yellow inscription, not blue. How did it . . ."

Her eyes circled around as if she could find an answer among the pots and shovels in the greenhouse.

". . . I put it away in my desk drawer."

"The lighter was found near where Gisèle froze to death."

She didn't answer right away, seemingly lost in thought. Then her eyes narrowed.

"Do you mean . . ."

Her face went stiff. She looked around. There was nobody near them.

"Gisèle must have filched it."

Clem didn't get it.

"Gisèle was at our place that day. I wasn't home, I was off with the dogs and some tourists. Duncan was in the house by himself. She is . . . She brought us some hash. It relieves my pain. Rheumatism. She wanted something else: she offered Duncan money to fix the dogsled race. Gisèle's boyfriend in Dawson was probably behind it. He's been dying to win the race for a long time."

"Cole Baker?"

"Probably."

Clem had heard about Cole's racing team. Cole had a reputation for working his dogs much too hard.

Alana sighed.

"Duncan had taken Booster into the house. He wanted to inspect her paws. Something on her right forepaw seemed to be bothering her. He filled her dish and went in to the kitchen to get her a tincture. He's convinced that Gisèle poisoned Booster."

Alana's eyes were moist.

And Clem's throat was constricted. Because the faint thought that had burrowed itself into his brain was growing louder. Pihuk Bart had seen Toria's red SUV in front of Alana's house that day. Pihuk hadn't uttered a word about seeing Gisèle. Something wasn't adding up.

"I'm packing up here," Alana said. "I don't feel so hot today."

Clem thought for a moment before asking, "Do you mind if I come with you and pick up Meteor?"

Duncan had taken his dog along as one of his team.

She looked at him. Her eyes were shadowed in fear.

She suspects what I suspect.

But she nodded and put her hands on the wheelbarrow.

Clem drove ahead, keeping Alana's green pickup in his rearview mirror. What he saw when he drove up to the house was no surprise.

The SUV parked there was red.

Alana got out, frowning. She didn't say anything. The dogs in their enclosures barked all the more frantically.

Nobody was in the mudroom. Alana didn't bother to take off her boots. She'd nearly reached the upper landing to the house when Duncan stumbled out the upstairs door.

"You're back already?" he asked.

Idiot, Clem thought.

"Where's Toria?" Alana's voice was strained.

"She's finishing her coffee," Duncan replied, without moving away from the door.

Alana whirled around.

"Clem, I'm sure there's enough coffee for you, too."

He suddenly saw in her the woman whose firm hand could tame an unruly pack of dogs.

Toria wasn't in the kitchen, where her parka was draped over the arm of a chair, or in the living room. She emerged from the bathroom without showing a shred of embarrassment.

"Hello, Clem," she exclaimed. "Is Valerie back from Tuktoyaktuk yet? She bought me a few things in Vancouver."

Several seconds of silence followed.

Then Alana got ahold of herself.

"Sit down, Toria, and have your imaginary coffee."

Toria declined with a hand gesture.

"Sorry, I have to take off, I just wanted to—"

"Sit down, Toria." Clem had also discovered his voice again. "There are some things going on here that require an explanation."

"Another time, I've really got to go."

Toria made for the door, but Alana got there first.

"Either you talk to us, or we'll talk to Helvin."

Toria gave a shrug.

"Well, OK, if that's how it's got to be—a kitchen-sink drama."

She glanced for a second at Duncan, who was leaning against the sideboard with his arms folded.

"If you mean that Duncan and me . . ."

Clem broke in.

"I think there's much more to it, Toria."

He shoved his cell phone with the picture of the lighter under Duncan's nose. Out of the corner of his eye, he saw Alana wince.

"'Booster Adventures.' A nice inscription. This was found near the place where Gisèle lay dead on the road. I wonder how it got there?"

Duncan stared at the picture and turned pale. He looked at Alana.

"Yes, I've told Clem everything," she said. "That Gisèle was here and what she did."

Toria butted in.

"What? What's on the phone? Show me!"

Clem held his cell up to her. She shook her head in disbelief, then reached for her parka.

"Phil Niditichie saw you with Gisèle, Toria," Clem said. "That night. You two had an argument. Beside Helv's truck."

"Phil's crazy, he couldn't have possibly seen—"

"Give up, Toria, it's pointless. Tell them what happened," Duncan urged.

Everybody stared at him. His movie-star face was sagging, defeat written all over it.

Toria's voice turned shrill. "You're crazy, Duncan! Nothing happened, absolutely nothing. I—"

Duncan interrupted her.

"We met Gisèle behind the arena. Toria wanted to buy a bit of hash off her. I wanted to call Gisèle out. I knew right away that she'd poisoned Booster."

Clem saw Alana standing as still as a pillar of salt by the door. But he had to pursue his line of questioning.

"Was Toria here earlier that day?"

"Yes, after Gisèle left."

"How did Gisèle get here?"

"By snowmobile. I don't know whose it was. Maybe she swiped that, too."

"Was Booster already . . . was the dog already showing signs of being poisoned while Gisèle was at your place?"

Duncan pondered for a long time.

"No, but afterward she began to foam at the mouth and writhe on the floor. It was . . . it was awful."

He wiped his hand over his lips and closed his eyes.

Toria came over to him and grabbed him by the shoulders.

"Shut your goddamn mouth, Duncan! You're making things a hell of a lot worse."

Duncan pushed her back.

"It'll all come out anyway, don't you see? Phil saw you arguing with Gisèle. Maybe he also saw her drive off in Helv's pickup. How convenient of you to leave the motor running."

Toria drove Helvin's truck to the arena, not her SUV, Clem thought. Things were starting to make sense: Gisèle didn't secretly follow Helvin to his office and steal his truck after he'd thrown her out of it in town. *Toria* had taken her husband's truck from outside his office, then driven it to the center of Inuvik to rendezvous with Duncan and Gisèle behind the arena. It was there that Gisèle took Helv's pickup *after* the quarrel and drove off. And Clem's boss was blissfully ignorant about it all.

Clem followed up.

"What was the argument about?"

Toria didn't answer.

"She showed you a gold nugget, didn't she? And said it was from Helvin for services rendered. Didn't she?"

That was largely speculation, but Clem instantly saw he'd hit a bull's-eye.

"Gisèle was angry that you and Duncan dumped on her," Clem continued. "Duncan accused her of poisoning Booster. And someone told you that Gisèle had been seen with Helvin."

Toria looked at him furiously without a reply.

Clem was now able to work out exactly what had happened.

"So you two followed her. You, Toria, because of the pickup. And you, Duncan, because you still had a score to settle with her. On account of Booster."

"Yes," Duncan admitted. "Gisèle drove onto the Ice Road. She'd told me she was supposed to meet a shaman. Maybe Pihuk, but he has an alibi, of course." He sucked in his breath loudly. "She drove much too fast and . . . hit a pile of snow beside the road. There was no way she was going to be able to back the truck out of it. We stopped and got out. Her motor was still running. We knocked on the window. But she wouldn't get out; she just sat there. We . . . nothing worked. Toria said, 'Let her stew in her own juice, that'll teach her.' And then we drove back."

"And the lighter?" Clem asked.

Duncan stared at the floor.

"We stopped before Inuvik because I almost shit my pants. That's when I must have lost the lighter."

"You simply left Gisèle behind?" Alana asked in a faraway voice.

Duncan threw up his arms.

"Christ Almighty, Alana, she poisoned Booster! She killed our best dog!"

"And I thought you were in the Crazy Hunter with Phil," Alana shouted back.

Clem intervened before the altercation could escalate. Toria was not moving an inch; her expression showed distress.

"So Gisèle didn't get out of the vehicle while you were there."

Duncan shook his head.

"Like I said, she was supposed to meet up with somebody apparently. We thought it was Pihuk. He would have hauled her out. Or somebody else would have."

Clem sat down at a nearby table and propped up his chin in his hand.

"She probably attempted to walk back to Inuvik after nobody showed up. Typical miscalculation for somebody with no knowledge of the area. And when she realized it was too cold and too far, she tried to get back to the truck. She underestimated the distance. On the way back she became exhausted, sat down, and froze to death. And in her desperation, she threw the package with the gold nugget into the snow."

Toria grabbed her jacket and shot daggers at Duncan.

"You see, it was Gisèle's mistake. And you put the blame on yourself, you moron. Just can't keep your mouth shut."

Clem banged his fist on the table.

"The police will see it differently, Toria. That poor woman paid with her life for your recklessness."

Toria flashed hate-filled eyes at him.

"You've just lost your job, Clem—you can bet on it. You've just gotta stick your nose into somebody else's business. And you know what? Your pal Phil bashed you on the head, I'm positive. He wanted to take you out of the race because he was afraid your new snowmobile was faster than his. He yakked about it everywhere."

Duncan stopped her.

"That's bullshit, Toria. Who can't keep her mouth shut now?!"

The irony was not lost on Clem. Duncan was defending his friend Phil. Phil, who'd spilled the beans and put Duncan in the hot seat without realizing it. Phil, who let Clem know he'd watched Toria and Gisèle arguing, which ultimately put Clem on Duncan's trail. Before he could play out the thought further, Toria bellowed, "You're such a wimp, Duncan! Sticking with your oh-so-sweet Alana like a lapdog. She doesn't care about anything but dogs! Dogs and gardens! It's so fucking ludicrous!"

Clem jumped up and looked her straight in the eye.

"You poisoned Booster, Toria, didn't you? It was *you*; you put the poison in her food."

"And what if I did?" Toria shouted. She pointed toward Alana. "She had it coming, the arrogant, snot-nosed bitch! A know-it-all who isn't even from these parts. She had it coming and more!"

Alana rushed at Toria, screaming, but Toria shoved a chair in her way and stormed out of the now-unguarded door.

CHAPTER 31

The musicians onstage inside the arena started playing; the jigging contest was now underway. A young pair hopped onto the dance floor to cheers of encouragement from the audience. The girl was in black leggings and a miniskirt; the guy had a baseball cap in his hand. They shuffled their feet in an old Scottish dance style to the strains of a guitar and a fiddle. The audience in their seats spurred the pair on with whistles and yells. After a few minutes, the next pair showed off their synchronized steps. Whites, Gwich'in, Métis, and Inuvialuit all took part in the contest. Valerie marveled at the ladies' boots of soft caribou skin, embroidered and bordered with fur. Children in miniparkas skipped around at the edges of the dance floor, frisky as Arctic hares. Valerie noticed that the trip on the Ice Road had triggered a wave of enthusiasm in her group too. They'd spotted a lynx and an Arctic fox on the ride back to Inuvik.

Glenn was the only one who seemed a little disappointed in the dance contest. Jigging wasn't his thing, apparently.

"I'd rather film something traditional, old Inuit parkas—or throat singing," he complained.

"That's coming," she consoled him. "The festival lasts for a few more days."

"Jigging's traditional, too," Paula chimed in. "Many of the early settlers in Inuvik were of Scottish descent. People here have danced the jig for centuries."

Valerie recognized a familiar face in the crowd. Poppy Dixon fought his way to her seat.

"Hello, Poppy! All tired out? You should be shaking a leg out there!"

Poppy grinned broadly, revealing his brown teeth, the consequence of chewing tobacco.

"I need a partner. Why don't you come with me?"

Valerie staved him off with a laugh.

"Afraid you'll have to find somebody else."

"I can do a jig," Carol shouted.

Poppy's face spoke volumes.

"I just knew I'd find a pretty woman willing to dance with me. Well, then, off we go!"

Carol followed Poppy to the line of candidates waiting for the emcee to announce them.

"I've definitely got to record this," said Glenn, who suddenly decided to go along with the festivities.

Faye looked at Valerie in amusement from the other end of the row.

Valerie pointed out a pair of dancers.

"Do you want to?"

She mouthed her words because it was impossible for Faye to hear her amid the hubbub. But Faye pointed to the arena's entranceway.

Where Clem Hardeven was standing.

Valerie acknowledged Faye's signal and crept away. Clem had already seen her. Her heart skipped a beat.

He's been looking for me.

"We're going to my place," he said right off the bat when he approached her.

They hardly talked on the way. Valerie suspected that something serious had happened. She hadn't come across Alana or Toria in the arena, unlike in previous years. And Duncan and Helvin were nowhere to be seen either.

Meteor gave them an animated reception upon their arrival. Valerie ruffled the fur on his head with repeated shouts of, "Not so rough, boy, not so rough!"

Clem took his time making tea and feeding the fire. Watching him, Valerie felt a fluttering in her stomach.

He has tea with me but vodka with Sedna, she observed silently but scolded herself at once. His serious expression made her nervous. He hadn't touched her even slightly so far.

"C'mon, I can't stand the suspense any longer," she finally exclaimed.

He sat down with her at the kitchen table and began to talk.

It was worse than she could ever have imagined. Gisèle and Duncan. Duncan and Toria. The Ice Road. Toria and Booster. Gisèle forsaken in death. Alana's unraveling.

When he'd finished, she sat there as if a bomb had gone off.

Then she stammered, "I can't believe it. Toria, I mean . . . I really liked her. She was always generous toward me. She . . . she opened doors for me in Inuvik. She was so helpful, I . . ."

Words failed her. She felt Clem's eyes on her.

"Why?" she asked.

Clem spun his cup around.

"Boredom? Jealousy? Envy? Dissatisfaction? Recklessness? Arrogance? A mishmash of everything?" He tossed his words out like a fisherman tossing bait.

He scratched his head.

"I dunno. What I *do* know is that she's unhappy in her marriage. And that she hates Alana's guts. Alana doesn't mince words when it comes to dogs."

"What will Alana do now? She must be devastated."

"She doesn't want to leave him."

Clem patted Meteor's head.

"And I unwittingly handed her the solution that could redeem him." He stared off into space. "Every truck and every pickup Suntuk Logistics owns is equipped with a satellite phone. Because we never know when we'll be on the Ice Road, and no one can risk forgetting a cell phone or leaving it in the office."

She peered into his exhausted face and thought: I really like him very much.

"I told Alana about it," he continued. "Now she's convinced herself that Gisèle could have called for help on the phone. And that Duncan isn't an accessory to her death. That he's innocent."

"Why didn't Gisèle use the phone?"

"There was no way she'd have known it was there, so she didn't look for it. Val, she's a girl from a village in Quebec. One winter in Dawson doesn't remake you into a local."

"Could that have happened to me, too, do you think?"

He looked at her with an indecipherable expression on his face and didn't respond.

I shouldn't have let myself be kissed; he'll break my heart.

"Do the police know?" she continued.

He nodded.

"Yes, Duncan and Alana went to the station right away. I don't know what Toria plans to do."

"And Helvin?"

"Haven't heard a word out of him. That's been happening recently, off and on."

She sipped her tea.

"How's it look between Duncan and Toria now?"

He shrugged.

"I don't want to condone what happened, Val. Still, I don't believe they meant for Gisèle to die. They were furious at her and wanted to teach her a lesson. Normally, a car or truck will come by out there. But not that night."

He cleared his throat.

Something was on the tip of Valerie's tongue, but she didn't say it. Instead she asked, "So is it true what Toria said, that Phil hit you on the head so you couldn't be in the race?"

Clem took his time with his answer. It was obviously hard for him to look that possibility square in the face.

"Even Duncan thinks it's possible. Phil was evidently seen near my house that night. Phil's a fanatic when it comes to snowmobiles."

He stopped talking and lowered his eyes. Valerie thought it wise to change the subject.

"Does the media know about Duncan's confession?"

"So far they don't. It won't stay that way for long, though. The cops need a win after they screwed up in Tuktoyaktuk and left Christine in the ice house after they found Roy. But they let you into the ice house, eh?"

"Yes. John Palmer was very accommodating." She waited a beat. "I bumped into Laz, who said you'd help him. He's trying to find a good lawyer for Tanya."

"We're working on it."

He sipped some tea, then went on. "I know it sounds strange, but I think Roy Stevens would be the best person to act as Tanya's lawyer."

"What? I don't get it."

"Roy understands the hopelessness many of the young Inuvialuit feel. A lot of them have no work, no future, nothing to do. They start drinking or smoking pot. Roy's often talked about it with me."

He looked at Meteor, who was stretched out at his feet, head on his paws.

"Roy wants to help them. He always says a synthesis of the traditional lifestyle and modern ways is possible if you just go about it right.

But parents aren't able to do that for their young sons and daughters. He says it's too much for them to handle. Roy says the most important thing is jobs, and I think he's right there. Training, work, making ends meet."

He gave a laugh that sounded like resignation.

"Right now, doctors and people in the hospital get work, and they're nearly all white."

Valerie couldn't hold back any longer.

"I think Roy was the boy who was with my parents."

Clem suspended his cup in midair.

"What's that?"

"His father is William Anaqiina, from Tuktoyaktuk. That's what Gary told me—he's one of the men who helped us at the ice house. William Anaqiina moved his family to Yellowknife thirty years ago. Just after my mother died."

She traced a finger over the tabletop.

"Like I said, John Palmer was with us at the ice house when I took my group there. He said that Christine Preston desperately wanted the police to tell me that Roy wasn't to blame."

She let her words hang in the air for a moment. She still wasn't sure why Christine had felt it was so important to send that message to her.

"I'll likely find out more when she can have visitors."

Clem took her hand. His touch on her skin was electric, but his tone of voice was calming.

"It will all be resolved someday. Someday you'll learn the truth. It looks like a tangled ball of yarn right now, I know. But it's only a matter of time."

His nearness almost pained her. Every fiber of her body was attuned to him.

Take me in your arms. Please, right now.

As if reading her mind, he got up and drew her toward him.

At that moment, she couldn't have cared less whether this was a smart thing to do. Or worried about his one-night stand with Sedna. Or that Meteor was jealously thrusting his way into their embrace.

A few minutes later, Lazarusie burst into the house, bringing the moment to a sober end.

"They brought Roy out of his coma," he reported.

CHAPTER 32

"Finders keepers, losers weepers," Poppy Dixon chirped, his face beaming. "So many customers in one day!"

Valerie and Faye exchanged glances. Valerie had originally planned to take the group on a dogsled trip with Booster Adventures. But for obvious reasons, Alana and Duncan weren't up to it. So she switched to renting snowmobiles from Poppy. Even Anika was keen to go on the excursion.

"I used to have a motorcycle," she confessed with a laugh.

Poppy patiently explained to them how the machines worked, while his son passed around the helmets. Valerie had drummed into them the importance of dressing warmly enough. The sun was shining, but it was still bitterly cold. If she took off her gloves, her fingers quickly went numb.

With Poppy in the lead and his son as the rearguard, they left Inuvik and crossed the frozen Mackenzie. Anika steered her vehicle amazingly well, and even Trish goosed her machine on the flat ice after some initial hesitation.

Valerie followed her lead. She felt like she was flying. She shed all her worries and anxieties and was seized by the intoxication of speed, which filled her with an unforeseen sensation of happiness. It quietly annoyed her that Glenn and Jordan kept stopping to shoot the snowscape. She wanted to race ahead until she'd fall off the snowmobile, exhausted.

They pushed along a snowmobile trail cut through a wooded area on the taiga. In half an hour, they came to a trapper's cabin, its windows boarded up with plywood. It stood on a hill sloping down to a small lake. They stopped there for a snack, which the group ate while keeping their gloves on.

The weather really was spectacular. Blue sky, sun, snow. Valerie saw delighted faces all around her.

They started on the way back shortly after noon. Glenn and Jordan didn't hold the group up for photo ops this time, and Valerie worried that her group was on the verge of taking too much risk with their snowmobiles. Glenn bombed over the wide snow-covered field. Or *was* it Glenn? She counted them off. Someone was missing.

She dashed ahead on her snowmobile and signaled for Poppy to stop.

They all took off their helmets, and Valerie scanned the faces.

"Glenn's missing. We've got to go back."

Poppy spoke up quickly. "I'll go look for him. Rory, you take the rest of them back, slowly. Very slowly, you hear?"

"I'm going with Poppy," Valerie declared.

Faye picked up the ball right away.

"No problem. I'll keep an eye on them."

Valerie could have hugged her at that moment.

Poppy took off through the taiga without waiting, and Valerie was hot on his heels. Then they slid more leisurely over the plain, surveying their surroundings and the tracks ahead of them.

They didn't see any place where a snowmobile could have turned off.

It seemed to Valerie that it took forever to reach the cabin above the lake again. A snowmobile was parked in front of it. And the door was open just a crack.

Poppy must have noticed it, too, because he stopped directly in front of it. Valerie followed him into the cabin. Her eyes had to adjust to the dimmer light.

An abrupt movement in a dark corner. Then she saw Glenn, kneeling before a crudely constructed bed. He turned to face them.

"She's not breathing! She's all cold!"

His voice registered disbelief. He stood up and walked a few steps away from the bed. Valerie stared at his horrified face. Her view of the person on the bed was blocked.

"She's dead!" he went on. "This can't be! How'd she die?"

Poppy composed himself and approached the bed. He bent down and felt for a pulse.

"We can't help her; she's gone," he said. "We have to call the police and an ambulance."

He walked over to Glenn.

As if led by an invisible hand, Valerie walked over to the bed. She instantly recognized the woman lying there motionless. Her face, framed by colorful strands of hair, looked peaceful, as if she were simply asleep. Valerie screamed.

"Sedna!"

"Who is she? Do you know her?" Poppy asked.

Valerie tried to speak but was struggling to breathe.

She heard Glenn's voice coming from somewhere.

"She's my sister."

Valerie gave a start. She was in shock. She saw Glenn in front of her, his face distorted with pain.

"What?" she wanted to shout, but her throat was blocked.

She shook her head.

"It's true, Valerie—Sedna is my sister. You won't want to believe it, but our mother was Bella Bliss. Bella Wakefield now."

Poppy was nervously pacing back and forth.

"What was she doing here? This is Pete's cabin."

Glenn ignored him. His eyes were unwaveringly fixed on Valerie.

"She deserted us to marry your father. She simply walked out on her children. Sedna and me."

Valerie shook her head again.

"That . . . that can't be. That . . ."

"We didn't know for a long time where our mother was. But Sedna sniffed her out. It came as a shock to Sedna. Our mother had left to become part of another family. A stranger's children were more important to her than her own children." He was yelling now.

Poppy interrupted him. "We mustn't waste time. We have to call the police and an ambulance!"

Glenn was absolutely frantic. "Someone killed her!" he shouted. He grabbed Poppy by the shoulders and shook him. "Who wanted her dead?"

Poppy extricated himself from Glenn's grasp.

"Cool it, man. The cops will figure this out. You can come back with us."

"Are you out of your mind? I won't leave Sedna here alone. Somebody killed her."

Poppy looked toward Valerie, his eyes pleading for help. She was the tour guide and responsible for her customers. But she didn't know what she could do to sway Glenn; she didn't recognize him anymore. He was a threatening stranger.

When she tried to speak, she could only croak.

"Glenn, we should take care of Sedna—you're right. We won't leave her here alone. But now—"

"She almost made it. She was going to tell the whole world. The whole world's going to know what a son of a bitch your father

228

was, Valerie. How he killed Mary-Ann Strong so he could marry our mother."

Glenn walked over to a little table that held a propane lamp, notebooks, and a bundle of papers. He grabbed the bundle and held it high.

"Here! It's all in here!"

Enraged, he threw it into a corner.

Poppy seized Glenn's arm.

"Don't touch anything. We need to leave everything just as we found it for the police. It's important."

Glenn pushed him down onto the floor. There was a tussle, and the next thing Valerie saw was a pistol in Glenn's hand.

Poppy dove for cover under the table.

But Glenn's eyes were trained on Valerie.

"You think you're untouchable, you and your family. A family of murderers. You killed Sedna because you were afraid the truth would come out. Now the whole world will know."

Valerie slowly backed away from him. Panicked, she looked for an escape, but Glenn was blocking the way out. She had to stall Glenn as long as she could.

"Why didn't Sedna ever tell me? We were friends. Bella never told us that she had children. It was impossible for us to know. And we were just children ourselves. What could we have done about it?"

"What could you have done about it? What could you have done about it?" Glenn's voice grew louder and louder. "You're right, Valerie. You were just kids, just like we were. Maybe none of us could have done anything about it. But we're not helpless kids anymore—we're adults now. Sedna and me . . ."

Something slammed into the outside back wall, startling Glenn. Valerie glimpsed a shadow diving by her. A figure came through the open door and jumped on Glenn. They fell to the floor.

The pistol landed at her feet. She heard steps. Somebody reached for the gun. Strong arms unceremoniously dragged her outside.

"Don't be afraid. You're safe," the figure said. "Get behind the snow-mobile for cover."

Even with the scarf that covered half the person's face and the beaver hat, Valerie recognized her: the caribou lady.

CHAPTER 33

She crouched all alone behind the snowmobile for what seemed like an eternity. Agitated voices came through the open door. The caribou lady ran around to the back of the cabin and seemed to be talking to the police on some device. Then she went back inside.

Valerie waited, immobile as a nearby fir tree in the sparkling snow. The sunshine struck her face. The edges of her ears turned numb. She pulled the thin head covering she wore under her helmet over her head. A wave of despair threatened to bury her. Sedna is dead. Sedna is dead. How in the world did it happen?

Suddenly, Marjorie Tama's words about her mother flashed through her mind.

"Her soul is still here. Talk to her, Valerie. She'll give you counsel and guide you."

And so she closed her eyes and called to her mother. Give me a sign that you are here, that you are standing by me. Do not leave me alone in these dark hours. I need your help, my unknown mother. Be with me with your love and counsel. Her eyes filled with tears that froze to her eyelashes. She blinked and blinked. And then she saw it. An Arctic fox was crouching just a few yards in front of her beside the fir. An Arctic fox! Valerie knew that these white foxes were common around Tuktoyaktuk. But not Inuvik. You'd only expect to see red foxes there.

The fox watched her with dark button eyes buried in white fur. It turned to look back and then again in her direction. They stared at each other for several long seconds. And in a moment of sudden intuition, it became clear to Valerie that life was a struggle for all, for this fox in the Arctic, and for her, and for all people. The one thing she could do at that moment was to accept that fact and face life as it was.

The fox twitched all of a sudden, then bounded off and disappeared. Somebody had come out of the cabin. Valerie could still hear men's voices.

"Come with me," the caribou lady said. "Let's go where we can talk in peace and quiet. The police will be here soon, but first I have to explain why we're here."

They went around the cabin, where Valerie saw three parked snowmobiles.

"I'm Ellen Sukova and my partner is Alex Firth. We work for a security firm in Vancouver. Your brother Kosta hired us to follow you and see to your safety. I'm sure that comes as a surprise; it might be best if you call your brother today and have him confirm it."

Ellen talked quickly and smoothly as if she'd long prepared for this moment. Valerie listened in silence.

"Kosta told us about Glenn Bliss's identity. He really is Sedna Mahrer's brother. And Bella Wakefield, also known as Bella Bliss, is Sedna and Glenn's mother. We know that Sedna sent the threatening letter to your brother. She and Bliss planned a tell-all book about your parents."

She halted her rapid flow of words.

"Do you understand what I'm saying?"

Valerie nodded like a robot.

"Good. Better stay put until the police come. We contacted them by satellite phone. We want everything to be carried out properly on our end."

She scrutinized Valerie, whose silence seemed to be unsettling her.

"You're probably asking yourself how we located Sedna. Somebody in Inuvik gave us a vital tip. We were here last evening but couldn't see any movement inside the cabin. No sign of life. We thought we might have the wrong place. This morning we tried it again. We knew from Poppy Dixon that your tour group was coming here today, including Glenn. We wanted to monitor everything so we hid behind the cabin. We—"

Valerie raised a gloved hand.

"Please, this is all too fast for me. It's . . . it's all so . . . inconceivable."

"Yes, yes, of course. I understand perfectly well." Ellen sounded very professional. "Please cooperate with the police when they arrive. We want all this tied up properly."

Valerie nodded. She screwed up her courage.

"How did Sedna die?"

Ellen's voice stayed businesslike, as if the question was just one item among many on a list.

"I don't want to anticipate what the police will say, but it might have been carbon monoxide poisoning. Sedna heated the cabin with a portable stove. The windows were boarded up, and the door was shut, so the cabin might have filled up with carbon monoxide; it's possible no fresh air could get in. She probably just dozed off and never woke up."

Ellen looked up.

"There's the police helicopter."

She put her hands on Valerie's shoulders.

"I know this is very tough on you. But you'll pull through, believe me."

Valerie nodded once more.

But Sedna didn't pull through.

CHAPTER 34

Five heads turned toward Valerie when she and Faye arrived at the group's table in the hotel restaurant. They were fortunately out of earshot of the other guests, just as she'd asked the maître d'. The day's events had dragged her down like lead weights. She kept replaying the images in her head. Paramedics loading Sedna's body onto the stretcher and into the helicopter. RCMP officials carrying out forensic work in the cabin. Her interrogation by John Palmer and Franklin Edwards, his colleague from Yellowknife, who once again intimidated her with his penetrating stare. Ellen Sukova and Alex Firth in animated conversation with the investigators.

And Poppy Dixon, who took her under his wing until they got to the hotel where Faye was waiting. They went to Valerie's room, and Faye listened to Valerie's hasty account and asked a lot of questions.

After she finished, Valerie burst into tears.

"I'll never be able to ask Sedna why she didn't just tell me everything," she managed to get out amid sobs. "We could have talked it out. Then she might still be alive today. I might have gained a sister—"

"Stop!" Faye broke in. "Stop right this minute. Sedna was free to make her own decision, and that decision had nothing to do with you."

Then Faye put her arm around Valerie's shoulder and let her cry until the tears stopped flowing.

Valerie took a seat at the table, acutely aware that her eyes were still red and swollen.

"Where's Glenn?" Paula asked.

"He's still at the police station," Valerie responded, surprised at how composed she sounded. "We found a dead woman in the cabin we stopped at. She was Glenn's sister. She was on vacation here, but Glenn didn't want to advertise that fact for whatever reason. She was staying at the cabin, and Glenn wanted to check on her."

Her eyes scanned the group until they landed on Jordan Walker, whose face showed the same bafflement as the others' did.

"How did she die?" Anika asked.

"It was probably an accident. It looks like she died of carbon monoxide poisoning. The door was closed and the windows were sealed, and she had a propane camp stove. The cabin had a woodstove, but she hadn't lit it; she probably tried to heat the place with the gas stove."

She decided not to mention the security people Kosta had hired and her own relationship with Sedna. Things were complicated enough as it was.

"Did you find Glenn in the cabin? With the dead woman?" Anika asked, sounding curious, not troubled.

"Yes. He was very upset, of course, as you can imagine. He . . . thinks somebody killed his sister. He must have felt threatened somehow because . . . he was distressed and waved a pistol around."

A wave of shock passed through the group.

"What? He had a pistol in his luggage?" Carol's jaw dropped.

Valerie raised both hands.

"Shhh. Not so loud. I don't want the other guests to hear. It wasn't a real pistol, the police told me, but a fake."

"Why did he have a fake pistol with him?"

"He's an American, and they're obsessed with guns. They constantly feel like they have to defend themselves against whatever."

They all looked at Jordan, who'd nonchalantly uttered the remark.

"Did you know about it?" Paula asked.

"Certainly not, or I'd have taken it away from him."

"How did he get the pistol through airport security?"

Jordan shrugged.

"I'd guess he bought it in Whitehorse, but I don't know. Glenn and I, we don't know each other all that well. We have the same hobbies—orchids and filming nature. We met at an orchid show. When he asked me if I wanted to see the Ice Road, I said yes."

A waiter approached, and Valerie motioned to him to come back later.

"When the police were searching the bus, Glenn seemed rather nervous," Anika said.

Valerie and Faye exchanged glances.

Trish spoke up in her warm, hesitant voice.

"I thought . . . the day I got lost . . . when I had to . . . to go. I went into the brush and Glenn used the outhouse. Do you think he's the one?"

"What one?"

"The one who followed me? Who scared me."

Now everybody started talking all at once.

Valerie thought back on the shaman's rattle that Trish had found near the outhouse. The rattle that Valerie recognized as the same one Sedna had shown her last summer. Of course. Sedna must have given it to Glenn! And he'd planted it intentionally to cause confusion.

But why did he want to scare Trish? Was that Glenn and Sedna's intention from the outset, to cause trouble for Valerie's tour? Or to hurt Valerie? To trip her up? Glenn had made a spectacular display of his hatred in the cabin. "A family of murderers," he'd screamed.

"Valerie?"

Faye's voice snapped her out of her musing.

"What's it look like for the rest of our trip? Can you tell us?"

"Yes, sure. We have two options: We retrace our route tomorrow on the Dempster back to Whitehorse. Or we stay here three days longer and fly from Inuvik to Whitehorse and then to Vancouver."

It was Jordan once again who spoke very calmly.

"I'd like to stay here and take care of Glenn."

Paula spoke up, her voice full of excitement: "I'd like to stay here, too, and do the Ice Road again before it's closed. And then go ice fishing in Tuktoyaktuk."

"Somebody has to take the Chevy back to Whitehorse," Trish submitted, looking at Valerie with a worried face as if the minibus were one of her children.

"We can definitely find somebody to do it. In the meantime, you all can think about it a little more."

They ordered dinner, and at the end of the meal, some lively discussion produced a decision. Three extra days in Inuvik.

Valerie could have hugged them all out of relief.

She entrusted the group to Faye while she went up to her room.

She longed to tell Clem about the day's events. But first she absolutely had to talk to Kosta; she'd already e-mailed him the basics.

She called his number, and he answered after the fifth ring.

"I can't believe everything that's happened," she said instead of a hello.

"Sedna's death shocked us, too. Have the police confirmed the cause?"

Kosta sounded as factual as ever. It was his modus vivendi. Valerie envied him for it at that moment.

"Officially no, not yet. The bureaucratic mills grind exceedingly slowly. Why did you keep so much from me?"

"To protect you. And to make your job easier. What would you have done if I'd told you?"

She reflected. Yes, what *would* she have done?

Would she have left Glenn behind? Confronted him? What would that have meant for her long-planned tour? Maybe it really was better for her *not* to have any idea about what she would have done.

"I can tell you a few things now," Kosta continued. "But first fill me in on the details."

She took a deep breath and started slowly, but then it all burst out of her full force. Kosta didn't say much, just an "oh" or a "really" or an "aha" now and then.

After she'd finished, he started his report, in a voice that struck her as lower than usual.

"Bella Wakefield's first husband was an American named Theodore Bliss. She married him in the US and had two children by him, Glenn and Sedna; Sedna's first name at the time was actually Iris. Bella was unhappy in her marriage. She met Dad at a sporting event she'd organized for top international athletes. They met again later when he was in the US. More meetings followed, a half dozen or so. At some point she decided to leave her husband because Dad was prepared to marry her. Evidently, it was very serious for them both."

Kosta's words rendered her speechless.

"Are you still there?" he asked.

"Yes, yes. It's all so overwhelming. Did Bella and Dad meet when our mother was still alive?"

"Yes, but they didn't get involved until after Mary-Ann's death. There's a lot more. Bella apparently tried to take her children to Canada with her. Illegally. But her husband prevented it at the last minute. Not one of Bella's better moves. She did manage to make it to Canada, but she had to leave Sedna and Glenn behind in the US. You can imagine how messy the situation became after that."

Yes, she could.

"Keep talking," she said.

"Theodore Bliss was able, through the American courts, to prevent the children from having any and all contact with Bella. He feared a kidnapping. His relatives, as well as Bella's strictly religious family, turned their backs on her. Nobody told the children where their mother had gone. She . . ."

"That must have been terrible for them."

"Yes, for them *and* for Bella."

"And we were completely in the dark."

"Yes. Apparently, Dad thought it was best to keep us out of it."

"My God, Kosta, how she must have suffered!"

He said nothing for a few seconds.

So she went on.

"She gave all her love and care, all . . . her maternal feelings to *us*, Kosta."

"She really was a good mother."

"Lucky for us, but for Sedna and Glenn . . ."

"It was an irreplaceable loss; you're right there."

Her thoughts whirled around in her mind like in a centrifuge.

"Wait, wait. How come you know all this? About Bella and all that?"

He cleared his throat.

"Do you remember how Bella always answered with the word *waterfall* whenever you asked her about Dad's diaries? I couldn't make any sense out of it until one day the penny dropped. You remember that painting of a waterfall in the music room?"

"Yes, of course."

"I talked to the people who bought Dad's house, and they let me check it out. We knocked on the wall where the picture used to hang. It had to be that spot. We opened up the wall and discovered a niche behind it. And there they were."

"What?"

"Bella's diaries."

"Oh my God! She wrote everything down?"

"Yes, and she concealed those records very well."

Valerie stood up and sat down again; then she stood up and walked up and down the entire length of the room and looked out the window. Suddenly, everything—the neighborhood outside, the snow, the persistently bright sky, the tangle of pipes on top of the permafrost—seemed unreal, like in a movie.

Kosta's voice came through like it was penetrating a fog.

"Bella tried and tried to find out where her children lived, but she never could. Bliss gave them different names and frequently changed addresses. Sedna began calling herself Sedna later. Probably to make you curious. An American colleague found that out for me."

A message appeared on her cell phone, but she ignored it.

"How in the world did she ever . . . how did Sedna find me?"

"A relative finally spilled the beans. You know how it is. Family secrets can't be kept forever. Sedna found Bella and visited her in the nursing home in Vancouver. Bella could only respond to her questions with bewilderment, as she does with us. She didn't recognize her daughter. A nursing home worker told me that."

"Sedna came too late. It must have been a great shock when she realized that."

"We've come too late as well. We could have shown her Bella's diaries. She would have known how much her mother loved Glenn and her, and how hard she tried to find them."

"I saw so much hate in Glenn's eyes, Kosta. He hated us for what happened to them."

"Perhaps . . . but I think it was more likely desperation. Hopefully, Glenn will come to understand."

The old question surfaced.

"Why didn't Sedna talk to me? We were friends. I don't get it, I simply don't get it."

More tears welled up.

"Maybe she was afraid we'd stop her from publishing the truth. She intended to write a book—you know that, right?"

"Yes."

"That book, Val, *you've* got to write it now. You've got to find out what happened and write about it, to make this story your own. Otherwise, other people will pounce on this, and we don't know what the upshot will be."

He paused.

"I think we owe it to our parents."

She waited before responding. She waited so long that Kosta asked, "Val, you still there?"

"Yes. I . . . I've got to think this over, Kosta."

"Of course, sister dear. By the way, Ellen and Alex are on the next plane to Vancouver. Their mission is over."

"That's OK. I can take care of myself, Kosta. But we've got to brace ourselves for the media."

"Yes. That's unavoidable at this point. And that's also why it would be a good thing for us to clear up the story of our parents as a family. Nobody's better suited to write that story than you, Val. James thinks so, too. We need to try to finally find out the whole truth."

The whole truth. She let Kosta's words flow back and forth in her mind like waves on a sandy beach.

Maybe she could sniff out a part of that truth. She had a hunch where.

CHAPTER 35

Clem heard the helicopter from his office as he was finishing his daily report on the Ice Road conditions. Helvin had made himself scarce—no surprise to Clem anymore—and didn't pick up his cell when Clem called.

Clem wondered if his boss had heard Waldo Bronk's radio reports on the explosion on the ice and the other peculiar events in the Arctic. Waldo hadn't been deterred by the vague justifications he'd gotten from government officials in Ottawa. The young reporter had found out that the explosion was one of many unexplained incidents in a long line of suspicious events over the last several years.

Waldo had turned up reports of mysterious submarines in the Northwest Passage; of soldiers from foreign countries who showed up in Inuit settlements and then disappeared; and of helicopters that were never identified, at least not officially. He added reports of armed vessels sailing through Canadian Arctic waters without Canada's permission.

Clem still heard Waldo's voice ringing in his ears: "We might ask what our country could do about this. Our Coast Guard is unarmed, their icebreakers are old and continually under repair. They can't break through very thick pack ice in winter. Our brigade of rangers is under-staffed and must patrol an unimaginably huge area. But is it right to simply sweep unsettling events under the rug because Canada is in no position to call a halt to potential attacks by foreign countries on our territory?"

Clem's esteem for Waldo took off like a comet after that. The guy's got guts, you've got to give him that. That report will either cost Waldo his job or make his career.

When Clem heard a chopper flying above the office, he immediately called the hospital. Had there been an accident on the Ice Road? They confirmed that the air ambulance was up but not flying to the road. While on the phone, he heard another helicopter above, so he called the RCMP. The woman at the station confirmed that their helicopter had nothing to do with the Ice Road either. She wouldn't say anything more. Clem pushed.

"I need more information—in case people phone in here."

The dispatcher knew him and gave in.

"A woman, a tourist, was found dead in one of the hunting cabins. That's all I can tell you, Clem."

Instant anxiety. Valerie had texted earlier to let him know her group was going on a snowmobile outing. He ran to his truck and drove to Poppy Dixon's. Poppy's son was there, and he was not reassuring: he said his father and Valerie had gone back to the cabin on Lake Fowler because a man from her tour had gone missing. She had sent the rest of her group back to the hotel. Poppy's son didn't know anything about a dead female tourist. Maybe the dispatcher was wrong—maybe the dead person was a man.

Clem put the truck into reverse and was about to drive onto the highway when a blue pickup arrived and stopped beside him. Helvin West lowered the window. Clem immediately noticed his bloodshot eyes. From sleepless nights or too much alcohol? He also noticed with some satisfaction that recent events had etched their traces in his boss's face; he looked haggard.

Clem told Helvin about the two choppers. "Probably nothing to do with the Ice Road," Clem said.

Helvin squinted at him.

"A dead woman in a cabin, you say? Doesn't that send your blood pressure through the roof?"

Clem didn't respond. He hadn't expected to find Helvin in a good mood, considering the recent revelations about Toria. Helvin's tone turned caustic: "Women shouldn't come up here. They know fuck all about life here. They only cause trouble for people. They're so irresponsible. Steal cars and push drugs. It's criminal."

Clem remained silent.

"So now we've got another dead woman," Helvin continued, his voice exuding sarcasm. "That's just fantastic. We couldn't wish for anything more. That'll pump up the tourist trade—you watch."

Clem stuck his elbow out the window.

"How are things with Toria?"

Helvin looked in the rearview mirror, then back at Clem.

"She's got a good lawyer. She's got nothing to fear. But I hear your pretty baby is Peter Hurdy-Blaine's daughter. That'll be red meat for the media. I guarantee you it'll be more interesting than Helvin West's wife. You can bet on it."

Clem heard a message alert on his cell. He withdrew his arm from the window.

"I'll give you a tip, Helv. Gisèle told Toria she'd gotten the gold nugget from you. For services rendered. You've got to iron that out with Toria. And the police."

He took off as he closed the window.

But his sense of triumph was short-lived. He couldn't shake off an unsettling feeling. Was the missing man from the tour dead? That could end Valerie's Inuvik tours. Good-bye to their annual meetings, dammit.

Fuck. Fuck. Fuck.

He remembered the new text message and stopped near the Great Polar Hotel to read it. He had two messages, actually. One from the boy he paid to walk Meteor; he'd brought the dog back home safely.

The second message took him by complete surprise.

"You got some time? Must tell you something. I'm in the church."

Clem instantly knew what church that was. He was close by. It had been months since he'd been at the igloo church. He wasn't Catholic, but a friend's wedding had taken place there. Soon he was standing before the circular building that drew people from all over the world, and he once again was struck by the extraordinary architecture: the outside walls made to look like rectilinear blocks of snow, and the silvery domed roof crowned by a small cupola bearing a cross.

He went through the door and along the pews until he came to a motionless seated figure. This was a good place to meet. The nave was otherwise empty.

"This is a fine place for peace and calm," he remarked as he sat down.

"Yes," Marjorie Tama agreed, "and now that we've collected enough money to cover the horrendous heating costs, we don't freeze in here anymore."

"So who should I pray for?" he asked.

"Maybe for the woman found dead in Pete's cabin."

"There's really nothing you don't know, is there? Who is she?"

"Pete rented out his cabin to a woman from somewhere near Vancouver. She called herself Sedna. God only knows why a white woman is named after an Inuit goddess."

"Sedna's dead?" His mouth turned dry.

"I don't know. But Pete rented his cabin to her."

"Good God! What happened there?"

"No idea. We'll definitely know more by this evening."

He shook his head in bewilderment.

"A bit too many corpses these days, don't you think?"

He looked up at the rosette in the center of the ceiling: a red flower with some white petals on a turquoise background.

"Do you think this will have a negative impact on Inuvik?" he asked.

She pursed her lips.

"We Inuvialuit have always lived with death. Death lurks everywhere. It's not death we fear but suffering. Our ancestors sometimes died of hunger. Nobody does now."

He didn't let her off the hook.

"Reporters will probably descend on Inuvik like locusts."

"Then we'll show them what we've achieved here. That we've taken our fate into our own hands. That we've got things moving, economically speaking. We can't allow ourselves to be cowed by fear. We have our pride. So bring 'em on! Sure, we'll tell them about death and disaster but also a story of beauty and self-determination."

He waited for several seconds. They'd been talking about other things because Inuvialuit thought it was impolite to come straight to the point.

"And why did you want to see me? What do you want to tell me?"

By way of an answer, she began to sing. A song in her mother tongue, Uummarmiutun. She sang softly, almost in a hum. Clem caught a few words, but that was all. He just sat there, waiting patiently, because if he'd learned one thing from the Inuvialuit, it was never to reveal impatience.

In the middle of her song, she started to speak.

"You asked me a few days ago about Pihuk Bart's story."

She sang a few more notes. Clem waited.

"A shaman lived in our area a while back. He called himself Qilalugaq Hupumiyuaq, Whale's Breath. He was a good shaman for a long time. Then he changed; people reckoned that the spirits took a dislike to him. They trusted his counsel less and less. And there was competition: a relative of his was becoming increasingly influential. That made Qilalugaq Hupumiyuaq mad. The people in Inuliktuuq were the only ones who still believed in him. He prophesized that a fire would destroy their houses. Maybe he meant Russian bombs. Until then, people here didn't have the slightest idea what went on in the rest of the world. But then they could see the radar towers and military bases with their own eyes. And so they knew about the threat from Russia. That got people frightened. Qilalugaq Hupumiyuaq stoked their fears in order to reestablish his power. And the people followed him to their death. They left one baby behind because he declared that the infant would bring doom. They were putting the world's doom behind them. That baby was Pihuk."

Clem expected her to go on with her story. But Marjorie said out of the blue, "I've heard that Valerie's father's diary has turned up. It's supposed to record the Dempster Highway Memorial Trek. The diary apparently disappeared back then, and the police searched for it without any luck; somebody must have hidden it all that time. You have to try to get it back before it falls into the wrong hands."

Clem was stupefied.

"Do you have any idea who has the diary?"

"Somebody you know. That's all I can tell you."

She resumed her singing. Her voice followed him as he rushed out of the church.

When he reached home, a second snowmobile was parked in front of his house. Lazarusie. Clem had given him a key.

Meteor was waiting for him at the door, panting. Clem looked around the kitchen, then in the living room. Lazarusie was asleep on the sofa. Meteor couldn't have been pleased; he labored under the false belief that the sofa was *his* sleeping place.

"Hey, wake up!" Clem shouted.

Lazarusie opened his eyes in a daze. Catching sight of Clem, he jumped to his feet with amazing agility.

Clem sat down across from him in an armchair. This time, he skipped the polite chitchat.

"Laz, do you know where Peter Hurdy-Blaine's diary is?"

Lazarusie looked at him, alarmed.

"What . . . why . . . ?"

"Has Tanya got it?"

Lazarusie shook his head.

"Do you know anything about the diary, Laz?"

"She was asking about it in the village."

"Who?"

"That woman, the one in the ice house."

"She asked about the diary?"

"She asked about . . . things to do with the Dempster Memorial Trek. She said there must have been a diary somewhere."

"Did Tanya get ahold of the diary?"

"No, she doesn't have it."

He seemed to want to say more but closed his mouth instead.

"Laz, that diary is important. Tell me what you know about it."

"She offered to pay for it. If I'd had the diary, I'd have sold it to her. Then I'd have the money to get my daughter a good lawyer."

Clem stood up.

"Laz, Tanya will get a lawyer from the Mackenzie Resource Corporation. For free. The organization exists just for the Inuvialuit. It's in the statute. I'm going to see about that diary. Stay here."

He went to the kitchen and called Valerie's number.

CHAPTER 36

The hospital's facade was a playful arrangement of blue, yellow, and red building blocks. Primary colors sparkled against the white of the snow, brighter than a Fisher-Price toy. Faye dropped Valerie off at the main entrance. The tour had a free day—but unfortunately, the weather wasn't great. A strong wind blew snow around in all directions, and visibility on the road was reduced to about fifteen feet.

Faye had heard in the hotel that some other tourists had nonetheless ventured out onto the Ice Road, hoping for a change in the weather.

"I wouldn't want to be in their shoes," she said. Valerie could only hope that the day would pass for her charges without any glitches. As for herself, she wasn't so sure. The receptionist told her how to navigate the hospital corridors, so she found the room sooner than she'd expected. Her heart was in her mouth as she knocked on the door and went in. One bed was empty; a pale woman lay in the other one, but Valerie didn't recognize her at first. She'd only met Christine Preston once, and that felt like a long, long time ago. But the patient said hello without missing a beat.

"Valerie! I've been waiting to see you for such a long time!"

Christine wasn't wearing makeup, and her hair lay flat on her head. But Valerie recognized the high, melodious voice.

"How are you?" she inquired.

"Much better. Much, much better. The people here are taking good care of me."

Pointing to a chair in the corner, she said, "Do sit down."

Valerie pulled the chair closer to the bed.

"How on earth could it ever have happened?"

"Insane, isn't it? Something you only see in the movies." Christine smoothed the covers with her thin, elegant fingers. "Roy Stevens wanted to show me something in the ice house. I trusted him implicitly—after all, he *is* a ranger. Then there was that business with the backpack. I was standing on the ladder when I suddenly remembered it. He went to get it . . . and never came back. Of course, now I know why."

"So you had no idea then what was happening up there?"

"No, I heard strange noises, and then the lid slammed down, leaving me literally in the dark."

"It must have been awful."

Christine nodded.

"Yes, I panicked in the beginning, naturally. Then I remembered that you and your tour group were coming to the cellar. I heard that from Roy. It could only be one or two days. You were my lifesaver, Valerie!"

"Clem Hardeven and Lazarusie Uvvayuaq saved your life."

"And my little warmers. I packed them into my shoes and gloves. And I prayed."

Valerie observed Christine with growing astonishment. She seemed very cheery. Some people survived traumatic situations better than others. Valerie took a chance and probed a little more deeply.

"Why did you come to Inuvik all by yourself in the first place, Christine?"

"I knew you'd ask me that. Fair enough. The answer's quite simple: my dear husband died of cancer, so I had time on my hands. First I paid a visit to my daughter. I had to do something after my husband's death to avoid falling into a depression. I never forgot Mary-Ann during all those years. I told you when we first met that she was my best friend. I never had another best friend after her. Friends, of course, but not the same close bond."

"Please excuse the question . . . couldn't you have just come with us on our tour?"

Christine smiled.

"Yes, I contemplated that possibility. Especially after I met you. Maybe you don't know this, but you resemble Mary-Ann a lot. Not so much in the face or the voice, but rather in your demeanor, your body movements. Your smile. Your gestures. It's almost weird."

She looked off into the distance.

A strong bond had held these two women together—Valerie understood that now. And it held still, even thirty years after Mary-Ann's death. But a man had come between them, an idol the masses worshipped, Peter Hurdy-Blaine.

Christine continued.

"I wanted to be alone. I wanted to relive my memories of Mary-Ann all by myself. To be intimately together with her once again. At least that was my dream."

Christine furrowed her brow, then smiled.

"You must think I'm peculiar. You know, people and experiences from our childhood sometimes have long-lasting effects on us. And at some point, you've got to face up to that. Look, I was against Mary-Ann's marriage to your father. I knew he would try to dominate her. I had a suspicion that he'd try to force her to live his lifestyle. I made no bones about it, and Peter Hurdy-Blaine heard about it one day. Mary-Ann and I argued as a result, and she broke off any and all contact with me."

Christine fell back on her pillow as if she'd been pushed.

Valerie shifted her chair closer. The right moment was now.

"Why did you offer to pay people here for my father's diary?"

Christine's face lit up; that wasn't the reaction Valerie was expecting.

"I'd have been so happy to do that for Mary-Ann—to acquire the diary. And for her daughter. For you, Valerie," she said in a tone of voice melting with warmth. "I'd heard rumors that somebody had hidden it. I heard it from Roy Stevens. Wouldn't it have been wonderful if I could have presented you with it? Alas, I failed."

Christine's eyes turned moist. "Roy told me everything," she said.

Every muscle in Valerie's body tensed up.

"About what happened back then? Please, please tell me."

Christine pulled herself up again.

"It was bad luck. Roy had his hunting rifle with him, and she wanted to show him that she was a good shot. The bullet ricocheted off a tree and came back like a boomerang and hit her."

She stopped, took several breaths, and collected herself.

"Your father saw the whole incident. And I must say I respect him much more now than I did then. In spite of his grief over Mary-Ann, he wanted to make sure that Roy—he was just fourteen—wouldn't be blamed. It was a bullet from Roy's rifle that was in her chest. But your father wanted to protect the boy at all costs."

The door opened and a nurse stuck her head inside.

"Everything OK?" she asked.

"Yes, everything's OK," Christine replied, and the nurse disappeared. "Really nice people here," Christine murmured.

Valerie couldn't get a word out but gestured her approval when Christine asked solicitously, "Shall I go on?"

The blizzard looked so heavy through the window that it wiped out the shape of everything outside.

"Your father paid for the boy's education and his family's move to Yellowknife. The Anaqiinas were apparently feuding with some relatives; that's why they wanted to move away. They . . ."

"So it wasn't hush money?"

Christine looked at her, confused, until she caught on.

"No, no. There was nothing to hide. Oh, maybe you don't know that there were witnesses. Another family was there en route to the caribou hunt. The three of them were not alone."

"Where is this family? Where can I find them?"

Christine sighed.

"Roy told me that the family doesn't want their whereabouts known. They have English names now and have removed all traces of themselves. Maybe your father pulled some strings for them. He wanted to preserve *his* privacy, too."

One last question was on the tip of Valerie's tongue. "Were you in the Whitehorse museum under the name of Phyllis Crombe?"

Christine hesitated momentarily before answering.

"Phyllis Crombe was someone I knew from Whitehorse. My late husband's cousin. She was with me in the museum. They probably remembered her name because she's from Whitehorse. Why?"

"Because a Phyllis Crombe let the museum director's secretary know that Peter Hurdy-Blaine's daughter would be coming to the museum with a tour group. Nobody knew my identity before that."

Christine closed her eyes and rubbed her fingers against them.

"That was my fault. I'm awfully sorry. I realized in retrospect that it might have been an indiscretion." She looked at Valerie. "But I promise you that from now on, I'll never make anything about you or your parents public without your permission. I can give it to you in writing if—"

The phone on the night table rang. Christine picked it up and after a few words handed it to Valerie. It was Faye.

"I'd like to come pick you up and bring you back to the hotel now; it might be impossible soon. It's getting worse and worse outside."

Valerie said good-bye to Christine quickly and promised to see her again in the next few days.

Faye was right on. The Chevy proceeded at a crawl. They were driving through a frightening, almost impenetrable wall; Faye called it "a white darkness." They were on edge, searching for the slightest indication of where they were.

They finally made it to the hotel parking lot, and Faye heaved a loud sigh of relief.

"You deserve a medal, my dear," Valerie acknowledged.

Faye nodded.

"Yeah, I think so, too."

She turned to Valerie.

"A man's waiting for you at the reception desk."

"Police?" She was thinking of Franklin Edwards, the police officer from Yellowknife with that funny stare.

"No. Glenn's lawyer."

Now it was Valerie's turn to sigh. She was about to open the door when Faye held her back.

"Before we go in, what's the latest?"

Valerie filled her in.

"I don't know what to think of all this," Valerie said. "There's an inconsistency in Christine's version of my mother's death. She says there were other witnesses—a family on their way to the caribou hunt. But Kosta didn't say anything about them. Something doesn't add up."

Faye agreed.

"It would be a good thing if the diary turned up. That would sure explain a lot." She pulled her hood on. "I wonder what Sedna found out."

Valerie shrugged. She couldn't tell Faye what she suspected. If Sedna had brought their father's diary or other important documents to the cabin—maybe they were among the papers that Glenn had thrown onto the floor—then Kosta's security people, Ellen and Alex, might have swept them up before the police set foot in the place. Maybe that was why they were so eager to cut and run.

CHAPTER 37

Valerie was in the bathtub trying to relax when her phone alerted her to a text message. After her long conversations with Kosta, Christine, and Faye, she desperately wanted to be alone. But as a tour guide, she couldn't disregard her phone. She wiped the moist film from the display in order to read the message: "It was a brutal day. Only you can save it. May I invite you to dinner?"

Instead of words, she sent Clem five exclamation marks.

She laid the phone down on the tile floor so she wouldn't drop it in her excitement. Then she ran some more hot water, as much as the small bathtub could take. Filled with expectation, she gave her thoughts full rein—beautiful and secret thoughts she would never have revealed, even to Faye.

She reluctantly got out of the bath and dried herself. She snuggled into her soft bathrobe and texted Faye: "Do you mind if I don't spend tonight with you?"

Her instant reply: "No, as long as you don't spend it with Jordan."

Jordan Walker? Valerie stared at the words, baffled. Then she couldn't resist a smile. The sly little bitch! And she hadn't even picked up on it.

She put on a long white sweater with glitter around the décolleté and picked out dark stretch pants. Clem was going to have every reason to call her Snowy Owl again. She blow-dried her chestnut hair and styled it so that her brushed locks fell over her shoulders.

The reward for all her efforts was Clem's admiring look when she opened the door. Compared to his full-bore Arctic dress, she felt like a summertime tourist.

"You'll need your parka," he declared.

She looked at him in disbelief.

"We're not going out in this storm?"

"Storm?" He laughed. "If you ever experience a real Arctic storm, you'll call this one a bunch of pretty, swirling snowflakes."

Five minutes later, he led her through the biting wind to his pickup.

She didn't have the slightest idea where they were going, but it was not to his place.

Clem put on soft country music.

"I was on the Ice Road today. Some Austrian tourists were stuck in a snowbank. The motor was still running, thank God. They had to wait four hours for the tow truck from Tuktoyaktuk because it was already towing a truck. It was pure chaos."

Valerie felt an instant chill.

"They could have frozen to death."

"Fortunately, they had several gas cans in reserve. And a satellite phone. Still, some of them were scared half to death when I talked to them."

"How did you manage to get there?"

"With my GPS and a plow."

He laughed and turned his bold face toward her. She warmed up at once.

The truck stopped, and Valerie could just make out a large shadow through the windshield. After hopping into the snow, she recognized the Inuvik community greenhouse.

"C'mon!" he shouted and showed her to the entrance with a flashlight.

It wasn't as cold inside as she'd feared.

"I've rented the whole place. A refuge for poor little plants like us." He threw her a mischievous grin. "Follow me!"

She felt her way through the hall after him. She caught sight of flickering candlelight out of the corner of her eye and turned to see a row of burning candles in aluminum bowls filled with water. He must have bought up all the wax candles in Inuvik. The warmth they spread was amazing. There were hide blankets on a platform of wooden boxes; paper shopping bags were bunched up beside it.

He took off his gloves and hat and made an inviting gesture.

"Make yourself comfortable."

She had to take in the scene first.

"Clem, I . . . this is . . ." She was at a loss for words.

"I thought maybe an igloo at first but couldn't find anybody fast enough to have one made. Besides, it would really have been a cliché. And hey, who ever heard of a greenhouse in the Arctic?"

He unpacked some white wine, fried chicken, cheese, olives, and tomatoes that looked impressively fresh.

"Bread straight out of the oven." Clem beamed, and Valerie glowed along with him.

She couldn't show off her glittery sweater and stretch pants because the parka and her ski pants were keeping her warm.

But there wasn't a chic restaurant in Vancouver that could beat this experience.

She sat down on the hide-bedecked platform, and Clem handed her a glass of wine. Not in crystal but in a kid's party glass decorated with colored balloons. Valerie never missed crystal glasses less than at that moment.

"Tell me how your day went," Clem said.

She recounted her conversation with Christine and her meeting with Glenn's lawyer. Clem didn't comment on Christine's revelations, which surprised her. But when she came to the lawyer, his eyes grew wider.

"His lawyer! He got to Inuvik fast."

"Yes, I wondered about that. Maybe Glenn has more money than we supposed."

She popped an olive into her mouth. The little green morsel had probably never dreamed it would leave the groves of southern France to end up in the Arctic, she mused. She resumed her narrative.

"The lawyer was eager to extricate his client from the affair with the least possible harm to Glenn. He let it be known he was ready to make a deal."

"And—what did you say to that?"

"That he should get in touch with Kosta. I can't make the decision all by myself."

Clem bit off a piece from a drumstick and said with his mouth full, "All the same, you must know what you want."

"I want Faye to get her money back so she can renovate her house. What was Sedna thinking?"

"I assume she wanted to spend some more time with Richard Melville. Maybe he talked her into it. Richard can sell refrigerators to the Eskimos, so they say in Dawson."

"Maybe she'd fallen in love with him, who knows?"

Clem chopped the tomatoes into small pieces with his pocketknife and piled them up on a plastic plate.

"You mean, love is blind?"

She raised her eyebrows in feigned indignation.

"I'd like something else," she stated. "I'd like to write up my parents' story, to do justice to all those involved. And by *all* I'm including Sedna and Glenn."

Clem bobbed his impressive head back and forth, chewing with relish.

She definitely had to get one more thing off her chest before the evening with Clem took off in a certain direction.

"I still owe you an answer," she began, the wine lending her courage. Clem looked at her, eyebrows raised.

"When you told me about you and Sedna . . . at first I was . . . well, not exactly thrilled. But I have enough . . . let's call it life experience, to know that things happen. When I wanted to leave my marriage—not because my husband was a bad man, on the contrary—I managed to do it in a not very decent manner. I . . . was unfaithful to him. And he didn't find out until I told him."

She looked at him before turning away. He fished a paper napkin out of a bag and wiped the grease off his glistening lips.

"If now is the hour for confessions, then I have some explaining to do, too."

He picked up the bottle and refilled her glass. For a second his face was very close, but she didn't dare kiss him. They hadn't even touched up to then.

"You mentioned once," he began, "that you'd heard the men up here—white men—have escaped to the North to get away from something."

He stared at the wavering candles, his head slightly turned away from her.

"That probably—no, that rather accurately applies to me. I worked in the Department of Foreign Affairs in Ottawa as an expert for the Middle East. I'm sure that will surprise you. I traveled a lot in the Middle East working as a hydrologist. From the sandy desert to the ice desert—how's that for a career arc?"

Valerie sensed he was masking his vulnerability.

"And wonder of wonders, who fell in love with me? The daughter of the foreign minister, Claude Duchéné. And I with her. Naturally, I was flattered. I admit she was enchanting, really pretty. She was also . . .

erratic. Unstable. Had violent mood swings. All that put a great strain on our relationship."

She felt his eyes on her as she listened to him in silence.

"To keep it short: I broke off our relationship. At first she was enraged and vengeful, which made it easier on me. Easier than if she'd . . . just been devastated. Three weeks later, she committed suicide."

"Oh, no!" Valerie gasped.

"Yes." He turned his glass around and around in his hands.

"It was hell on wheels. I felt guilty, of course, and had to live with the fact that I was almost instantly persona non grata in Ottawa. A leper. It was clear that any plans for a career in foreign affairs were down the drain. I was treated like a pariah. I found out later that she'd been suicidal as early as sixteen. By then, I was living in Inuvik."

Valerie looked at him, trying to fathom his expression. She decided to take the bull by the horns.

"Are you afraid that I'd do something to myself if . . . if, say, you don't want us to see each other again after I leave Inuvik?"

He reacted so forcefully that he almost spilled his wine.

"No, Val, no! I don't mean anything of the kind. For God's sake, no."

He crept closer until he was kneeling before her.

"What I'm most afraid of at this instant is that I won't see you for a whole year." The next moment, he was gently kissing her mouth. "I don't want to be with anyone but you."

His voice sounded rough, raw.

She felt his eager, searching lips on her face, on her mouth, on all the bare places he could reach in spite of her parka.

They sank onto the covers, and she heard him say as if from afar, "I scared up some caribou hides. They'll keep us warm."

CHAPTER 38

This was his chance.

He had to do it.

The weather gods couldn't have been more propitious for him and his plan. A clear, sunny day.

The Ice Road was open. The plow had cleared the ice, and the grader had roughed up the surface to help prevent skidding. That guy Hardeven sure did good work. He'd heard that yesterday some Austrian tourists had turned a deaf ear to Clem's warning.

He'd started out early, before the sun melted the thin film of snow off the road and turned it into a playground slide. He felt the tires gain traction on the road surface.

Time was running out. A few more days of this intense sun, and the Ice Road wouldn't be safe anymore. But that wasn't the most driving force. Valerie Blaine had booked a return flight for her group—he had exactly two days left.

Sometimes you needed that kind of pressure to force yourself into making a decision. The events of the past few days had accelerated everything. He couldn't avoid it any longer: fate had caught up with him.

After deciding to take the plunge, his mind was more at ease, completely sharp. He was at peace with himself and his resolution. Nervous, but ready to go.

He saw the pingos looming up on the horizon, and the radar towers on the DEW line a little farther on.

He parked his truck near the ice house. He'd pictured this moment time and again in the hours and days before. Now everything was occurring like in a dream. After all, he did know the place well. He unlocked the door, lifted the lid, and tied the rope to the post by the entrance. Then he tied the other end around his upper body. His headlamp cast a comforting beam over his surroundings. He'd brought along a small pickax that dangled from his belt.

Caution was his number-one rule. Even if somebody shut the lid and closed the door—as had happened to Christine Preston—he'd be able to get himself out by hacking through the wood. He slowly descended the icy rungs, one after the other. Had he ever guessed he'd be back here so soon? Maybe subconsciously. It wasn't Christine Preston's terrible experience but Sedna Mahrer's death that had forced him to face the consequences of that long-past tragedy.

It couldn't continue. All of a sudden, it became crystal clear.

No more dead bodies.

He knew what he had to do.

He felt his way forward in the headlamp beam. He knew the number on the chamber door. He knew it was empty but for a barrel of seal oil. Behind it he found the ice-encrusted object.

He pulled out the ax and hacked the iced-over clump away from the ground. Then he took a plastic bag from his jacket pocket and put it inside.

He couldn't wait to see her face when he handed her what he'd just cut out from the ice.

CHAPTER 39

Valerie couldn't believe how long Jordan and Faye were sticking it out in minus-twenty-two-degree weather. From the warm Chevy bus, she watched them conferring. Jordan and his camera were set up on the Ice Road; Faye held the tripod. They wanted to be ready to shoot the end of the dogsled race. Jordan had to cope without Glenn. What was going on inside him? And inside Glenn?

She felt for Glenn in spite of the threat Sedna's brother could pose to her family. He not only had to deal with the legal jam he was in but with Sedna's death as well. There was hardly a minute in the day that Valerie didn't think of her, but it had hit Glenn all the harder.

She stuck on her hat and was out of the car in a second.

"Don't you want to get in? It'll be another half hour or more. The race is fifty miles long!"

She felt the ice-cold air immediately stick to her skin and eat its way through her clothing. She retreated into the bus. Faye and Jordan came tramping back too.

Valerie understood Jordan's plan. The dogs would quite suddenly appear out of nowhere. Maybe there'd be a fight for first place just before the finish line. Jordan would certainly want to capture that on film, but without Glenn's help all sorts of things could go wrong.

She wished for nothing more fervently than for Alana to win. She'd seen the musher just before the start, hugged her, and wished her luck. She knew what the race meant to her, especially since everything else in her life was beginning to wobble. Duncan was nowhere to be seen around the starting line. But Valerie did bump into Clem. The intimacy of the previous night made them both a bit sheepish.

They exchanged stolen glances and tried to keep people from noticing. Conversations were virtually impossible anyway because of the dogs' frenzied yapping. Faye was discreet; she didn't ask questions. She also didn't disclose anything to Valerie about how her night with Jordan had gone.

Marjorie Tama was there to start the race off. Pihuk Bart appeared. Valerie automatically recalled that he'd predicted beauty and terror for her this year. She could only hope that the terror half of it was history and that only the beautiful part lay ahead.

In calmer moments, she consoled herself with the knowledge that her group seemed to be eminently satisfied with the trip. True, the news of Sedna's death had shocked them all even though they didn't know her, and they felt sorry for Glenn and his agonizing loss. They all thought Sedna and Christine Preston were foolish to travel by themselves. They were reminded every day of how risky a sojourn in the Arctic was.

With Faye's help, Valerie poured hot chocolate from thermoses for the rest of her troops, who also came for the race. When she turned her head, she saw a man standing outside the driver's side window. She opened the window a crack.

"May I speak to you for a minute?" Franklin Edwards asked.

Valerie looked at Faye, zipped up her jacket, pulled her hood down tight, and stepped out.

"You're not in uniform today?"

He seemed older and stockier than he had in his police uniform.

"No, it's my day off. If it's all right with you, shall we sit in my car?"

Valerie had an uneasy feeling. Can he be doing police work on his day off?

She got into Edwards's pickup. He reached into a door pocket for a small object wrapped in a cloth and handed it to her.

"This belongs to you."

She looked at him, unsure of herself.

"Open it."

Oh, no, not another gold nugget!

She took off her gloves and unwrapped the cloth.

Inside was an antique chain holding a round medallion with a filigree metal lid. It looked like an old-fashioned pendant.

"You can open the medallion."

He showed her how and gave it back to her.

She raised the lid. And froze.

She recognized the photograph. Three children's faces. Valerie, James, and Kosta. The twins were eight years old at the time; she was just two. There was a copy of the picture in her personal photo album. A blowup in a silver frame had graced her parents' living room table for many years.

"This pendant was your mother's. She was wearing it when it happened."

When it happened.

She looked him straight in the eye.

"Did the RCMP have this in storage until today?"

"No, somebody else took the medallion."

"Who?"

"I'm not sure exactly. But I found out where it was ultimately hidden. Roy Stevens knew where. Probably someone in his family hid it there."

He stared through the windshield, lost in thought.

"You see, it was chaotic right after it happened. Two families from Aklavik were nearby and helped tie your mother to a sled. And they packed up a second sled with your parents' tent and belongings. The bush plane they called for landed some distance away. Everyone was in shock; it all happened so fast. Somebody must have removed the chain from your mother's neck. Not to steal it, but to examine the bullet wound, I'm guessing. And then they packed it away somewhere."

"How come you know so much about what happened?"

"Because I was there. With your parents."

"You . . . you were with the families from Aklavik?"

He shook his head.

"No, I accompanied your parents."

"But that was Roy Stevens. His name was Siqiniq Anaqiina at the time."

"No, Roy wasn't there. Originally, he was supposed to go with your parents because they explicitly wanted to see the caribou herd. But he took sick. His father and older brother had already gone out on the caribou hunt. The Anaqiinas didn't want to disappoint your parents, so they asked me to go in his place."

"So *you* were the boy who was with my parents?"

Edwards nodded.

"Roy sometimes plays fast and loose with the facts. He loves to tell fanciful stories about himself . . . he loves the effect they have. Especially on tourists. Otherwise—I mean in his work—he's a reliable guy. He just sort of likes to be seen in the best light. He'd like to be regarded as a hero."

Valerie was spellbound.

"So the story isn't true, that my mother wanted to show Roy she was a good shot and the bullet ricocheted off a tree and killed her? That's what he told Christine Preston. But I thought even then that something didn't add up."

"Did he say that? Typical Roy." Edwards shook his head. "No, that's not at all how it played out. Roy was telling a real tall tale there."

Valerie hoped she'd finally learn what had really happened.

"Please tell me everything, very precisely," she asked, her voice hoarse.

Edwards turned down the noisy heater in the truck.

"I wasn't exactly enthusiastic about going with your parents. I really wanted to go hunting with my father. He'd left a few days before with my brother and cousin to get the winter camp ready. But the Anaqiinas told me that Peter Hurdy-Blaine was a famous hockey player and I'd get to be in a film."

"What film?"

"Your mother made some films."

One more thing her father had concealed. Where were those films?

"Your parents thought I was Roy, who, as you said, called himself Siqiniq back then. I didn't tell them my real name for a long time because I was scared they'd send me back. Because in the end, I did want to go. Your father didn't find out until after . . . after the tragedy who I really was."

Valerie was mesmerized.

"Everything went well the first few days—no storms and only a little snow. Your father was very friendly; he showed me his equipment and how it all worked. I liked that. I was also allowed to drive a snowmobile; I didn't have one of my own so your parents managed to find one for me. Your mother . . . she kept a notebook. And made some drawings. Sketches. She gave me caramel candies as a present. They were frozen but turned soft in my mouth. I spotted caribou on the fourth day. I was happy because that meant I'd soon see my father and brother. We'd already made it to their winter camp that morning, but nobody was there. Your parents were very excited about the caribou. They wanted to shoot some films and then go on alone after leaving me with Dad."

Edwards cleared his throat. Valerie couldn't look at him. Who else had he told this to? Probably very few people over the years. And he would certainly never in a million years have imagined that he'd be telling it to Mary-Ann Strong's daughter someday.

"I saw the herd coming from some distance off, on an angle to us. I had my hunting rifle with me. I felt the thrill of the hunt. Caribou are very important for my people. They give us so much: meat, hide, leather, sinews, bones, antlers. They are our lifeblood. Your mother had gotten everything set up for her film shoot. Somehow I didn't really fully appreciate what all that meant. I wanted to prove to my dad that I could kill a caribou. I was fourteen, but I wanted to be a real hunter. So I crept up toward the herd, my rifle at the ready."

He paused to take a deep breath.

"Suddenly, she jumped on me. She tried to take away my rifle. I didn't understand what was happening. I held on to my gun tight. It was *my* gun. I was proud of it. I didn't know what she wanted. I heard your father shouting at her, 'Mary-Ann! Mary-Ann!' Then a shot."

Valerie saw her group pouring out of the Chevy and moving toward the racetrack. The dogsled race felt miles away now. She was in the snow-covered tundra, with three people, one of them fatally struck by a bullet.

"She didn't die right away. We carried her into the tent, and your father attempted to give her first aid. She tried to say something but couldn't. It was too late. I knew before he did that she had died."

His voice cracked.

"He was calm, composed. He said we had to get her to a hospital. He called for help on his satellite phone. He didn't break down until he saw that any attempt to save her would be hopeless.

"Before the plane landed, my father and some other hunters and their families joined us. Your father told them that it was an accident. Nobody was to blame. If anybody was, he was, he said. He told the police that as well."

Valerie tried to thread her way through his story, to make some sense of it.

"My mother was about to shoot her film, and she knew your shots would frighten the caribou off. She couldn't shout that to you because the caribou would have heard her. So she tried to take your gun away from you instead."

"That's how your father saw it, too."

"And you?"

"Everything was incomprehensible to me at the time. And everything that came afterward was, too."

"The police investigation?"

"Yes. And your father helping our family out. And paying for my education. He wasn't mad at me, even though his wife was dead."

"Did you want to move away from Aklavik?"

"My parents did. There was a conflict brewing with some relatives that was making life difficult for them. I'd rather not talk about it— I'm sure you'll understand. I wasn't thrilled with the move at first. It's hard for a fourteen-year-old to leave his friends and home. But look at me now: I'm doing well; I have a job and a family I love. And it was good for my parents and brothers and sisters."

Valerie studied the photo in the medallion.

"How did you know where this pendant was hidden?"

"From Roy, indirectly. He'd gotten it from a relative who was there when your mother was taken away. They'd given it to him as a consolation, since Roy was sick and couldn't go on the trek. Crazy, eh? But after Roy was attacked, he finally told his father about it; his dad thought it was best to go straight to the headquarters in the capital, so he contacted the Yellowknife police. My colleagues passed the information on to me because that's my department."

"Does anybody else know who you are? Sedna Mahrer—did she know? Or people in Inuvik?"

"No. My father Anglicized our family name. He wanted nothing more to do with those relatives or Aklavik. They treated him . . . rather badly."

He got out a tissue and noisily wiped his nose.

"Nobody recognized me here. No wonder—the whole thing took place thirty years ago."

"May I pass this information on to my two brothers?"

"Yes. And if you publish anything, then please change my name. I wouldn't want my identity revealed. Promise?"

Valerie stopped to think. Edwards had taken a big risk by confessing everything to her. At the same time, he wanted to offer her certainty. Certainty about her mother's fate.

"Yes, I promise. That's what my father would have wanted. He wanted to protect you. And my mother probably would have, too."

Outside, she heard yelling and loud cheers. Valerie saw a dogsled flit by. Then another. A purple jacket caught her eye. Alana.

She rewrapped the medallion in the cloth.

"Thank you, thank you for everything. I hope we'll keep in touch."

"Of course. Here's my card with my home address. Just a minute . . ." He took a plastic bag from between the seats and laid it in her lap.

"No way I should forget this."

She took the bag with her somewhat clammy fingers. It contained a narrow cardboard box; inside was a leather-bound book.

She opened it. Diary entries and sketches. All in pencil. She turned toward Edwards, puzzled.

"Your mother's travel diary," he explained. "I found it in the police archives. It's just been declassified. It had been packed onto a sled along with your mother's other things, but the police confiscated it. Maybe because of rumors that she'd been an American informant. I'm glad her daughter has it now."

He placed both hands on the steering wheel.

"I think somebody's looking for you."

"I . . . don't know what to say." Valerie's throat tightened and tears came to her eyes.

In a husky voice, he said, "You can get in touch with me anytime."

Valerie saw Faye nearing the truck. She stuffed the plastic bag and the book under her jacket and slipped outside with a curt good-bye. The cold hit her with brutal force.

"C'mon, we've got to celebrate!" Faye called. "Alana came in second!" She linked arms with Valerie and whispered, "Everything OK?"

"Yes," she said. "A-OK."

Alana was surrounded at the finish line by a good number of spectators offering congratulations. Valerie came across Clem holding a bottle of champagne. She worked her way over to him and shouted, "Don't I get some, too?"

His face morphed into a happy grin.

"Do we have something to celebrate?" he joked.

Poppy Dixon came up behind him with plastic cups.

"If you don't drink it soon, you'll have ice instead of champagne!"

Clem didn't have to be told twice. He filled the cups, emptying the bottle in next to no time.

He bent down close to her.

"Come on," he said. "I have to let Meteor out of the truck. He gets to celebrate, too."

As they walked over to the pickup, Valerie said, "I heard you were one of the winners."

Clem stopped and stared at her. Then he got it.

"We both won, Val," he corrected her. "The two of us."

CHAPTER 40

Vancouver Times: Valerie Blaine, your book, *In the Arctic's Magic Circle*, has been a sensation. It's been on the best-seller list for weeks. Did this enormous interest in your parents' story surprise you?

Valerie Blaine: Yes and no. My father was idolized across the country back in the eighties and even later on. And not only in the sports world. But yes, I suppose it does surprise me somewhat that he still has a place in people's hearts after all these years.

Your mother and her tragic death are central to the book. Was it difficult to reprocess these events?

I wanted to retrieve Mary-Ann Strong's death from obscurity, to bring it into the light, and I hope I did that. But there was more: I wanted to shed light on her *life*, too, which was all too brief, sadly. Thanks to her travel diary, I was able to find my way to a woman I never knew. She was a courageous, exciting person, and it's a shame she wasn't granted the time to fully realize her potential.

And *your* book is courageous as well, Ms. Blaine. You don't shrink from exploring painful and controversial facts in your family's

history. For example, the realization that your stepmother, Bella Wakefield, had two children you knew absolutely nothing about.

My brothers and I were very moved by Sedna Mahrer's fate and tragic end—she was Bella's daughter, as you know. Sedna and her brother, Glenn, were raised believing that their biological mother didn't want to have anything to do with them. That must have been terrible. We're in regular communication with Glenn Bliss now. In the meantime, he's come to see his mother differently; he now knows the whole truth behind her absence in his life. But it's too bad my book comes out too late for Sedna, and for Bella, who's got Alzheimer's.

You say in your book that Mary-Ann Strong's film footage is lost. What do you think happened to it?

If I only knew! Maybe it was squirreled away in a police archive, and now nobody knows anything about it. Or else it was destroyed. It's a great mystery.

You used to be in journalism, and since then you've led numerous tours to the Arctic and other places. Will you still be writing books in the future?

We'll see. I do still have my tour company, but my business partner, Faye Burton, who's also in the book, is mainly in charge of running it now. I travel with Clem Hardeven, who currently works for Parks Canada. We get to many of Canada's national parks.

For years, you strongly resisted immersing yourself in your parents' story, and yet you regularly returned to the Arctic, where the disaster took place. Was that a coincidence?

It certainly wouldn't have been a coincidence according to Inuit mythology. But there's a huge interest in Arctic tourism today. So it was only a matter of time before I got up there. But you're right: it pretty much took the force of circumstances to get me involved with my parents' history. I'm pleased today that it happened.

Will you go to that part of the Arctic again?

This will surprise you: Clem Hardeven and I are planning a Dempster Memorial Trek. We want to bring my parents' project to a fitting conclusion. We're already preparing for it. We're bringing our dog, Meteor, and a second one that we've named Sedna. Two Gwich'in guides are coming with us since nobody knows the territory—*their* territory, I mean—as well as they do.

The revelation of your family secrets has been fascinating for your readers. Are they all now out in the open?

Let's just say that I've included everything that my readers need to know in order to understand my parents' tragedy and how it impacted anyone connected with them. The few remaining facts are merely of family interest. I would never make them public. I think there are limits, and that's where you have to stop.

Many thanks for this interview, Ms. Blaine.

EPILOGUE

February 14, 1985

Cold. Cold. Cold.

Fifty-four below.

Kept the little woodstove in the tent going all night.

The caribou hides are warmer than our sleeping bags. We mustn't tell our sponsors that.

Little icicles hang down from Peter's mustache.

How can the sun be shining and it's still so cold? We can't wear sunglasses because they'll freeze to our faces in seconds.

Wish we were alone in the tent, without Siqiniq. We can deliver him back to his father in a few days. Peter wants to go on afterward, just the two of us. Without a local guide.

Crazy.

Talked last night because the cold kept us from sleeping.

We talked about what might have happened to us if we had never met. One of the rare relaxed conversations we have had. Peter is irritated and frustrated most of the time.

I told him about Kenneth, who used to chase me and today makes millions from a soft drink factory. "You would have been a trophy wife," Peter said.

Isn't that what I am now? Everybody admires Peter Hurdy-Blaine, but nobody knows Mary-Ann Strong. Not yet.

Peter talks about a woman named Bella he knew in the US. Very pretty, he says, but very domesticated. "She's not adventurous, like you."

Well, this Bella didn't give up college the way I did to marry Peter. I haven't got a profession, and I have three kids I miss badly. Left them with his parents so he can make his dreams come true.

But that will soon change.

February 15, 1985

We had a lost day. Furious winds.

It's loud in the tent. Tried to listen to music on my Walkman, but the batteries are dead. Too cold. Peter laughed and laughed at me.

He never misses a chance to mock me when I make a mistake.

Had trouble finding wood for the stove.

Siqiniq and I put up the tent with Peter. He swore and complained.

What did he expect? Sunshine every day? We could have bad weather for two weeks. Easily possible.

Peter calls me paranoid. I always prepare for the worst-case scenario. It's only realistic. Weather. Dangers.

Peter has one bad moment after another. He's in pain. I don't see how many pills he takes. Sometimes he grimaces with pain. Osteoarthritis. Rheumatism.

He doesn't talk to me about his health problems. A hockey player is old at 45. But he refuses to believe it.

Maybe old injuries are showing up now.

February 16, 1985

Gorgeous night. A sea of stars in the firmament.

Magical.

We made good progress today. Got to the winter camp of Siqiniq's father. Nobody there. Probably out setting traps.

Siqiniq says the caribou are not far off.

How does he know?

We moved on, Siqiniq with us. I'm more used to having him around. Still, I'd prefer an adult guide to a fourteen-year-old. A teenager with a hunting rifle.

Peter thinks nothing of it. But it makes me nervous.

Peter does not take my concerns seriously.

Have my suspicions why Peter doesn't want an adult guide. He's not used to sharing the spotlight.

He tolerates me shooting films just because Peter Hurdy-Blaine is in every shot. We shall see if he's in the credits. After all, I'm doing all the work.

February 17, 1985

Woke up early. Filled with anticipation.

The caribou can't be far away.

I asked Peter again last night if he'd explained to Siqiniq that he has to keep absolutely still during my shoot.

Peter had forgotten again. Intentionally? He doesn't want me to tell Siqiniq directly that he shouldn't interfere with the filming. Peter says I don't understand their culture and that you have to approach Siqiniq with tact and sensitivity and caution. As if I didn't know how to do that! But I don't want tensions to flare up between us. So I keep my mouth shut and cut Peter some slack. He promised to make up for it. Why didn't he do it days ago? I have the feeling he wants to sabotage my film work.

Those mood swings. Not a good sign. The exertion is simply too much for him. He's not physically able to get through this trek. He'll never admit it. So *I* will be the one to do the wilting.

When the caribou are in the can, I'll pretend I'm sick. He can save face, but I'll have my film regardless.

I know how to do it. I'll be very convincing. He won't have any choice but to go back to Inuvik as fast as possible.

Perhaps this is Peter's last trip to the Arctic. But he doesn't know that yet.

Siqiniq is back from scouting. I asked Peter if he told the boy not to move while the camera's rolling. Peter said yes. Didn't sound convincing. But what can I do?

Today's my big day. Here we go!

ACKNOWLEDGMENTS

Some years ago, I traveled the same route as my heroine, Valerie Blaine—an unforgettable journey I highly recommend. The communities along the road, especially Dawson City, Inuvik, and Tuktoyaktuk, inspired this novel. While some of the settings I describe do exist, none of my imaginary protagonists live in them.

Throughout my trip, I encountered many interesting, helpful, independent, and impressive people. Inuvik is a real multicultural community with all sorts of inhabitants; it's admirable how they make this remote Arctic town a diverse place to live, creating a unique meeting space. I can only tip my hat out of respect.

I hope that some of my readers will succumb to the temptation to travel to the Arctic Ocean and come away as fascinated as I was. To be sure, they won't meet anyone like Clem Hardeven, Helvin West, or Marjorie Tama. It was a great pleasure to invent these fictional characters. My description of places like Inuvik and Tuktoyaktuk hew close to the originals; but just as much they sprang from my imagination, as people who know those towns can easily verify.

I would first like to thank the people who helped me revive, correct, and amend my memories and knowledge of Inuvik and Tuktoyaktuk.

They showed much patience, although it couldn't have been easy for them to respond to all my questions.

Beverly Amos from the Inuvialuit Cultural Resource Centre in Inuvik gave me indefatigable assistance with indigenous names, local dialects, and customs, from animals' ranges to deciphering expressions like *Alappaa-Brrr* ("I am cold," in Siglitun). She also taught me how to translate "Thank you" into Inuvialuktun, which comes in handy right now: *Quyanainni*, Beverly.

It is important to state up front: I myself am accountable for any errors that may have crept in despite my intensive research. I have allowed myself some freedom in many aspects, particularly in the portrayal of shamans and Inuit myths. The myths mentioned in the novel are not specific to the Inuvik region or the Western Arctic. I hope I'll be forgiven for these creative deviations.

Amie Hay, who worked for three years as a speech therapist in Inuvik, filled me in on many interesting experiences from her time there. Dr. Grant Zazula, a Canadian paleontologist at the Ministry for Tourism and Culture in Whitehorse, gave me some insight into the Beringia era during the last Ice Age, when people and animals from Asia migrated to North America over a glacier-free land bridge to the present-day Yukon Territory. Beth and Peter Lamb refreshed their memories to tell me about their fascinating life during the couple of years they and their two children were in Inuvik. Margot Grant's oral reports of her two trips to Inuvik and Tuktoyaktuk as a journalist provided valuable enrichment that supplemented my own travel experiences.

The enthusiasm of my test readers relieved me of hidden fears by contributing highly valued insights and suggestions toward the completion of the novel. Big hugs to Peter Stenberg, Erika Imhof, Gisela Dalvit, Oswald Abersbach, Margot Grant, and Susanne Keller. As we say in Canada, you rock!

I must also thank the Swiss photographer Rudolf Grütter, who provided me with fantastic pictures of the Ice Road. I was accompanied in the Arctic by *my* tour guide, Benno Jaeger, a Swiss-Canadian, and I am grateful to him for one of the best adventures of my life. The sharp eyes, the admirable feeling for language, and the infallible logic of my editor, Gisa Marehn, made this book what it is today. A fine editor like her is heaven-sent.

Die Fremde auf dem Eis would not exist in its present form without Franz Edlmayr, who acquired and produced it for Amazon Publishing in Munich. He saw my fifth book through with the right measure of goading and patience to bring the baby safe and sound into the world. Thanks to the efforts of the magnificent Amazon team, my crime novels have been a success.

The award-winning translator, Gerald Chapple, has repeated the miracle of my story's rebirth in English, using powerful and seductive language that never fails to impress me immensely. It is always such an honor and blessing to have Gerald Chapple on board.

My editor, Lauren Edwards, at AmazonCrossing has impressed me over and over again with her passion, dedication, and efficiency. She showed such a good intuition for what an author needs. My warm thanks go to her, and to the developmental editor, Susan Hulett; the copyeditor, Lindsey Alexander; and the proofreader, Monique Vescia; who suggested so many excellent changes to this book.

To all the people who have supported and inspired me, I express my heartfelt gratitude.

AUTHOR'S NOTE

Regarding the mysterious explosion in the Canadian Arctic: About nine years ago I read a brief article in a major Canadian newspaper that captivated me at once. It referred to an explosion in the Arctic at the end of July 2008 that several Inuit hunters claimed to have observed at the tip of Baffin Island. The article said the Inuit reported a black cloud above the explosion and found a number of dead whales on the shore. It went on to say that an indigenous army volunteer of the Canadian Rangers submitted a similar report.

The Canadian military stated they would be sending a long-range airplane, a CP-140 Aurora, to the area to look for evidence.

I waited eagerly to read more about this extraordinary incident in the Canadian media. I waited and waited. But there was no follow-up.

As a journalist, I decided to pursue the matter. I called many agencies, from the Ministry of Defense to the RCMP to officers in Yellowknife to the Ministry of Fisheries—only to be passed on to other agencies that promised to return my calls but never did. I finally gave up my research and worked the mysterious explosion into the present novel.

I read in later news agency articles that a helicopter was sent instead of an Aurora, from a Canadian Coast Guard ship one week later, but no traces of an explosion or any dead whales were found.

An anonymous government source was quoted in the *Calgary Herald* on August 9, 2008, as saying that any indications of an explosion over a week old would have long disappeared and that polar bears could have eaten the whale carcasses.

So what did happen in the Arctic that summer? Was it an unidentified submarine? A foreign military power? Illegal whale hunters with explosives? There are no limits to the imagination on this point. The explosion remains unexplained to this day—at least officially. This is why I have not given a final explanation for it in this book.

One of my favorite figures in this story is Pihuk Bart, the shaman. Shamans have always played an important role in the lives and history of the peoples living in Arctic regions. I was told by an Inuvialuk that there were (and are) good shamans but also bad shamans. Pihuk isn't a bad shaman, although he's a bit quirky. But he must have liked Valerie Blaine, who respected him. And he was correct in his prediction for her.

An Inuit from Nunavik in Northern Quebec told me an old myth about shamans: A long, long time ago, there were two shamans fighting each other. As the Inuit didn't like people fighting, they sent the shamans to the moon. There they kept on fighting, so mightily that they dug in their feet. That is how craters appeared on the moon.

I have always been fascinated by another partly factual story of a shaman named Qitdlarssuaq on Canada's Baffin Island. In the nineteenth century, this shaman committed murder and fled with a group of about fifty Inuit in order to escape revenge. The group traveled all the way across the Arctic to northwestern Greenland, which took years. They arrived in Greenland around 1863, and there they stayed and had quite a decent life. When the shaman grew old, he wanted to return to Baffin Island. Around 1873, he took a group of twenty or so people with him. The shaman died around 1875 on the journey. Only five of the group survived the arduous and dangerous trip; the others starved to death. The survivors returned to Greenland two years later and stayed. This stunning odyssey is partly oral history, partly documented, and can be read in the Canadian Encyclopedia: http://www.thecanadianency-clopedia.ca/en/article/qitdlarssuaq/.

I invented the story of the Inuvialuit hamlet of Inuliktuuq, whose inhabitants followed their bad shaman to their deaths because they were more afraid of not following him than of the dangers that lurked beyond their territory. Nothing like this ever really existed. The reality is very different: The Inuvialuit have taken their fate into their own hands: in 1984, they signed a comprehensive land claim agreement with the Canadian government that makes them "equal and meaningful participants in the northern and national economy and society" and that helps to preserve the "Inuvialuit cultural identity and values within a changing northern society" (from the Inuvialuit Regional Corporation website: http://www.irc.inuvialuit.com/inuvialuit-final-agreement).

ABOUT THE AUTHOR

Photo © 2015 Kim Stallknecht

Bernadette Calonego was born in Switzerland and grew up on the shores of Lake Lucerne. She was just eleven years old when she published her first story in a Swiss newspaper. She went on to earn a teaching degree from the University of Fribourg, which she put to good use in England and Switzerland before switching gears to become a journalist. As a foreign correspondent, she published stories in *Vogue*, *GEO*, and *SZ Magazin*. After several years working with the Reuters news agency and a series of German-language newspapers, she moved to Canada and began writing fiction. *The Stranger on the Ice* is her fourth novel to be translated into English, following *Stormy Cove*, *Under Dark Waters*, and *The Zurich Conspiracy*. She lives near Vancouver, British Columbia.

ABOUT THE TRANSLATOR

Photo © 2018 Nina Chapple

Gerald Chapple is an award-winning translator of German literature. He received his doctorate at Harvard and went on to teach German and comparative literature at McMaster University in Hamilton, Ontario. He has been translating contemporary German-language fiction, poetry, and nonfiction for over forty years. His recent renditions into English include Anita Albus's wonderfully idiosyncratic book, *On Rare Birds*, and one hundred poems by Günter Kunert. Of his six novels translated for AmazonCrossing, three were by the Swiss-Canadian author and journalist Bernadette Calonego: *The Zurich Conspiracy*; *Under Dark Waters*, set in British Columbia and the Canadian Arctic; and *Stormy Cove*, another novel of suspense placed this time in northern Newfoundland. He lives in Dundas, Ontario, with his wife, Nina, an architectural historian. When not translating, he can usually be found studying birds, butterflies, and dragonflies; reading; listening to classical music; or enjoying life with his children and grandchildren in New York.

WORKS CONSULTED

Berton, Laura Beatrice. *I Married the Klondike*. Madeira Park, BC: Harbour Publishing, 2005.

Billington, Keith. *House Calls by Dogsled*. Whitehorse, YT: Lost Moose, 2008; now Madeira Park, BC: Harbour Publishing.

Jones, Charlotte Foltz. *Yukon Gold: The Story of the Klondike Gold Rush*. New York: Holiday House, 1999.

Lanz, Walter. *Along the Dempster: An Outdoor Guide to Canada's Northernmost Highway*. Vancouver: Oak House, 2002.